I0553807

The Quest for the Chalice of Power

The Rixey Files Book Two

Hugh Richard Williams

Published by Rogue Phoenix Press, LLP
Copyright © 2020

Names, characters and incidents depicted in this book are products of the author's imagination or are used fictitiously. Any resemblance to actual events, locales, organizations, or persons, living or dead, is entirely coincidental and beyond the intent of the author or the publisher. No part of this book may be reproduced or transmitted in any form or by any means, electronic or mechanical, including photocopying, recording, or by any information storage and retrieval system, without permission in writing from the publisher.

ISBN: 978-1-62420-456-2

Credits
Cover Artist: Designs by Ms G
Editor: Sherry Derr-Wille

A Word from the Author

This is the second book in The Rixey Files series. Once I changed genres from zombie apocalypse to detective thrillers, I felt like the person with a bag of Jay's potato chips: It was impossible to stop at just one. I began this story while I was still working on *The Rixey Files: The Quest for Caesar's Medallion* as I had a terrific opening scene for this story and didn't want to forget it. I have found it's best to strike on writing while the fire is hot.

This book would have been impossible without the valuable help of my team of Beta readers. Grant Elliot Smith and Geoffrey S. Jade Barrett gave me incredible insight into the importance of pacing. Bree Pierce, Kathy Dinisi, Stephen W. Smith, Pam Bingle Finch, Mary Brueckner, Elizabeth Holman Collins, Christopher Manny, Shirley Nanos, Sarah Moskowitz Hocking, Elizabeth Stuart, and Linda S. Goersch also provided me very valuable ideas and pointers. Also, thanks to the many friends, too numerous to mention, who I discussed the book with and who gave me great ideas about situations.

Finally, though my books are in fiction genres, I do my best to make them believable. This is achieved by doing research on the various locations my characters visit as well as the items they use. Sit back now and enjoy.

Hugh Richard Williams March 12, 2017, Carbondale, IL

Chapter One

"Nothing is impossible, the word itself says 'I'm possible'!" Audrey Hepburn.

Breathing in the warm salty smell of the ocean, I guided the dinghy as silently as possible in the darkness of the evening and the overcast skies hiding the stars. Since my childhood, I've always enjoyed the ocean smell, though I could have really done without on this caper. I felt as if I were in a silent and empty void.

While I've never been a big fan of silent and empty voids, at least tonight I should be. The current condition made it harder for me to be seen from the ship I was heading to. Maybe then I wouldn't have been so annoyed with the sudden sensation of the cold raindrops hitting me. Punishing me for my lack of appreciation, the ocean took it upon itself to grow a little rougher. Next time I embark on some maritime adventure, I will make a small offering to Poseidon, like chicken soup. It might not have helped, but it couldn't have hurt. I swore at myself as the harsh spray dented my face while the little craft crested and fell with each wave. As if someone from above didn't think I was having a tough enough night, the cold raindrops turned into a crisp sheet of water descending from the sky.

The combination of the now heavily-falling rain and saltwater spray really stung. I pulled a mirror out of my jacket pocket and checked the blacking I'd applied to my face a bit too liberally. I'd always been a lousy makeup artist. The spray hadn't affected my camouflage at all. At least that precaution went according to plan.

Ten minutes out from my evening's target, I found myself distracted on how I came to put myself in a situation that was rapidly becoming a much more dangerous than I planned. Again.

This caper began like most. It started with a phone call from a man who would eventually become my client. He'd possessed a Fabergé egg. This one was called the Hen's Egg. It had been delivered to Tsar Alexander III and was given to his wife to celebrate their anniversary. It had been stolen and the police seemed powerless to get to the bottom of the crime.

The egg was a white enamel shell that concealed a matte golden-yolk filling. The egg is worth between thirty and forty million dollars. It was insured by a famous insurance company, whose name need not be mentioned here. The company and I agreed on a suitable retainer as well as a finder's fee and I began work. The wetter I got, the more I believed I'd undercharged them. I shook my head. Perhaps my mom had been right about me. Maybe I was a little too reckless and adventure seeking. Taking this assignment was undoubtedly a bit of both.

I knew my intelligence was right. I'd spent enough on it and had gotten it from the best research company in the world, Kaplan Cleaning Company. I'd used them before and they were always very reliable. In case you're wondering about their name, in addition to their intelligence work, they are professional cleaners. Got a body you need moved or otherwise disposed of? They will do that task. Of course, for a fee.

During their research, they came across quite a bit of chatter on the dark web and various intel agencies about the egg as well as other high-line robberies that had been occurring. The theory that had the most legs concerning the theft was it was part of a scheme by the North Koreans to raise hard currency.

Why? That was still unknown, and some of the guesses were bizarre. All of the intel suggested the Hen's Egg was steaming to Hong Kong via a tramp freighter, or more accurately a spy ship disguised as a tramp freighter, named the *Jin Teng*. The ship flew a flag of convenience from Liberia in an attempt to conceal its North Korean identity. North Korean ships were generally not allowed to dock in many countries, thus the need for subterfuge. Kaplan had added an interesting fact: "The vessel changed names eight times the past two years. I guess this was all part of the concealment game. The thieves chose not to risk a flight to Hong Kong for fear of a crash." A ship, while slower, was indeed safer.

This turned out to be a mistake as it cost them their head start. It gave me time to fly to Hong Kong the day before it was to be transferred to another, more formidable ship headed to North Korea.

Upon my landing in Hong Kong, Kaplan sent me the names of three possible ships to take the Hen's Egg to North Korea. A little leg work and some American dollars later, I had the name of the vessel.

3

As I neared the ship, I smiled to myself. I mean what could possibly go wrong? I was in a foreign city that is controlled by the People's Republic of China, who, if they found out what I was illegally doing in their domain, would take a dim view of me. Add to that I was boarding a vessel that was controlled by the most ruthless regime in the world and I faced almost certain death, if I were lucky, if my mission failed and I was captured. Perhaps my mom was right about me being too reckless and adventure seeking for my own good. Maybe I just had a screw loose. I was already regretting the fact I hadn't charged nearly enough and allowed myself to be talked into the caper. A cold wave coming over the bow of the boat woke me from my reverie and brought me back to the dangerous present.

I looked behind me and felt reassured. I still was able to make out the lights from the Hong Kong harbor. I wasn't too worried. If the ocean got rougher on my return trip, I wouldn't care about stealth and I would open the engine up. For now, slow and silent was the agenda. Up ahead, I saw my mark, a ship, despite the fact it was flying a Liberian flag, that was owned by North Korea, called the *Dae Song*.

Making sure the crew wouldn't see my approach, I tethered my little craft to the side of the ship. I took a cleansing breath to calm myself down and relax. I knew I would need my wits about me if I were going to survive the night. I adjusted my dark leather jacket and picked up the rope. It was time for me to board the *Dae Song*. As silence was at a premium, I took care to muffle the sound of the hook by wrapping it in cloth. After hearing it catch the railing, I pulled hard on it to make sure it wouldn't slip. It didn't. I removed two small shaped charges from a backpack and

4

placed them on the hull near where I was standing. I began my ascent up the rope and froze in terror.

I heard what I assumed was Korean spoken by two sailors who were on watch. They stopped for a moment, and I saw two burning embers being tossed overboard. I heard the strike of a lighter as they lit new cigarettes. This was another break in my favor. The light from the lighter would destroy their night vision for a while. I smelt the odor of their cigarettes. An announcement came over a speaker in a language I didn't understand, then I heard the retreating footsteps of the sailors as they continued on their watch. Now was my chance! I finished climbing up the rope and before I cleared the gunwale, I peered up and down the outside corridor. All clear. Once over the rail, it took me a few moments to get my bearings. I knew from the map I committed to memory the Captain's cabin was supposed to be toward the stern. Staying as low as possible, I headed toward the stern. I planted two more shaped charges on doors I passed as I slowly made my way to the Captain's cabin. I was going to put my last shaped charge where it would do the most good. It was being saved for the door to his cabin.

Why had I bothered with the shaped charges? They were a backup in case my plan went a cropper. Setting them off if things went to hell would hopefully cause the crew to lose interest in shooting me and become more concerned about their ship sinking than me.

I was soon standing in front of the door to the cabin of the Captain. I listened carefully, and hearing no sounds coming from the cabin, I placed the final shaped charge on his door. I turned the handle. It didn't turn. I looked up and down the corridor and all was still quiet. I reached into my jacket pocket and pulled out my custom-made set of graphene lock picks. They never break as they are two hundred times stronger than steel and the material can cut diamonds. There was just enough light to allow me to see the keyhole on the knob. Seconds later, I heard the satisfying click as the tumblers fell into place. I put my lock picks back in my pocket and tried the handle again. It gave way and I was soon in the cabin. I closed the door behind me.

The ambient light in the room made finding the safe easier. I saw the safe was already partially open. This struck me as odd, but I'm one never to look a gift horse in the mouth.

I looked inside the safe. I saw about a six-inch stack of hundred-dollar bills, bundled with a strap from a bank. I didn't understand the writing on the strap. There was also a half dozen glassine bags containing a white powder, a stack of passports, a pistol that looked like a Glock 17, my weapon of choice and what currently was strapped to my hip. I saw a purple bag that had the shape of tonight's reason for me being here.

I removed the purple bag from the safe. I opened it up and feasted my eyes on The Hen's Egg. I carefully placed it in a special container and *then* attached the bag securely around my neck. Not a chance I was going to lose this baby. *Miller, I think, your plan is pure genius. Nothing can go wrong now.* Oh, how we deceive ourselves. Moments after congratulating myself on a job well done, there was a wail of alarms going off and red lights flashing everywhere. I felt a burst of adrenaline hit me like a hammer. I realized there was a great chance this whole plan was probably ending badly for me. I stopped for a moment and took another deep breath and collected myself. This was not the time to act irrationally.

I stepped out of the room and began to head back toward where my dinghy would be waiting for me. Gunshots rang out over my head. These people were seriously pissed at me. I heard cursing in a language I was pretty sure was Korean. After all, I was on a ship owned by North Korea. I made it around a corner of the boat. This offered some protection for a few seconds. I pulled my pistol and returned fire. I heard screams of agony and bodies thud as they hit the rusted metal deck. The sirens had been shut off by now, so I was able to hear better. I oriented myself and knew I was less than thirty seconds away from where I was hoping my dinghy would be. Only now, I realized I should have known the safe was protected by a pressure alarm. Once the weight dropped, the signal would go off. I cursed my stupidity for not having been more careful, but the time for recriminations would come later. At least, I hoped there would be a later.

I panted as I debated my next move. My clothes were soaked with sweat and I felt my heart racing. Not for the first time, I promised myself I would quit smoking and begin working out at a local gym. The plan that came to mind was a simple one. I would make a mad dash to where the dinghy was tied off and dive over the rail. I needed to see how the sailors were lined up. If maybe only one or two might be able to shoot at me, I might have a chance to survive the night.

Reluctantly, I took a quick glance around the corner. I was in luck. I saw ten sailors armed with AK-47s and a man dressed in a uniform holding a bullhorn in one hand and a pistol in another. He would be hard to forget. His face was screwed into a look of anger and a jagged scar running from his ear to his mouth on the right side of his face made him even more memorable. The way the sailors were lined up on the narrow deck corridor, only one with an AK-47 and the leader with a pistol would be able to shoot at me without risking shooting their comrades. I was in luck. The sailors put themselves in the worst possible position in terms of getting the most people to shoot at me.

One of the sailors began firing his AK-47. I heard a shot from the pistol and listened to the weapon clatter as it hit the deck, seconds ahead of the thud of the body.

I was startled when I heard over a bullhorn, this time in English: "You are trapped. You have to surrender. Drop your weapon and gently lay down the People's property you have stolen. We will be fair in our dealings with you." I also heard what I was sure was the same message repeated in French and German.

I smiled to myself and remembered the kid who got fifteen years at hard labor for merely stealing a banner in North Korea. I'd boarded their vessel, taken something worth a lot of money, and probably shot and killed a few of the crew. I didn't even want to think about what would happen to me. I was encouraged by the use of three languages. They didn't know who I was. If I was able to get away chances where they wouldn't be able to follow me. I felt my jacket pocket for my detonator. It was still there. I moved it to a more secure location in my pants pocket. I knew I was going to need it to get out of this alive.

When I didn't respond, the firing began again. I heard another command and the shooting stopped. They probably didn't want to take a chance on damaging my prize. I couldn't blame them. After all, the item I now possessed was worth a lot in hard currency.

I made my decision then and there. Now that I knew they were afraid to shoot for fear of damaging the egg, I made a mad dash for the rail. I dove over the side and landed near the dinghy. They began firing as soon as I struck the water. I imagine it was out of frustration. Their concern for the Hen's Egg had evaporated. I knew, as they did, the best chance for recovery was to shoot at me and hope they could remove the egg undamaged. If I got away, the egg would be gone forever.

Moments after hitting the water, the dinghy was ripped apart by what sounded like automatic weapons fire. *Crap*, I thought, *time for swimmies.*

I took a deep breath and dove as deep as possible. I heard bullets bouncing off the water above me. I reached into one of my pants pockets and pulled out the detonator. I knew it was necessary to take a chance and get the detonator above the water for it to work. I needed a clear path to send the electronic waves to set off the shape charges. I hoped the darkness would give me cover to at least stick my hand with the detonator out of the water without it being shot off. I raised my hand above the water. I pressed the button and prayed it worked. If it didn't, I was going to be in a lot of trouble. I was rewarded with a series of explosions. Nothing too serious, but the crew would have more interest in finding out why their ship began blowing up and less interest in shooting at me. The gunshots stopped, I surfaced, and I heard more cursing. I kicked off my shoes and wiggled out of my leather jacket. I realized I couldn't swim back to safety being in shoes and weighed down in a heavy leather coat. My poor fedora was long gone. At least my prize was safe and sound. I saw the lights of Hong Kong off in the distance. I was fortunate enough to find a piece of wood floating in the harbor. I grabbed it and was surprised when it supported me. I began kicking my way back to dry land and relative safety.

I was regretting not having thought out my plan better. What did I think when I sneaked aboard the tramp freighter? My project made perfect sense when I was planning it out back in my hotel room. I acquired a motorized rubber dinghy with a silent running motor so I'd be able to quietly travel out to the freighter, anchored about a half a mile from Hong Kong. I knew where the ship captain's room was. I knew where the safe was that contained the item I was hired to recover. My mistake was lying to myself. It's something Willard long lectured me about. I let the finder's fee, while considerable, cloud my judgment and tell myself the safe wouldn't be alarmed. I was wrong. I did one thing correctly: I planted some small distractions on board. The explosives worked and were the only reason I was still alive and not heading for a prison in North Korea. Even a blind pig does on occasion find an acorn. At least, I keep telling myself that.

I made it to a wharf about twenty minutes later. I was exhausted. The combination of the physical exertion and the adrenaline rush leaving my body left me in pretty bad shape. I forced myself out of the water and climbed up the side and was back on dry land, where I promptly collapsed. I rested for a few minutes then, with great effort, got to my feet.

I felt my pockets, no wallet, no money, I did have my badge from the Bishop Agency and, fortunately, the First Hen's Egg. I remembered a hotel Willard told me about where he stayed many times when he was in Hong Kong. It was called the Ancient Cloak Hotel. I was in luck as it was nearby. I headed toward the hotel and safety, hopefully. I must have looked a sight when I stumbled into the most elegant hotel in Hong Kong: no shoes, looking like a drowned rat, doing my best to keep myself upright as I staggered like a drunk into the hotel.

A doorman looked at me strangely as he opened the door for me. His reaction was nothing compared to the looks I received from the people in the lobby and finally the front desk. I heard myself squish and saw myself dripping water all over the very nice marble floors of the hotel. Okay, people, I know I am not looking good. Give it a rest.

A young Chinese man standing behind the front desk, looked at me quizzically. "May I help you? There is a shelter about six blocks from here." He smiled.

"Is Mr. Chen working?"

The clerk sniffed. "What business do you have with Mr. Chen?"

I looked perturbed. "Not really any of your business. I've been through a dreadful night and I need to speak to Mr. Chen."

The clerk shook his head. "Perhaps you have an appointment?"

Just then an older Chinese man approached the desk. "Did I hear my name being called?"

The man behind the desk said something to him in Chinese. The older man looked at me strangely and smiled. "How can I help you, sir? My name is Mr. Chen. You were asking for me?"

I pulled out my badge from the Bishop Agency. "I'm afraid I had a rough night and this is the only ID I have on me. I lost my wallet someplace. Mr. Bishop told me if I was ever in a spot in Hong Kong, I can always count on this hotel's hospitality."

The clerk clucked disapprovingly at me and reached for a phone as if he was getting ready to call the police. The older man, Mr. Chen, held up his hand and the clerk put down the phone with a look of disgust. I breathed a sigh of relief when the phone went back into its holder. I knew I didn't have a good explanation for why someone in my condition possessed one of the rarest Fabergé eggs in the world.

The older man looked at the badge and said something in a very harsh tone to the clerk. He told me. "Willard was a terrific friend of mine. He saved my life one time. And you would be?"

"Miller Rixey, I am running the Agency. Mr. Bishop has retired."

He nodded. "Please accept my humble apologies for your rather poor treatment." He glared at the clerk. He turned to the clerk and barked an order. The clerk lowered his eyes and began working frantically.

I laughed. "Don't worry about it. I don't blame your clerk. I just need a room, some food, and a change of clothes. I will be making some phone calls to replace some missing items. I assume I can use this address for them to be delivered?"

"This little misunderstanding will not be a problem, Mr. Rixey."

I saw him look strangely at me. I felt like I was flashing a sign saying I have a multi-million-dollar artifact on me.

"Am I correct in saying a search at customs might result in, shall we say, an embarrassing situation?"

I nodded.

"Based on the scuttlebutt I have heard, there was an incident involving the *Dae Song*. Lots of gunfire and explosions. You wouldn't happen to know anything about those goings on, would you, Mr. Rixey?"

"No, sir. I just took a misstep and fell into the harbor. This is how I came to your hotel in this wretched condition."

He pondered the situation for a moment. "You will not be searched at customs then. I will make a phone call to take care of your problem. Would you like some friendly advice, Mr. Rixey?"

"Yes, I would."

"Hong Kong is a truly wonderful city. There is so much to see and do. One might live here a lifetime and not do everything there is to do here. Take this advice as you wish, Mr. Rixey. I would advise you to stay clear of Hong Kong for the next, oh, shall we say, ten years or so. I would also make certain by this time tomorrow night I was out of our wonderful city. Do we understand each other?" he asked pointedly.

"Very clear, Mr. Chen."

Mr. Chen barked another command to the clerk and accepted an ornate box from him. He turned to me. "I suspect you are without protection. Allow me to help you, Mr. Rixey. All we ask is you leave it in your room when you check out."

I nodded. "Yes. I doubt it would clear airport security." There was no need to look into the box. I knew what was in there.

Mr. Chen laughed. "Same sense of humor as Mr. Bishop. Your accommodations have been taken care of, Mr. Rixey. I will not be here in the morning. Please do me the favor of saying hello to Mr. Bishop for me."

"It will be the first thing I say to him when I see him, Mr. Chen."

As we waited for my room to be found, Mr. Chen asked me. "So how has life in general been treating you, Mr. Rixey?"

I grinned. "Just doing my best to survive, Mr. Chen."

He nodded and smiled wanly. "Have a good evening, Mr. Rixey."

Checking out the next morning was relatively painless. I looked like a totally different man from the one who had walked into the hotel the night before. I was dressed in a very nice suit and tie. I do clean up well if I may say so. I exchanged my ornate box for another one from the front desk. I opened the new box and saw another diplomatic passport, some cash, and a one-way ticket from Hong Kong to St. Louis. I walked outside, grabbed a cab, and headed for the airport. My prize was still intact and, if Mr. Chen were a man of his word, I would soon be back in Carbondale, Illinois. He was.

Chapter Two

"You got to look on the bright side, even if there ain't one." Dashiell
Hammett.

Two days later

Everything went well. I was able to leave Hong Kong and made it back in one piece to Carbondale. Mr. Chen's contacting whoever he contacted plus my diplomatic passport meant only the most cursory search. My client in America had quite a bit of influence and I went through no search when I landed in the United States. He had my name placed on a list. When I showed my passport, I was sent right through. He'd gotten a diplomatic passport delivered to me at the Ancient Cloak.

I had decided to hire an intern much as Willard had hired me. Hopefully, whoever my new hire was, they would be a quick learner and eventually become a full-time employee of the Bishop Agency. I was growing much too busy to handle the routine cases and, to be honest, after my most recent experiences, they bored me. Had I become spoiled by the excitement generated by working for particular clients? The answer to the question seemed clear.

I was gone for a week. This meant there was a backlog of projects to catch up on. Willard was out of the country for six months, taking a well-earned vacation and was incommunicado, so it was all on me. I had been having Ms. Nickels refer the more mundane cases to various PI agencies. Never hurts to build up goodwill in your professional community.

I sat at my desk going through the mail deemed important enough by Ms. Nickels for me to read, and I checked my bank statement online. My fee for the rescue of the Hen's Egg had just been received. The owner would be sending over a courier service to pick up the artifact and send it back to her. I wasn't in the mood for a cigar, so I lit a cigarette to go with my first coffee of the day. The phone rang a few times, but I wasn't in the mood to answer it. It was time for me to reflect on my earlier adventure.

I sat back with feet on the desk and was replaying what happened to me on the *Dae Song*. I knew I made some mistakes. The biggest one was taking the caper for what I'd agreed to. As Willard told me more than once, everything should run smoothly while you're planning it. Once you're in the field, that's when the shit hits the fan. Those pesky things called variables come into play. The weather was worse than I'd planned on and I hadn't considered the Captain's safe was alarmed when I saw it open. I'm a hard-headed kind of guy. There were no set of circumstances that would have allowed me not to try for the egg once I'd agreed to. I'm not built that way.

I saw a light flash on my phone and then heard a crackle from the office intercom. "Mr. Rixey, there is a Mr. Chen on the phone. He claims to know you from your vacation in Hong Kong. Shall I put him through?"

"Yes, please do, Ms. Nickels. Please put him through and hold my calls until I tell you otherwise."

I punched the flashing light on my phone and picked up the receiver. "Mr. Chen, so nice to hear from you. I wasn't sure I adequately thanked you for the help you gave me in Hong Kong. I'm sure a man of your influence and power didn't simply call me to chit-chat. What can I do for you?"

"Think nothing of my previous help, Mr. Rixey. I am always glad to help friends or friends of friends. I have a question for you, Mr. Rixey, that embarrasses me. Is your phone line secured?"

"Yes. We take security very seriously at the Bishop Agency. Please call me Miller, Mr. Chen."

"I knew it was. It was an unfortunate question I needed to ask. I hope I didn't offend you, Miller."

"Not at all, Mr. Chen." I heard a long pause at the other end of the line. "Mr. Chen?"

"Sorry, something came up here. I am aware of your skills at locating and retrieving items that, shall we say, have been misplaced or lost," he said as delicately as he could.

I nodded, then realizing he couldn't see my nod. "Yes." I strummed my fingers on the desk, hoping Mr. Chen was going to get to the reason for the call.

"I was contacted by an individual, an old friend actually, who works for your government. He asked me if I knew of someone who was capable and discreet at recovering items. I suggested you."

I laughed. "I'm not sure how discreet I was in Hong Kong. I am capable. You said he works for the U.S. Government?"

"Yes. He claims there are some security breaches in the government and he cannot be sure who to trust. Apparently, the group involved is very big and powerful."

"With the number of leaks our government seems to spout, I'm surprised America somehow manages to stay afloat. Did he bother telling you anything about the case?"

Chen's tone took a serious turn. "He thanked me for giving me your name and told me he held concerns about government security."

"Thanks for the referral. Any idea when I can expect your friend?"

"What time is it there?"

I looked at my watch. "About ten A.M. By the way, what is the name of your referral?"

"Mr. Andrew Stuart. He will be there between two and four P.M. I need to go now. I wish you the best of luck, Miller. He has assured me it will be a simple assignment. Just zip in and zip out. I need to go now. Best of luck."

I groaned inwardly as the mention of a simple assignment. I thought about my last two assignments described as simple, the Medallion and the Egg.

I clicked on my intercom. "Ms. Nickels, did I miss anything?"

"No, Mr. Rixey. A couple of cases came in and I have already referred them."

"Great. I will be gone till one. I have a special client coming in around two. His name is Andrew Stuart. If he gets here before I make it back, please show him to my office."

"Very good, Mr. Rixey. You have some appointments scheduled for later today. I will go ahead and cancel them."

I grabbed my hat, coat, and slid my pistol into my shoulder holster. I had some errands to run and now seemed like the time to do them. As I opened the door to my office, I saw a tall, thin, and partially-bald man frantically gesturing at Ms. Nickels. A client perhaps? From the look of his suit, he seemed well-heeled.

"And who would this gentleman be?"

Ms. Nickels started to tell me but the man interrupted her. "I'm Agent Jude Lewis from the Department of Finance and Professional Regulation." He flashed his cred pack at me. "You must be the famous Miller Rixey who is never in his office."

I chuckled, which seemed to infuriate Agent Lewis. He looked familiar but I couldn't place him. "What seems to be the problem, Agent Lewis?"

"The problem, Mr. Rixey, is I have a laundry list of complaints against you and your firm," he snarled.

It came to me like a lightning bolt. Willard had dealt with this guy before. He was merely an ineffective bureaucrat who despite all of his efforts couldn't pull our licenses or shut down the Agency. Apparently, in another life, he'd had his own firm and Willard aced him out on a very high-profile and high-ticket case. That was ten years ago and once his firm failed, he began working for the state. It seemed like his goal in life was to harass the Agency and anyone connected with it.

"I'm warning you, Rixey, I have a laundry list of complaints against you and your firm. At a minimum, we have you and your agency for practicing detective work without a license. You did work on cases in New York, Argentina, and Colorado at a minimum. Your time is done."

"Listen, Agent Lewis, you've been trying to pull our license for the past ten years and all you've gotten is a big laugh. I advise you to head your dumb ass back to Springfield and don't darken this office anymore." I pointed to the door. "You know the way out."

Lewis turned purple and sputtered. "I'll close you crooks down one way or another." He turned on his heels and stormed out of the office.

I looked at Ms. Nickels. "Whenever Willard calls in tell him about this." I looked at my watch. "I need to know how this guy seems to know so much about the Agency. I've wasted enough time on that fool. I'll see you about one."

Chapter Three

"May you live in interesting times." Unknown.

I made it back to the office at one. I heard Ms. Nickels' voice from behind her office door. It sounded like she was dealing with a telephone solicitor. I knew there was nothing for me to do until my two o'clock. It seemed like a good time to enjoy a cigar. I opened my humidor and selected a Monte Christo. I smiled when I squeezed it and heard no crackle. *Perfect,* I thought. I quickly lopped the rear off, ran my lighter's flame over it, popped it in my mouth and lit it. I poured myself a cup of coffee, looked at my watch, sat back and relaxed. I wondered what the meeting would reveal.

I heard a crackle on my intercom. "Mr. Rixey, your two o'clock is here. Shall I send them in?"

I looked at my watch. It was one thirty. *Better early than late,* I thought. "Please send them in, Ms. Nickels, and hold my calls."

I heard a knock on the door.

"Please come in."

In walked a powerfully-built man. I was guessing he was six foot four and maybe two hundred pounds. He had a full head of black hair and was dressed in a very nice suit. He was accompanied by a tall and thin woman. She looked like she was in good shape and was doing her best to hide her body in her expensive suit. Her horn-rim glasses did not do much for her either. She looked as if she had never smiled before in her life. Since my last case, I had added a recording device to my office. I nonchalantly pressed "record."

I rose to my feet and extended my hand. "Miller Rixey. You would be Andrew Stuart?"

He nodded as he shook my hand. "Yes. Glad to meet you. Joseph has spoken highly of you. He says you are very capable and very discreet."

I nodded and then turned to the woman. "And you would be?" I extended my hand.

"Dr. Eve Kendall. I am Chairwoman of the Department of Antiquities at Minnesota State," she responded in a voice that dripped ice. Her nasal-sounding eastern accent reminded me of nails on a blackboard. She ignored my hand.

"Before we begin, I need to make certain you don't have any listening devices which have been planted on you." I ran my wand over both of them and was happy to discover neither of them was bugged. I looked over at Stuart. "I'm sure you understand." He nodded, as did Dr. Kendall. "The rest of the room is secure. It's swept twice a day and I have anti-bugging devices on the windows."

"Almost done. Now, Mr. Stuart, all I need to do is some ID and we can begin. Please take a seat," I said as I pointed to the two seats in front of my desk.

Dr. Kendall gingerly sat down in her seat while Stuart flopped down in his.

Stuart reached into his jacket pocket and pulled out a set of credentials and handed them to me. I saw a badge, his photo ID, and discovered the agency he worked for, the Office of Artifact Retrieval (OAR). I raised an eyebrow when I saw this version of the alphabet soup. I never heard of them. I relied on Mr. Chen knowing they were really from the American government. Doing my best to appear nonchalant, I handed the credentials back to him. I sat back in my chair. "Can I get either of you anything before we start?"

Stuart said, "A cigar would be good."

Dr. Kendall shook her head no.

I handed a cigar to Stuart and waited.

Dr. Kendall leaned forward in her chair. "Tell me, Mr. Rixey, what do you know about Marco Polo?"

I grimaced as I thought. "Let's see, famous Italian merchant and explorer. Traveled to China in the late thirteenth century." I stroked my chin. "He and his family were court favorites of Kublai Khan? I don't remember anything else from my history classes in college."

She turned to Stuart. "My, he seems very well informed."

She turned back to me and I swear she was actually smiling. "Very good, Mr. Rixey. Let me tell you a tale. Originally, Marco's father and uncle made a trip to what we call China. They met Kublai Khan and became fast friends. Khan asked them to return with some items, most notably some sacred oil from Jerusalem and letters from the Pope explaining the Catholic religion. They returned to Italy fifteen or so years after they left for China. It was the first chance for Marco to see his father. His mother realized she was pregnant with him a month after his father left for China. He wanted Marco to come along on the return trip and Marco agreed on one condition."

"What was the condition?"

"He knew Khan's son was about his age. He wanted to make him a special present."

I saw Dr. Kendall was becoming flushed with excitement as she continued. "They commissioned a famous alchemist, Taddeo Alderotti, to construct a golden chalice. According to the description of the chalice found in his journal, it was eight inches high and encrusted with the finest jewels money might buy. A fitting gift for the son of an emperor. Alderotti called it the Chalice of Power. About a year into the trip, the Chalice began to glow and vibrate. To the emperor's son, this merely added to the mystery of this wonderful gift. What happened to the Chalice is lost in the sands of history. When the Polos returned to Venice some twenty years later, they sought out Alderotti to find out why the Chalice behaved in such a manner. Unfortunately, he had died a year earlier and nothing in his papers indicating why the Chalice did what it did. The Polos suspected the Chalice held some hidden power, but no one figured out what it was."

I nodded as I poured myself another cup of coffee. "Question, why did the Polos go to an alchemist instead of a jeweler to have the Chalice made?"

"They were patrons of Alderotti. He was much more than an

alchemist. He was reputed to be one of the greatest scientists of his time. He was always working on projects far ahead of his time in several fields. Alderotti's incredible skills when it came to making and designing jewelry were well known. He was quite often in trouble with the Catholic church for some of his work. He was accused of witchcraft as some of his projects included flying, astronomy, and even time travel. His views clashed with the Catholic church ideology. Usually, such views are inevitably fatal; only his powerful patrons such as the Polos kept him from being burnt at the stake. We could not be sure if the Polos knew what ability Alderotti imbued the Chalice with." She shrugged as she sat back in her chair.

"Very interesting to say the least. Now, what does all of this have to do with the Bishop Agency?"

Stuart turned to Dr. Kendall. "Would you mind waiting in the reception area? Mr. Rixey and I have some business to discuss."

Dr. Kendall frowned and slowly rose from her seat.

I pressed down on the intercom. "Ms. Nickels, Dr. Kendall will be coming out of my office shortly. Would you please see she is comfortable and get her whatever she wishes?"

"Yes, sir."

I rose from my chair. "So nice meeting you, Dr. Kendall. I hope you have a good trip home." I extended my hand and this time she took it and shook it. I watched her as she left my office, appreciating the way she walked out.

I turned my attention to Stuart. "You're right, we have some things to discuss."

Chapter Four

"It is not in the still calm of life, or the repose of a pacific station, that great characters are formed. The habits of a vigorous mind are formed in contending with difficulties." Abigail Adams.

After the door shut behind Dr. Kendall, I angrily spoke to Stuart. "Okay, this thing stinks. You think I don't know Chen is Chinese Intelligence? I'm guessing Ministry of State Security (MSS)? You come to me claiming to represent some organization. An organization, until a few minutes ago, I didn't realize even existed. You must think I'm an idiot."

Stuart put up his hands to placate me. "Far from it, Mr. Rixey. We know of your previous work and your previous work was well done. Look, it was necessary to go outside the government on this one. If you were as smart as Joseph said, we realized you would know Chen was MSS. He told me he was pretty sure you figured it out when he was able to get you so smoothly out of Hong Kong." He paced the room. "We know several moles are working for the group controlling the Chalice of Power.

We needed to go outside, I mean way outside, the government on this one." He laughed. "You can't get much further outside of the government than the MSS. You see my point, don't you? Now let's sit down and we can discuss the problem I need you to solve."

"How do you know there are people in our government working against your interests in recovering the Chalice? I mean, you have to agree your claim is pretty bizarre?"

I fumbled for a cigarette and finally lit it. I really wanted to hear the explanation for what he told me. I knew it would be interesting.

"We sent agents to Venice to investigate the group and to find its headquarters. We never heard back from them. Their bodies were found floating in the canals of Venice. It seemed pretty clear to us they were betrayed."

I frowned. "A hard point to argue, Mr. Stuart. So, what is it? Dr. Kendall claims the Chalice is lost in time. From your story, it sure doesn't sound like it."

I sat down at my desk and pushed the intercom. "Ms. Nickels, a bottle of Macallan and two glasses, please."

"Yes, Mr. Rixey."

I looked at Stuart and he nodded his approval.

Ms. Nickels entered and placed the tray on my desk. "Anything else, sir?"

"Yes, take Dr. Kendall out to lunch. Mr. Stuart and I might be a while."

Stuart nodded in agreement. We both watched Ms. Nickels leave the office.

"To answer your question, Dr. Kendall was here to provide you with historical background. She is totally unaware of what I am about to tell you. It's way above her pay grade. As far as she knows, everything she told you is the truth. She is an excellent researcher and what she discovered is the traditional research."

I opened the bottle and poured both of us two fingers, recapped the bottle and passed a glass to Stuart. I took a good belt to oil the brain cells and then began. "I know all the alphabet agencies and I have never heard of your office before, Mr. Stuart. Can you explain how a well-informed individual has never heard of you?"

"Our money is appropriated under the Smithsonian budget. We are a black budget organization." He paused momentarily. "We are not your conventional intelligence agency."

"What the hell is a non-conventional intel agency?"

"We monitor cosmic ley lines for possible disruptions in the cosmos. We also monitor the time continuum for possible disruptions. You know time operates in a linear fashion and disruptions, even minor ones, are easy to spot. Some minor disruptions have been found."

After the explanation, my brain cells were going to be in more need of lubrication. I reached for the bottle and poured myself another two fingers of Macallan. I grabbed another cigarette, lit it, and inhaled deeply, enjoying the burn. "You have my undivided attention, Mr. Stuart."

Stuart placed the folder he had been carrying on my desk. He opened it and handed me a picture. "Here is the most recent picture of the Chalice. It was taken in 1977."

I glanced at it. "Very impressive. Where did you find this?" I handed the picture back to him.

"The picture was part of an auction catalog from a small auction house in New York City. The suggested price range on the item was between five hundred and a thousand dollars. They clearly did not understand what they possessed. Gold was going for roughly one and hundred fifty dollars an ounce at the time. I mean, the value of the gold in the item was worth a lot more. Very sloppy work."

"How did you find this picture?"

"At OAR, we have a computer program capable of scanning thousands of pictures, descriptions, books, catalogs, you name it. We started with catalogs from the 1900s and after about one hundred false positives, we came across this. Based on Alderotti's description in his journals, we became convinced this is the Chalice."

As I listened to Stuart, I picked up a pen and began twirling it as I was thinking. "Okay. I'll give you the fact the picture you showed me is the Chalice. I might even give you the fact the Chalice has some special powers. You claim there have been minor disruptions on the timeline continuum and some link between the Chalice and the disruptions." I shook my head. "Also, are you saying no one noticed the Chalice glowing like Dr. Kendall described it?"

"Fair enough. To answer your last question first, nothing ever showed up anywhere about a glowing Chalice. We checked news sources for the past fifty years. The Chalice was finally analyzed correctly and its true value was estimated between one and two hundred thousand. The new value was reported in a lot of the newspapers about five years ago.

The Chalice was donated to the Art Institute of Chicago about six years ago and was added as part of the museum's medieval collection. Again, this made the news. Both news coverages, we believe, attracted the interest of a secret society. Two years ago, the Chalice disappeared. We know it was taken in a burglary and it was the only thing taken in the burglary. The minor disturbances in the timeline continuum began shortly after the burglary. We are terrified the people who stole the Chalice will be able to achieve their aims by figuring out how to get it to work at full capabilities. Only one group is powerful and well-funded enough to perform the burglary. Have you ever heard of a group named Ordo Templi Orientis (OTO)?"

"Yes, a few times when I have watched conspiracy theory movies. I just assumed they were either not real or not what they were made out to be. If you knew the Chalice was this important of an artifact and was capable of causing all of these problems, why didn't your group simply commandeer it?"

"We didn't realize the Chalice still existed until the robbery at the Art Institute."

"Sounds like some very sloppy work on your end. Now go ahead and tell me about the group."

"Ordo Templi Orientis was founded in the early 1200s. Their practices involved the use of ritual and the use of the occult. Elements of the Catholic Church tried many times to show their link with witchcraft. They were unsuccessful. The patrons of the group were much too powerful and influential even for the church back then. Alderotti was a member of OTO. The purpose of the group is to collect their members' creations and use them for some insane plan for world domination. To be honest, despite their claims otherwise, I doubt their goals have changed over the centuries. You can imagine what a huge weapon time travel would be in the hands of a group like OTO?"

I nodded. "So, let me see if I have this straight. Your group is afraid there will be a leak if you use your agency or any other governmental agency to find the Chalice?"

Stuart nodded.

I shook my head in disgust. "Pretty sorry state of affairs."

Stuart turned red. "Yes. I am afraid it is."

"The way this is going, I'm guessing you have no idea where the Chalice is?"

Stuart tugged at his collar. "Well, not exactly. I mean we don't know where it is now. We do know the places the Chalice has been used in the past. I mean, wouldn't it help to give us a way to narrow down where the item is?

"How so?"

"We were able to correlate huge power drains with the breaks in the timeline continuum. It seems as if the Chalice generates a tremendous amount of power when it is used. The power drains and time breaks did not start until after the Chalice was stolen. By the time we locate the source of the power drain, the Chalice and everyone is gone."

I poured myself another drink and offered the bottle to Stuart. He waved it off. I was having a hard time wrapping my head around this fantastic story. I lit another cigarette and stared at Stuart. "I don't imagine you or any of your agents have ever been in OTO headquarters?"

Stuart reached for the bottle and poured himself a generous drink. "To be honest, Mr. Rixey, we don't even know where their headquarters are. All we know is they have an office in Venice and they use a facility in Mexico City for yearly meetings."

"I take it none of the power surges have been traced to either Venice or Mexico City?"

The phone rang and I immediately sent the call to voicemail.

Stuart looked thoughtful and reached for my humidor to pull out a cigar. "There have been some occurrences in Venice. When we get there, we discover, just as in the other instances, the building they have used for whatever they have tried to do with the Chalice is empty." He reached into his folder and pulled out a piece of paper with the dates and locations of the power surges and the time continuum interruptions. "I brought this. I figured you would be interested in it."

"You figured right." I looked over the list. "Four surges linked to one location in Mexico City all occurred on November 2. They all occur every year. Did you investigate the building?"

Stuart shook his head. "It was well secured. Quite frankly, it was apparent the only way into the building was with the help of the Mexican government. This is a project we cannot even trust our own government on."

I nodded. "Understood. So, you couldn't find anyone in your organization to break into the building and check it out?"

Stuart chuckled. "Our organization is made up of academics, computer geeks, and nerds. There isn't a field agent among them. We normally rely on other agencies to do our heavy lifting when it comes to field work." He shrugged. "This project is unique because the organization controlling the Chalice is so powerful. The only way we are going to recover the artifact is to hire an agency as effective as yours seems to be. The recommendation from Joseph was solid. You and your agency have an excellent reputation besides the recommendation from Joseph. I would like to hire you to recover the Chalice."

I thought the offer over for a moment. "I'm flattered. Here is what I need from you and your organization: A one-hundred-and-fifty-thousand-dollar nonrefundable retainer and fifty thousand to cover expenses. There will be an extra fee if the Chalice is recovered."

Stuart didn't blink an eye. "Anything else?"

I smiled. "Oh yes. How much is the artifact worth, would you say?"

"It's priceless."

I stood up from my desk and walked around the office as I thought about asking what my fee would be for recovery. "The last priceless item I recovered, my finder's fee was three million dollars, tax free. Can you accommodate my modest requests?"

Stuart frowned. "I'm limited to a million-dollar expenditure on this project. Can you lower your reasonable request a little?" He coughed. "What this means is eight hundred thousand is the most I'll be able to pay to you after paying your initial retainer and expenses. Your payment would be tax free, of course. Is my offer acceptable?"

"It will be fine providing you can do two more things. First, I have a perfect person in mind to work with me on this case. She is a colonel in the DIA. I have worked with her before and she is very competent. You need to be able to get her temporarily assigned to OAR. Can you make the transfer without attracting attention?"

"I don't see a problem there. You said two things, what is the second thing?"

"I can't make it through customs in Mexico carrying a weapon. I need a Glock-17, with five loaded magazines, and a Sig Sauer P 229-Legion with the same five loaded magazines along with two bulletproof vests. Also, a couple of extra boxes of ammunition for each weapon. You will leave them in a briefcase in a locker at the airport and when you send me the money the locker key needs to be with it. They have a lot of lunatics down in Mexico City and I include the members of OTO. They will all be armed. I do not want to be unarmed any longer than necessary. I'm sure you can understand my reasons?"

Stuart nodded. "Quite clear and all imminently reasonable. Very thorough and very well thought out. I would expect nothing less from you. All I need is the name of the person you wish to be transferred to OAR."

"Morgan Burke."

Chapter Five

"Knowledge is power." Sir Francis Bacon.

Stuart nodded knowingly as he wrote down her name. "Yes. I know you two worked together in Argentina. You did a very commendable job."

I stood there dumbfounded. Was there anyone who did not know about my finding Caesar's Medallion? The case was supposed to have never happened, in a country, according to official records, I was never in?

"Anything else, Mr. Rixey?" Stuart extended his hand.

I took his hand and shook. "Today is October 22. I have some research to do. Naturally, there will be no written contract. Some of my clients prefer things done in this manner. No embarrassing paper trails."

"Yes, I understand."

"When can you overnight the money and the key to the airport locker to me?"

"We can overnight the money and you will have the key in a

couple of days. Are those conditions acceptable?"

I nodded. "Yes. Let's hold off for a day on the transfer of Colonel Burke until I have a chance to finish my research and to call her to make sure she is interested."

"Excellent. I will be expecting the package on the twenty-fourth. Until then, I have work to do."

I heard a buzzer as someone opened the door to the outer office. "Sounds like Ms. Nickels and Doctor Kendall have returned from lunch. Thanks for your business and we will be in touch." I stood there as I watched Stuart gather his belongings and head out the door. I sat at my computer and, on a map website, punched in the address of the building in Mexico City. I then checked for a hotel near the address of the building and was able to find one right across the street. I checked the website for the hotel and much to my surprise, rooms were available for the dates I wanted. I punched in arriving October 31 and checking out November 3 and paid the equivalent of about eighteen hundred dollars. I booked a flight from St. Louis to Mexico City and was relieved of another fifteen for my round-trip ticket. I was glad none of these costs were coming on my dime.

I picked up my phone and dialed the Kaplan Cleaning Company. I heard the phone ring twice and then, "Kaplan Cleaning Company. How may I direct your call?"

"The Bishop Agency, the password is umbrella 2231."

"Yes, Mr. Rixey, how can we be of assistance?"

"Research division, please?"

"Yes, sir. Your new password will be included in the sent

materials."

"Thank you."

"Research. How can we help you today, Mr. Rixey?"

"I need information on a Dr. Eve Kendall who claims to be Chairwoman of the Department of Antiquities at Minnesota State, Andrew Stuart who claims to be affiliated with the Office of Artifact Retrieval, an item called the Chalice of Power, a group named Ordo Templi Orientis, and the *Dae Song*, a freighter of Liberian registry. I don't need a schematic of the ship. I am more interested in the background of the captain of the vessel. Also, I need a set of plans for the three-story building located next to the El Grande Hotel. Its map coordinates would be 212.155.217. Finally, do you have access to a device capable of monitoring the timeline continuum?"

"Yes, Mr. Rixey, we do. What are you looking for with the timeline?"

"Send me a list of breaks in the continuum for the past two years. Should I think of anything else, I will contact you again."

"Very good Mr. Rixey. How do you wish this information to be delivered? Email or courier?"

"Courier. I still don't have a lot of faith in the internet."

"A wise precaution, Mr. Rixey. We can have it for you by the close of business on October 24."

"Yes. Very good. Thank you. I expect your invoice will be with the documents?"

"Yes, Mr. Rixey. Is there anything else we can get for you?"

"No. I cannot think of anything right now."

"Very good, then."

I pressed on the buzzer to Ms. Nickels' desk.

"Yes, Mr. Rixey?"

"I will be expecting two deliveries on the twenty-fourth. One will be from Mr. Stuart and one will be from Kaplan. If you are caught up, please take the rest of the day off. Also, thanks for keeping Dr. Kendall busy while I talked with Stuart."

"Thank you, Mr. Rixey. Anything else before I leave?"

"Yes, if you would make me up a pot of coffee before you go."

"Very good, sir, one pot of coffee with your usual sugar and cream will be there shortly."

I sat back in my chair and thought. I knew I would have the necessary background information from Kaplan. The information I received would give me a fighting chance to succeed. What I did with the report was going to determine how this case was going to turn.

About ten minutes later, Ms. Nickels knocked and came into my office. She set the tray down with the coffee pot, cream, and sugar. "I'm leaving now. I'll be sure to secure the front door."

I smiled at her. "Thanks."

She left the office and soon I was alone with my thoughts. I poured myself a cup of coffee and reached for my phone. I dialed a number and heard a voice on the phone after two rings. "Defense Intelligence Agency. How may I help you?"

"Colonel Burke's office, please?"

I heard some typical waiting-on-the-phone music for a few moments.

"Colonel Burke's office. How may I help you?"

"I need to speak to Colonel Burke if you would. Tell the colonel it's Miller Rixey calling."

"I am sorry, Mr. Rixey, Colonel Burke is currently unavailable."

Chapter Six

"The secret of getting ahead is getting started." Mark Twain.

I sat there stunned. What the hell did that mean? "Um, can you tell me what happened to her?"

"I'm sorry, sir. I am not at liberty to discuss her whereabouts."

I was rapidly losing my patience. "Do you have a supervisor?" I growled.

"Yes, Mr. Rixey. I will get her on the line. Please hold."

I was put on hold for a moment and then heard a new and feminine voice. "This is Bree Pierce, Colonel Burke's confidential secretary."

"Ms. Pierce, this is Miller Rixey. I'm looking for Colonel Burke. I was told she was unavailable."

I heard a giggle on the phone. "Oh, Mr. Rixey, it's so nice to finally meet you. Colonel Burke has spoken very highly of you. She left instructions not to be disturbed. The person who answered the phone did not know who you were. I am sure she would want to talk to you. Please hold."

"Thanks, Ms. Pierce."

"Not a problem, Mr. Rixey."

"Miller, long time no see or hear. How have things been?"

"Oh, come on. It hasn't been so long. Things have been exciting as usual and going well. The reason I am calling is I received a visit from someone who claims they work for the Office of Artifact Retrieval. I never heard of the group before."

"I've heard of them. What was the person's name? Did you meet him or her in person?"

"It was them, Dr. Eve Kendall and Andrew Stuart."

I heard some clicking on a keyboard as I was sure Morgan was pulling up their files. Her description of them matched the two people I talked to.

"I'll send you the transcript of my discussion with them as well as my itinerary. Anyway, they want me to go down to Mexico City to investigate and attempt to recover an item called the Chalice of Power. As you will see, they are concerned about moles in the government and why they want to go outside the government to recover the item. I asked Stuart if he'd be able quietly transfer you temporarily from DIA to OAR on the down low. He said he'd see to it."

"Great, the transfer will be a nice break from my boring routine. Being an analyst is not nearly as exciting as being in the field. Safer for sure, but very boring. I take it this is more a get-together like Argentina and not D.C. When do you need me down there?"

I laughed. "More like Argentina and November 1. I'll be down there on October 31. I have some work I need to do before November 2.

Anyway, read the transcript. It will tell you all you need to know about the artifact and what has been happening."

"Sounds good. I am amazed you were able to find someplace to stay so soon in Mexico City before the Day of the Dead."

The phone began ringing during my call. It was from the 212-area code. I pressed a button to send the caller to voice mail.

I laughed. "Very knowledgeable. I am impressed. Apparently, the group the OAR believes has the Chalice of Power meets every November 2 in Mexico City. There is a good chance we will be on the streets for the parade, so bring an outfit that will blend in. Also, don't worry about a weapon. As you will read, I have arranged a weapon for you."

"How soon before you send the transcript?"

"Give me ten minutes to format it and to send it to you. Call me when you get there. I will be staying at El Grande Hotel. The address will be in the information I will be sending you."

"I know where it is. It will be great to see and work with you again, Miller." I heard a click as she hung up.

I prepared the transcript of the Stuart and Kendall interview as well as my itinerary and sent it speeding to Morgan. I pulled a cigar from my humidor and, after the proper rituals, lit it and sat back in my chair with my feet up on the desk. I enjoyed the quiet of the office. I sat back up and poured myself a cup of coffee. I leaned back again and sighed contently.

It would be great to see Morgan again. During the time we spent together in Washington D.C. after we found Caesar's Medallion, we made all of the promises to keep in touch. Unfortunately, our respective jobs kept both of us much too busy. Outside of a couple of postcards and a few phone calls, we really hadn't done a very good job at keeping in contact

After a few minutes, I finished my coffee, sat back up in my chair, and placed my cigar in an ashtray. I was debating what to do next when I heard the phone ring again. I looked at my caller ID and saw it was the same number that called while I was on the phone with Morgan. Might be important, I thought. Reluctantly, I picked up the phone. "The Bishop Agency, this is Miller Rixey. How can I be of assistance?"

The call was from Zogg Incorporated. It was crucial.

Chapter Seven

"Knowledge is of no value unless you put it into practice." Anton *Chekhov.*

My plane landed at JFK International Airport the next day. The client seemed frantic to secure my services. I did my best to make unreasonable demands, asking for a round-trip first-class ticket, two nights in a five-star hotel, and a nonrefundable retainer of one hundred fifty thousand dollars for merely agreeing to make the trip to talk to him. As quickly as the now client agreed to all my demands left me wondering if I had asked for enough.

I grabbed a cab and directed the driver to the address. The cab stopped in front of a magnificent-looking ten-story building displaying the sign Zogg Inc. on the front. I left the cab and entered the building. The door swung open as I stepped on a pad with the swooshing sound one would hear when a door opened or closed on Star Trek. *Nice touch,* I thought. What immediately caught my eye were the various oil paintings on display in the lobby. The pictures were a who's who of the old masters.

I approached the marble reception desk and was greeted by a comely young lady, probably in her twenties. She was pretty tall and was a brunette. If I was lucky enough to have any spare time, I might have given some thought to asking her out. She was dressed in a uniform identifying her as Ms. Thompson. Her face told me she was all business.

"Mr. Rixey here to meet with Mr. Lothar Zogg."

Ms. Thompson nodded. "Let me check." She looked up smiling. "Yes, Mr. Rixey, I see you are scheduled for with a meeting with Mr. Zogg." She looked impressed. "No time set, you are to see him as soon as you arrive here."

I nodded. "Yes, he said he wanted to see me right away."

She handed me a tag with Visitor and a picture of me on it then said, "Let me get you an escort." She picked up a phone and said something I couldn't make out. Less than a minute later, a huge man dressed in a black uniform appeared by my side. He wore a gold badge and a nametag proclaiming he was head of security and his name was Jack Torrance. He also carried a 9 mm I saw from the bulge under his suit coat. These people seemed to take their security seriously. I wondered what the problem was that Zogg wasn't able to discuss over the phone. Something was bothering him as he agreed to my ridiculous demands for even meeting with him.

"If you will follow me, Mr. Rixey," he said as he pointed to the elevator banks.

"Aren't you going to search me?" I asked more out of curiosity than anything else.

Torrance smiled at me. "You walked through a scanner when you entered the building. When you fail the screening, we have a much different conversation."

The elevator door opened with a swoosh. I saw him place his hand on a panel inside the elevator. His hand was scanned for a moment, then a metallic voice said. "Floor number please." Torrance pushed P for the Penthouse and we were off. *How very space age,* I thought. Less than a minute later, the voice spoke again. "Now arriving at Penthouse." The door slid open with the same swoosh I heard when I first entered the building.

Torrance pointed to the open door. "I am not cleared past this point. Mr. Zogg is in the first door on the left." I stepped out and heard the door close behind me.

The corridor was well lit and well carpeted. As I walked down the hall, I noticed oil paintings by the masters hanging from both walls as well as display cases housing rare artifacts and old books. I knew Zogg was a collector, but I never imagined the depth of his collections.

I finally came to the first door on the left and saw on the door: Mr. Zogg—Private. I knocked on the door and heard a male voice with a strong Boston accent. "Come in."

I opened the door and saw Lothar Zogg sitting at a huge desk. He looked exactly like his pictures. He was pale, balding, thin, and wore glasses. He was just finishing up a phone conversation and slammed the phone down on its stand. He looked up and saw me enter. Zogg, still looking a little frazzled, stood and extended his hand and I accepted it. He forced a smile and, after we shook, sat back down.

"Pleasure to meet you, Mr. Rixey. Can I get you something to drink?"

"A coffee with plenty of cream and sugar, please."

Zogg pressed a buzzer and relayed my order to someone. He sat back in his chair and relaxed. A thin young woman with a dour look on her face entered the office and placed the tray with my coffee on the desk. She was quickly gone.

I picked up the coffee. "Now perhaps you can tell me what was so urgent and so secret you were unable to discuss it over the phone?"

As I talked, I glanced around the office. It was beautiful. Nice oak walls, Zogg's desk, two chairs in front of the desk. The walls were covered with shelves containing books and a table behind Zogg with three computers on it. There were a couple of windows on the left that I am sure offered a panoramic view of Manhattan.

"Very good, Mr. Rixey. I am glad to see you are a man who does not want to waste time on small talk. You are from what I have been told a man of action."

"Who told you about me?"

Zogg smiled. "I am not at liberty to reveal who told me. Shall we say, you seemed like the perfect person for this assignment. I know you are familiar with the world of numismatics."

"Yes. I have a nice collection. I am sure nothing like what you have amassed. Now if we can get to the reason for this meeting, I have a flight back to St. Louis leaving in four hours."

Zogg waved his hand. "Nonsense. I own a dozen jets and I will see you are flown back home." He pressed a button. I saw the shelving holding the books shudder and then slowly begin to move to reveal a blue-glass wall, the outside layer of a hidden room. There was also a door located in the center of the room and a number pad next to the door.

He reached over the desk and handed me a piece of paper.

I looked over the list. It was impressive. 1804 Silver Dollar, 1933 Double Eagle, 1913 Liberty Head Nickel, 1804 Eagle, and a 1794 Silver Dollar. I nodded as I handed him back the list. "Very impressive. Rough guess is twenty-five to thirty million?"

"Closer to thirty-three million, a decent guess nonetheless," Zogg conceded.

I nodded. "I'm guessing this list is why you called me?"

"Yes. I discovered the coins were gone yesterday. I contacted you the day I discovered the coins were missing."

I shook my head. "I can't help you. I don't get involved in ongoing police investigations."

I heard the panic in Zogg's voice. "It's not ongoing. I never reported it."

I grimaced. "And now you're going to tell me why you didn't report a thirty-three-million-dollar theft?"

"Mr. Rixey, the public humiliation would be too much for me to bear. I really don't want the police prowling through my offices, pawing and gaping at my precious objects. And, my God, the press reports. People would be laughing at me. This is a potential disaster. I'm not worried about the value of the coins, but I have developed a strong sentimental attachment far exceeding their value. I'm sure you understand as a fellow collector?"

I pulled a cigar from my pocket humidor. When I saw Zogg's

obvious look of disapproval, I refrained from lighting it. "Yes, I do. Very understandable, Mr. Zogg. You did have the coins insured?"

"Yes. The money isn't the issue. I want my coins back. I haven't even contacted the insurance company for fear of the publicity."

I played with the cigar as I thought. "Let me guess, the coins were located in the same place as your other treasures, yet the coins were the only thing missing?" I pointed to the room. "The other items in the room would be impossible to sell in a public auction or to a legitimate collector? Those are high-profile items that would attract a lot of attention?"

Zogg said eagerly. "Yes. I have one of the finest book collections in the world housed in the room. For example, I have Shakespeare's First Folio and a complete Gutenberg Bible as an example. My most valuable book is Leonardo da Vinci's Codex Leicester. My book collection has been estimated at between three hundred to five hundred million dollars. I also have other rare coins in there. Naturally, nothing on the scale of the coins that were taken. The books were kept in a special section, temperature controlled and requiring a key to enter."

I nodded as I walked around his office. "What kind of security do you have here, after hours?"

Zogg gulped. "Why, nothing special. I mean, I am on the tenth floor. My security team patrols the building after hours. They check every office in the building, including mine."

I frowned. "So nothing on the windows or any type of electronic alarm system or any kind of video surveillance?"

Zogg shook his head.

I pointed to the windows. "Do those open?"

"Yes. They only open from the inside."

I walked over to the windows and tested them. One of them was loose. I turned to Zogg. "Somehow someone was able to force this window out of its framing and make their way in." I looked out the window. The wall seemed to be totally sheer. I didn't see any hand holds. I thought to myself, you would have to be a human fly to get in this office. I quickly analyzed. "The people who stole your coins were very sophisticated, very professional, and I suspect very high tech. I also suspect this was an inside job. It was someone who was able to access the schedule of your security patrols. You did say security checks your office as part of its regular rounds?"

"Yes, I did. Why do you say very professional?"

"They knew exactly what they were here to take and how to make the most efficient use of their time. They were stealing to fulfill a contract. I'm sure you have cameras all over the place. I am also certain the robbers will not show up on any of the videos. They knew where and where not to go. They wouldn't have made an exit the same way they made their entrance. I need to check one more thing." I walked to the door of the blue-glassed room and knelt down to get a good view of the pad.

"This is state of the art for these types of devices," Zogg said proudly.

"Straight numeric pad? I would have been in here in about sixty seconds with the right equipment. It's clear to me the right equipment was used." I turned to him. "I'm going to need a list, pictures, and background information on all your security employees. I will also require their Social Security numbers and current addresses if those aren't currently in their file. Can you run the information from here? I would prefer no one other than you or I knew about it. I also have some security recommendations for you to follow."

"The company who installed it told me there were over one million permutations of the combination. It would take days or even weeks to figure out the code."

I nodded. "Companies will tell you anything to get you to buy their products." I pulled a small leather case from my jacket pocket. I opened the case and took out what looked like a tiny computer. I attached the machine to the keypad and turned it on. The seven-number code appeared within thirty seconds. I removed the device, put in back in its case and back in my pocket. I punched in the code and the door swung open.

I heard a gasp followed by some words you would not hear on a Sunday in church coming from Zogg. You didn't have to be a master detective like I am to figure out he was pretty unhappy.

"Sorry, I was wrong, it was thirty seconds." I entered the room and saw one of the finest coin collections I ever laid eyes on. It put the collection at the Smithsonian Institute to shame, even missing the five valuable coins. I saw the section for the rare books. I took out my lockpick kit. After about ten minutes of struggling, I finally gave up. *A very impressive lock,* I thought. I turned to Zogg. "I can normally pick any lock in under a minute, this lock is excellent."

Zogg finally smiled.

While Zogg was gathering the information I requested, I began to work out what may have happened. I didn't like what I was coming up with. I was becoming bothered by the similarities between the stealing of the Fabergé egg I had recovered and the coin theft. Both cases involved similar amounts of money being stolen. Also, in both cases, the thieves left behind valuable items and took only a specific item or in the case of the coin robbery, items. This showed me the group or groups were extremely disciplined. Whoever did these crimes, and I deduced both offenses were committed by the same group, were top flight and, if they were working with the North Koreans, very dangerous.

I wrote an extensive list of my recommendations for changes in his office and building security. He gratefully accepted them.

Mr. Zogg was a man of his word. He was kind enough to fly me home in one of his jets. I left his office with a signed contract and a thick sheaf of printouts detailing every member of his security force.

Chapter Eight

"We are all born ignorant but must work hard to remain stupid."
Benjamin Franklin.

I spent the night in St. Louis and drove back to Carbondale the following morning. I looked up some friends and enjoyed dinner and drinks with them. I suppose I might have driven back the same day. Flying usually takes a lot out of me. It was a good chance to get caught up with old friends. All of our lives had changed for the better since college. This trip was no different. Nothing could be done with the employee files Zogg gave me until I made it back to the office, so I put the time I was going to be spending in St. Louis to its best possible use.

The trip back home was pretty uneventful, just the way I liked it. I rolled into the office about seven thirty A.M. and was not surprised to see Ms. Nickels beat me in. I pulled around the back and parked my SUV. Just out of curiosity, I put my hand on Ms. Nickels' car. The engine was stone cold. I gathered the employee records and headed into the office. I unlocked the door, heard the familiar tinkle of the bell, and saw Ms.

Nickels come out of her office.

"Good morning, Mr. Rixey. How was your trip?" she said with a smile.

"We have a new client. Lothar Zogg."

"I've read a few stories about him in the papers. There is some talk about him running for President. What does the case involve?"

I shifted the sheaf of papers from one hand to another. "It's another high-end burglary, similar to the Hen's Egg. Same MO and everything. They took certain items, in this case, valuable coins, and left behind other valuable things." I shrugged. I held out the sheaf of papers. "I have some work for you to do." I saw the smile leave her face. Ms. Nickels has been in the office for a long time, I think she knew what was coming.

I held out the bundle. "These are the files of the seventy employees who currently work on Zogg's security team and ten employees who once worked security, no longer working for Zogg. These files go back ten years…" I looked helplessly at her. "You know what to look for, I know. I really need your help on this."

"Credit reports, bank accounts, real estate holdings, and vehicle purchases? Also, I am guessing you want to check their immediate families?"

I nodded. "Spouses, their children, their parents, and any siblings. Thanks. I'll be in my office."

"Oh, yes, before I get on this, Mr. Rixey, your package from Mr. Stuart is sitting on your desk."

I entered my office and as I always did when I arrived at the office and when I was gone for a while, I swept it, trying to locate electronic devices. Finding none, I sat down at my desk.

Inside the box, I saw a wire transfer to the Bishop Agency Account for one hundred and fifty thousand dollars and ten bundles that according to the wrappers, each contained five thousand dollars. Under the last stack of bills, I saw a white envelope taped to the bottom of the box. I opened it and an orange locker key fell into my hand. I dialed the combination to my safe, heard the tumblers click, then inserted a key into the lock and the safe door swung open. It might seem like I was being too cautious, perhaps even a bit paranoid. In my line of work, a little paranoia is a good thing. It keeps you sharp and keeps you on your toes. After placing the money and the locker key inside, I closed the door, spun the wheel, and double-locked the safe with my key.

I grabbed a Diet Coke from the office fridge, lit a cigarette, and then sat down to plan the rest of my day. I knew the files I requested from Kaplan would be here in a matter of hours. My phone rang and I stole a glance at the caller ID. To my surprise, it was Willard taking a break from his globe-trotting.

"Sending you my regards from Cairo, kid," the familiar and husky voice of Willard Bishop boomed over the phone.

"Great to hear from you, Willard. You tired of being a world traveler yet?"

A hearty laugh came over the phone. "Not a chance, kid. I am having too much fun to come back just yet. How are things going with the Agency? I'm sure you are carrying on with the good reputation I left it with."

"I met an old friend of yours while I was on assignment in Hong Kong. His name is Joseph Chen. He sends his regards. He helped get me out of a jam I couldn't avoid."

"He is a good man. You realized he was MSS? If you see or hear from him again, give him my best."

"Yeah, I strongly suspected he was. He had to be as he was able to get me out of Hong Kong without having to go through customs."

"Just be careful in your dealings with him. We have helped each other in the past, but remember he is a Red."

"Gotcha. He recommended me for a job and the client visited and retained me. Believe it or not, I'm working with the Feds again. You ever heard of a group called the Office of Archive Retrieval? I know I hadn't heard of them until we met. It seemed like Morgan was familiar with them. I guess the fact she was shouldn't have surprised me."

Willard chuckled. "You're right, she is on top of most things in the intel business. They really need to work on getting some good field agents. They are all eggheads and analysts."

"Yeah, well that's what the client, Andrew Stuart, said. He is worried about some leaks in the government concerning an item he is trying to get back. So, he hired me. I was able to get Morgan temporarily assigned to OAR and she will be working with me on this case."

I heard his smile over the phone. "Good. You two work well together. I'm sure you will be able to handle any problems that will come your way."

"I also was recently retained by Lothar Zogg. Seems like someone broke into his office and took his five most valuable coins. Worth was about thirty-three million dollars."

I heard a groan. "Not one of my favorite people. I guess his money spends. I know you know enough not to get into an active police investigation. Why didn't he report it?"

"He didn't want any publicity associated with the robbery, and he didn't want the cops roaming around in his building. I gave him some security suggestions and got a list of his current and former security employees. I am pretty sure it was an inside job. Ms. Nickels is running the employees through almost every database there is. I'm betting whoever was their inside man did something stupid with the money."

"Good theory."

"You know why I was in Hong Kong."

"You were working on a recovery for a client. I heard the recovery went quite well."

"Yeah, thanks. This crime is identical to the Hen's Egg caper. The place is broken into; a particular item is taken and other precious items are left untouched. In both cases, a high level of technical ability was shown. These people are terrific. There was no trace of them ever seen on the office cameras and they entered through a tenth-floor window."

"Be careful, Miller. It sounds like the North Koreans are involved in both robberies. They are either running a gang or having their agents from the Reconnaissance General Bureau (RGB) pulling off these heists. They are fanatical in their loyalty to their country and their leader. If bad news were a term, you would see a picture of their agents. This sounds like the type of operation they would be capable of."

"RGB? I never heard of them."

Willard further explained. "They are responsible for overseas clandestine operations. They have six bureaus. They are divided into operations, recon, technology, cyber, overseas intelligence, inter-Korean talks, and service support."

I inwardly groaned. First Nazis and now North Korean secret agents. I began to wonder how Willard survived as long as he did. It seemed like my job was doing its best to try to kill me. I was not about to allow my premature death.

"I got some things to do, so I better sign off now. Good hearing from you. I'll say hi to Morgan for you."

"Good talking to you, Miller. You should have my number on your caller ID. Don't hesitate to call me if you need me."

"Thanks, Willard. I feel better." I clicked off just in time to hear the office intercom buzzer.

"Mr. Rixey, I have an Ian Thomas Hardin out here. He claims he is from the NSA and his cred pack seems to be legitimate."

I wondered what the good people at NSA wanted with me. "Thank you, Ms. Nickels, please send him in." I hit the record button on the office recording device. I was ready for whatever was going to happen, at least I hoped I was.

The door burst open and standing in front of me was a tall and wiry-looking character sporting wire-rim glasses and a beard. He was dressed in a cheap sports coat and a button-down shirt. His outfit looked like it may have seen better days, going by the fraying cuffs. He completed his look with a pair of well-worn corduroys. The sports coat did little to hide the bulge under his arm. He flashed his cred pack at me, guessing I would be impressed, then put in in his pants pocket. He flopped down in a chair in front of my desk.

"I'd offer you a cigar or a drink. You aren't going to be around for very long," I growled.

"What does your comment mean?" Hardin asked angrily.

"You're in Intelligence, try to be intelligent."

I was in no mood for what I knew was going to be more government bullshit.

He waved away my comment. "Listen, Mr. Rixey, I know all about you. It seems as of late, every time you are overseas, an international incident occurs." He held up his hand and ticked off on his fingers. "Argentina, Hong Kong, and God knows where else. You are a walking disaster and a threat to national security."

I pulled a cigarette out of a pack and lit it.

Hardin waved his hand and began coughing. "Would you mind not smoking?"

"As a matter of fact, I would. My office, I do what I want. I looked at my watch, now if you are finished, I am busy."

Hardin stood up. "We know about your newest client, Lothar Zogg. I strongly advise you to drop the case, in the interest of national security. There can be consequences if you don't."

The phone began to ring. I knew Ms. Nickels was busy doing something important. I pressed a button sending the phone call straight to voice mail.

I placed my cigarette in an ashtray. "Look, you go ahead and do what you want. You aren't the first government goon to try to screw with me and I am sure you won't be the last. The last guy got nothing and I got a good laugh. You are heading for the same."

Hardin's face turned purple. "We will see."

"And for God's sake, learn how to dress. You look like a street bum."

Hardin left my office, slamming the door on the way out. It was all I could do to restrain myself from laughing until he left the office. I shut off the recording device and sat back down, shaking my head. I called Bobby Layne. He seemed to be the person I knew who was the most influential with the government higher-ups. I told him about my meeting with Hardin, and he assured me the problem would be taken care of. I clicked off and went back to work.

A few hours later, I heard a knock on the door.

"Come."

The usually reserved Ms. Nickels entered holding a couple of sheets of paper, her face flushed with success. "Mr. Rixey, I know who the inside man was in the Zogg robbery." She handed me the sheets. "I will finish my search. I'll be shocked if this guy isn't the insider."

Chapter Nine

"I used to advertise my loyalty and I don't believe there is a single person I loved that I didn't eventually betray." Albert Camus.

I quickly flipped through the papers Ms. Nickels gave me. "Hartley M. Baldwin, single, checking account balance three hundred and fifty dollars, three maxed-out credit cards totaling roughly sixty thousand dollars. Now, all the cards are paid off and he has a healthy balance in his checking account of thirty thousand dollars." I shook my head as I read on. "It gets even better. Until one month ago, the condo was in foreclosure, now up to date and, finally, was in default on roughly fifty thousand dollars student loans, now paid off." I drummed my fingers on my desk. "Pretty amazing on a salary of seventy-five thousand a year. Either this guy is the insider or he got an inheritance." I smiled. "This guy needs a course in hiding bribes. Sheesh, he did everything wrong he could have."

"I checked local court records, sir. Nothing indicates his name being mentioned in any probate court anywhere, and I checked back on his family and no recent deaths. Based on my level of analysis, this is the guy," Ms. Nickels said triumphantly.

"Great work, Ms. Nickels. Please get Mr. Zogg on the phone. He's going to want to know about his employee, Mr. Baldwin. He most certainly is going to want me to talk to him. I'm going to be out of town. Do you have a problem waiting for Kaplan? I'm not going to be able to wait around for their delivery."

Ms. Nickels smiled. "Not at all, Mr. Rixey, and I will get Mr. Zogg on the phone and transfer the call to you."

I sat at my desk waiting for the call and grabbed the receiver as soon as the phone rang.

"Rixey, did you discover anything?"

"Mr. Zogg, I have the information you wanted. The suspect's name is Hartley M. Baldwin. We looked through his credit history and discovered he recently paid off his credit cards, his student loans, got his condo payments up to date, and has a balance of about thirty thousand dollars in a checking account where his average balance was about five hundred. He didn't go out and buy flashy things. He used his money to settle his debts. He squared some high-balance credit cards, got his condo out of foreclosure, and paid off his student loans. It's almost like he wanted to be caught.

"Any chance he got the money through an inheritance?"

"No. We checked into the possibility and were unable to locate him in any probate court records and when we looked at his family, no recent deaths. He was very sloppy in the way he used his money. I'm afraid he may be at some risk when his employers discover this. If you can get a plane to the airport in Marion, I can be back in New York pretty quickly. What I recommend you do is put a tail on him immediately. Don't go through normal channels when assigning his tail. Get me a letter from your attorney saying I am working for him. I am not licensed in New York. Also, get me a conceal-carry permit. I will be bringing a pistol with me. Can you arrange a license for me?"

"Yes, not a problem. The letter and permit will be ready when you get here. I can have a plane in Marion, Illinois in an hour. Can you make it by then?"

"Yeah. No problem. You sure you don't want the Feds or the local police involved in this? I'd recommend it."

"No, Mr. Rixey, you have done a great job so far. I'm staying with you."

There wasn't much to pack. I did not plan to stay the night. I checked my pistol in my shoulder holster and took it out to screw on the suppressor, grabbed a few cigars from the humidor, took a pack of cigarettes from my desk, and a couple of magazines for my pistol. I put on my jacket and hat, and, after telling Ms. Nickels my plans, I was off.

I was greeted at LaGuardia by the head of Zogg's security team, Christopher Manny. Manny was a pretty big guy. He did not look like someone I would like to mess with. He was dressed in business casual to make himself blend in better. He was friendly enough and told me he was originally from Illinois.

After we exchanged greetings and handshakes, I asked Manny for an update.

"We have been watching Baldwin's apartment since we got your call. I have my best man tailing him. He called in sick with the flu then left his apartment and went to the gym. He didn't stay long. Makes me wonder if he kept a place where he would stash his valuables in the gym. Anyway, he is back now."

I nodded and chuckled. "There is a lot of the twenty-four-minute flu going around. I think he is planning on taking off."

"Yeah, we thought so, then he went back to his condo and hasn't left since. One unusual thing. He left for the gym empty-handed and came back with a gym bag. Seems like you would take a gym bag both ways, right?"

"Does seem odd. Maybe he was using a gym locker to hold some things he wouldn't want to be discovered that he would need fast access to. Is the gym open 24/7?"

"It sure is."

The drive to Baldwin's condo didn't take very long. It was located in a twenty-story building in Manhattan. This was the high-rent district to be sure. We were able to find a parking spot in front of the building. When we went inside, we were greeted by an attendant who was seated at a desk. The attendant was an older balding man dressed in a typical doorman's uniform with a name tag identifying him as D. Jones.

"How may I help you?" came the rasping voice.

"We're here to see Mr. Baldwin," Manny replied.

The doorman started to pick up the phone and Manny stopped him. Manny shook his head and wagged his finger.

"We'd like to make it a surprise. I brought one of his old college friends who's in town," Manny said pointing at me. Then I saw Manny slip the doorman a bill. The doorman broke into a big grin and the bill vanished right before my eyes. It must have been magic.

"Very good, sir," Jones said as he picked up the bill and stuffed it in his pocket. "Have a nice visit." He pointed us toward the elevator banks and, just as we left, another person entered the building.

We walked into the elevator and pressed fifteen. I pulled out my pistol, pulled the slide, and held it by my side. Manny did likewise. We arrived at fifteen quickly and our presence was announced by a ding as the door opened. We stepped into the hall and saw a man lying on the floor.

"You know him?" I asked.

"Crap. Yes. He's the man I assigned to watch Baldwin." Manny bent over the prostrate body and felt for a pulse. He looked relieved. "Still alive."

I looked up and down the hall and saw nothing. "What's Baldwin's number?"

"1501."

"You wake up sleeping beauty and I'll go check on Baldwin."

Manny nodded.

I made it down to the end of the corridor and saw 1501 on a closed door. I tried the handle but it was locked. I put my ear to the door and heard the television playing. By then Manny got the other man up and I saw Manny head toward me and the other man disappeared into the elevator. I shrugged my shoulders as if asking what we should do next. He shrugged back. I pulled out my lockpick kit. The door unlocked in about ten seconds. *Why bother with locks?* I asked myself. I slowly pushed the door open and I took a peek through the door. I saw a man lying face down on the floor with a puddle of blood forming around his head. I heard the sounds of someone moving around in the condo.

I slowly opened the door wider and Manny and I snuck into the room. We couldn't see anyone, but we did hear the sounds of someone ransacking the place. The living room looked like it had been thoroughly tossed. The furniture in the living room was slashed and turned over. Whoever was searching this place was not worried about people finding his handiwork. Suddenly, an Asian male came out of one of the rooms. I aimed my weapon at him. He reached for his but was too slow. I fired two rounds at him, both struck him in the chest and he went down. His body jerked for a moment then went still. I quickly searched his body. I found a wallet, a card key, and a few hundred dollars in cash. Everything went into my pocket. On an impulse, I checked his clothing, no labels. I pulled out my phone and snapped a picture of him.

I stood up and looked at Manny. "Now what? I mean we should just relock the door and leave. I am concerned about the doorman remembering us."

Manny stood up from searching Baldwin's body. He jiggled a safety deposit box key on a chain. He wore a strange smile on his face. "Don't worry about it. I sent the guy I revived downstairs to collect the tape of our visit. The doorman has a son in college and is being informed his son will be receiving an internship with the Zogg Corporation this summer and the doorman will be starting his new job at Zogg in a few weeks. We just need to go out the back way. After we got your call, we researched what we were able to find about the setup at the condo."

I nodded. "I'm impressed. When you have as much money as Zogg, you can make things happen. I still want to try to find the gym bag. He had the time to hide it and the assassin hadn't been here long enough to find it. I guess I interrupted his search."

Manny smiled again. "Exactly. Let's finish tossing this place and then get the hell out of here. We caught a break. His was the only occupied condo on this floor. We won't have to worry about another resident seeing us leaving the condo."

I nodded. "One less problem to deal with. Good. I didn't want to be answering questions about two bodies and I'm sure you didn't either."

Manny smiled again. "Exactly. Let's finish searching this place and then get the hell out of here. I don't know what the guy was looking for, but..."

I wasn't too thrilled about staying in the condo any longer than needed. I realized we would never get a second chance to search this place. On a hunch, I went to his bedroom. I looked under the bed and there was the gym bag. It was stuffed with banded hundred dollars bills. I quickly counted and came up with fifty thousand dollars. I handed the bag to Manny.

"This money's really your boss'."

Manny replied, "Yes, it is. I'll see he gets it."

We finished the search, not sure what we were looking for and, in fact, never found anything, which seemed to be very promising, other than what we discovered on the bodies. We left by heading down the stairwell and going out an unmonitored back door. We circled around the building and made it back to Manny's vehicle and drove directly to the airport. I handed over the results of my body search of the assassin to Manny. I knew when I got back to Carbondale and ran the picture I took of him through a vast face-recognition database I had access to his identity would no longer be secret. Manny promised to send me the results of what was found in the safety deposit box as well as any intelligence we gathered from the two bodies.

Zogg's jet was waiting for me when we arrived at the airport. Four hours later, I was back in Marion.

Chapter Ten

"The terrorist uses surprise and stealth, and the only way to defeat that is by having accurate and timely intelligence." Bill Nelson.

I dialed the office as soon as I got back in my SUV.

"Hello, Mr. Rixey. I trust everything went well in New York City?"

"Yes, it did, Ms. Nickels. I should be in the office in thirty to forty-five minutes depending on traffic." I looked at my watch. "You don't mind waiting until I get back?"

"Not at all, sir. By the way, while you were gone, Kaplan stopped by with the research you requested. They said they placed your new codeword in the usual spot. Per our standard procedure with Kaplan, when you are out of the office, I allowed them to enter and place the files on your desk. I already wired them their fee."

"Outstanding. Any other calls come in?"

"Two calls. One was for some divorce work and the other was from one of your regular law firms concerning possible fraud in a worker's comp case. They have already been referred to the usual detective agencies. I somehow didn't think you would have any time soon to get to them."

"Very good. I'll see you when I see you." I clicked off. Despite the usual heavy construction on Route 13, the traffic flowed well and the trip was uneventful.

Twenty minutes later, I pulled into the office parking lot and parked my SUV next to Ms. Nickels' vehicle. I hopped out and bounded into the office. I opened the door, heard the traditional bell ringing, announcing my presence.

Ms. Nickels looked up. "Glad to see you back in one piece, Mr. Rixey. Now, if you don't need me anymore, I am meeting my daughter and my granddaughter for dinner."

I fished out the few hundred dollars I'd taken off the man who murdered Baldwin. It wasn't going to do him any good, so I handed the money to her with a smile. "Make dinner on me."

"Why, thank you, Mr. Rixey. You have a full pot of coffee waiting for you in your office. I'll lock up and set the alarms. It looks like you have some reading to do." She set the alarm and locked the door.

I went to my office and saw the files sitting on my desk. I poured a cup of coffee and opened up my humidor. I saw my new code word covering my cigars and after memorizing it, destroyed the piece of paper. With that finished, I helped myself to one of my cigars and, after cutting the end, roasting the end, and lighting it, I blew out a big cloud of smoke. I reached into my pocket and removed my phone. I went to the photos section and emailed myself a copy of the picture of the dead man I took in Baldwin's apartment. Once I got my email, I downloaded it to my computer, called up the facial recognition program, inserted the picture, and began running it. A bell would ring when it hit a possible match of any value. I then turned on my outside cameras. It was another safety precaution I installed after an assassin paid me a visit during my hunt for Caesar's Medallion. I don't like tempting fate.

The first file I picked up was labeled Kendall, Eve. As I suspected, nothing too exciting in it. The only thing of any potential interest was she did a postdoc appointment in Venice for a year. She indeed went to the right schools. She had a B.A. Magna Cum Laude in History from Columbia then got her M.A. and Ph.D. from Georgetown in Medieval History. She had authored a dozen books and articles about the Polos. She was hired at Minnesota State and gradually worked her way up the food chain. I flipped her folder aside.

The next file I selected was labeled Stuart, Andrew. His folder was almost as dull as Kendall's. He had received a B.S and M.S. in Archive Studies from Georgetown. Stuart had worked at the Smithsonian for a few years before being recruited to OAR. His current position was Deputy Director. He had worked at OAR since the inception of the group. I tossed his file on top of Kendall's. I frowned. No new information to be gained from his or Kendall's folders.

So far, everything was as it seemed. Kendall was a professor and Stuart really worked for OAR. I was hoping I would find some information that would justify the money I spent on this research.

I picked up the folder labeled Ordo Templi Orientis (OTO). Stuart had already covered most of what was in the file except for some key items. The folder included a very rare picture of the usually camera-shy Eldor Jamieson Crypt. Crypt was Chairman of the Board of OTO. According to his dossier, he stood six foot seven, weighed three hundred pounds, had jet black hair, wore glasses, and was olive-skinned. He also only dressed in a white suit, black shirt, and red tie. He would be hard to miss in any size crowd. I knew he would be wearing a mask to blend in with the crowd celebrating the Day of the Dead. It wouldn't matter. His body structure would easily stand out even in a large crowd, mask or no.

Stuart's group listed four power surges in Mexico City in the past four years. According to the file, OTO had made a habit of meeting in Mexico City annually for the past fifty years. It was always on the same day, November 2, All Souls Day in America and Día de Muertos (Day of the Dead) in Mexico. The surges all occurred on November 2 and at the same location each year. I guessed the mysticism of the day, combined with the vast crowds present, appealed to the covert nature of the group. They would never be noticed.

The final fact was apparently unknown to Stuart or perhaps he didn't think it was important enough to mention, the members of the board of OTO all wore unique rings to identify themselves to each other. The ring showed a dragon wrapped around Earth. I removed the picture of Crypt, along with a picture of the dragon ring, and then tossed the OTO file on top of the other files. Just for the information about OTO's leader and the confirmation of their yearly meeting in Mexico City on the Day of the Dead, the money I paid Kaplan was well worth it.

The file on the *Dae Song* made for interesting reading. It flew the flag of Liberia. If it flew the North Korean flag, it would have been excluded from many ports. For Liberia, the Flags of Convenience program they ran accounted for roughly seventy percent of their government's funding. According to the ship's papers, the company who owned the *Dae Song*, Eastern Shipping Ltd., was headquartered in the capital city of Liberia, Monrovia. My report said the *Dae Song* was, in reality, a spy ship, patterned after the so-called Russian trawlers. I didn't see any evidence of it being a spy ship while I had been aboard. Then again, I wasn't aboard the ship to carefully examine, merely to recover what my client lost and get the hell out of there. I turned to the section discussing the captain of the ship.

The skipper of the *Dae Song* was a Korean named Pong Jon-Ho. My intelligence listed him as a Colonel in the RGB. I removed his picture from the file and studied it. It had been a moonless night when I first saw him, but I had little doubt he was the man I saw on the ship who I took to be the captain. At a minimum, what I read so far gave me a pretty strong link of North Korean involvement in the Hen's Egg heist. It was something I already suspected. Now it looked as if some very solid proof existed.

I reviewed the plans for the building. The first two floors consisted of small offices and storage rooms. Hardly the place for a meeting of what I was guessing would be at least ten people. I wasn't sure how many people would be on the OTO board. I was sure they wouldn't want to meet in a small office. Plus, they would want to have some space to operate the Chalice. On the third floor, I found a room labeled 'library and conference room.' The library would be my target. I'd make sure to slip a few listening devices in the place on November 1. I wanted to give the OTO as little time as possible to locate them.

The list from Kaplan about the power surges and the timeline continuum breaks was more extensive than the list Stuart showed me from OAR. Use of the device had become more frequent in recent days. Something big was brewing. Exactly what was brewing? Your guess is as good as mine.

I put the pictures I pulled into an envelope. I then put the *Dae Song* file, the plans for the building in Mexico City, the information dealing with the power surges, and the envelope with the pictures back in my safe. I shredded the other files as they were no longer needed. I sat back thinking about what I had read. Just then, the facial recognition program beeped. The beep meant the program found a match of more than ninety percent probability. It hit a match to the picture I fed to it. I looked over at the computer screen. The reading of 99.7 meant I found my man. His name was Jung Chan Wan. I pressed another button and his file appeared. His nationality was North Korean. Wan worked for RGB and specialized in black-bag jobs. He held the rank of major. Seemed like a perfect choice for leading both the robbery of my client and the robbery of Zogg. I was a little confused as to why he didn't send an underling to murder Baldwin and to search his place. I guess he got careless. In his line of work as well as mine, it can be a fatal character flaw.

I was even more confused as to how he even got into the country. He was wanted for crimes in a half-dozen countries, was on the no-fly list in the U.S. and was also on our terrorist watch list. Someone with some influence had cleared the way for him to enter the country. Maybe Stuart was right about the leaks in the government. I already knew the crimes were connected. To what end? I thought of two possibilities. First, with all of the sanctions against North Korea, it was impossible to import many things. Perhaps they were doing these high-end robberies to bring hard currency into their country? A hard currency like U.S. Dollars can overcome any types of sanctions. Our country never seems to learn the lesson. It was a lesson we should have learned from Iraq.

I sat back down at my computer and did a search for recent and unsolved large robberies. A regular crime wave had been occurring the past few weeks: Ten burglaries of a similar nature to what happened to my Hen's Egg client and Zogg. The thefts followed the same MO as the two I was aware of. Break-in at a super-secure site and only certain items taken, leaving valuable items behind in every case. I added up the estimations of what was taken, and it came to almost half a billion dollars.

I heard the roll of thunder, the crack of lightning, and a staccato of rain against the windows as I sat at my desk contemplating what I learned. I then heard a thud at my front door. I looked up at the monitor and saw a body huddled against the door as if it was trying to get protection from the storm. I couldn't make the figure out. The occasional lightning flashing did little to help me identify who was in my doorway.

This will never do, I thought.

I stood up and pulled a suppressor from a desk drawer and screwed it into the barrel of my pistol. I then pulled the slide back, slamming a cartridge into the chamber. I grabbed my hat and coat, put them on and was ready to leave. I carried my pistol by my side, but by the time I made it to the outer office, the figure was gone from the door. I went back into my office and changed the monitor setting to up and down the street. Still no figure. I shrugged and headed to the door.

I stepped into the storm. The rain was really pouring. I saw the streets beginning to flood. They claim these storms of this severity are one-hundred-year storms, meaning they only occur every one hundred years. I would say once a year storms was closer to the truth. The city needed an excuse for their failure to maintain its sewer system, and the public continued to buy the one-hundred-year storm line.

I walked toward my SUV. I would have preferred to run. I still had no idea where the figure I saw lurking at my office door was. Slow and steady was the order of the day. I would have hated to be shot because I was not paying attention to my surroundings. A little rain never hurt anyone, but knives and bullets sure can. I still hadn't seen anyone as I headed toward my SUV, then it happened. I heard a gunshot followed by a loud scream of agony. I raised my Glock and sprinted toward the direction of the scream.

Chapter Eleven

"Tough times don't last, tough people do, remember?" Gregory Peck.

I saw a small, thin, and I was pretty sure, male character sprinting from my SUV. As much as I wanted to chase him, I knew there wasn't a chance I'd be able to catch him. Besides, I didn't want to abandon the person who laid by my SUV bleeding and moaning. I knelt down and instantly realized the person lying there, it was my old acquaintance, Banner. Banner was a street person who served our country in the Army. He never recovered from his tour in Afghanistan. He was a victim of PTSD and his problems associated with the condition made his reintegration into society difficult. To help him out, I gave him some jobs to do around the office. He looked like he was bleeding badly and I had no way to stop it.

"Hang on, Banner."

He nodded weakly.

The rain continued to pour harder. I was afraid to move him out of the rain for fear of causing more damage.

I pulled my phone and dialed 911.

"This is 911. Please state your emergency."

"I have a gunshot wound victim. Do you need the address?"

"No, sir. We are locked on to your location."

"I'm in the parking lot behind the Bishop Agency."

"What is the victim's condition?"

"He's bleeding a lot. He was shot in the arm."

"We have already sent an ambulance and a squad car to your location."

I heard the sirens blasting away in the distance. "I'll stay with the victim until they arrive." I clicked off.

"Oh, man, this really hurts," Banner moaned, his speech badly slurred.

"I know it hurts. I got help on the way. So, what were you doing around here on this type of night?'

He went on a coughing jag for a few seconds. "I needed a place to stay and I was walking around and when it began raining, I was sure you wouldn't mind if I took cover in your doorway." He coughed again. "Mr. Rixey, do you have a smoke on you?"

I nodded, pulled out a pack of cigarettes, lit one and placed it between his lips.

Rejuvenated by the smoke, he continued. "Anyway, I saw this guy go behind your building. I decided to follow him and I saw him messing around with your vehicle. It looked like he was trying to get it open. I yelled at him to stop, I even grabbed him by one of his hands and he shot me."

Hugh Richard Williams

I nodded. "Good job, Banner. I got your medicals on this, don't sweat it. I'll have someone bring you some clean clothes while you're at the hospital. Swing by here after you've checked out of the hospital, I'll make sure there is some cash waiting for you. Ms. Nickels will make a hotel reservation for you. I want you off the streets for a while. Anything else, Banner?"

He opened his left hand and I saw a ring in it. "I guess I pulled this off the guy. Might be a clue?"

I bent down and quickly pocketed the ring. The ambulance and the police just pulled into the parking lot. "Tell the cops everything you told me, just don't mention the ring. Got it?"

"Sure thing, Boss," Banner said with a laughing croak.

The EMTs were quickly out of the ambulance as were the two police officers. I pulled a business card out of my pocket and scribbled something on the back of it and then handed it to one of the EMTs. "Call this guy. He's my doctor and one of the best. Understand?"

The EMT I handed the card to nodded. "Sure thing, Mr. Rixey."

The other EMT examined Banner. "He got lucky, it's a through and through. He'll be fine. I'll call your doctor as soon as we get the victim in the ambulance."

I nodded my thanks.

Both EMTs lifted Banner, placed him on a gurney and wheeled him back to the ambulance. A couple of minutes later, with sirens blasting, the ambulance headed toward the Carbondale Hospital.

"Care to give a statement, Mr. Rixey?" asked one of the policemen.

79

I looked at one who asked me the question. He wore sergeant's stripes on his sleeves, looked to be middle-aged, and seemed like he was in pretty good shape. His nametag said Presley.

I pointed to an overhang to get us out the rain and they joined me as I walked there.

"Well, Sergeant, I really don't know too much. I heard a scream and when I got here, a guy was running away. I didn't bother to try to chase him as he was moving and I wanted to tend to Banner. He told me the guy was trying to break into my car. He yelled at him and grabbed him. The perp shot him." I shrugged. "I don't think either of us got a very good look at the suspect except he was short and thin."

Pressley nodded as he wrote.

Pressley handed me what he just wrote. "If there is nothing else, read it and sign it, please. Once you do, you can be on your way."

I did as he asked and a few minutes later, they were gone.

I wasn't going to be going home until I examined the ring Banner took from whoever tried to break into my SUV. Once I was seated at my desk, I pulled the ring out of my pocket.

I hefted the ring a couple of times. It was heavy for its size. As the ring was gold colored, it was more than likely it was real gold. In the center of the ring was a design with a crown and a cross. The crown looked like it was a ruby. Those two parts of the design gave the ring a Templar flair. The design was surrounded an inscription in Latin, '*In Hoc Signo Vinces.*' I logged onto the internet and found a Latin to English translation program and punched in what had been engraved on the ring. The translation came back: 'In this sign, you will conquer.' To make things even more confusing, on the right side of the ring, there was a Masonic symbol. On the left side of the ring, there were two words engraved: '*Miles Scientia.*' The translation was 'Soldier of Knowledge.' I looked at the inside band and made out the name of the ring owner. His name was Phillip Vandamm. Considering the quality of the ring, I would have been surprised if an item of such obvious value and quality didn't have someone's name engraved on it. I mean, when I got my college ring, I got it engraved and dollar-wise it was not even close to the value of this ring.

The storm's intensity increased. I heard a steady staccato from the rain as it pounded on the windows. I enjoyed the sounds in my quiet office. I set the ring on my desk. The coffee was still warm, so I poured myself a cup and lit a cigarette. I needed to do some heavy thinking and caffeine and nicotine always helped me think. It was one of my bad habits from college. I sat there contemplating what I had learned from the files I'd gotten from Kaplan, what I had learned from the new client, Zogg, and the ring Banner had found.

I heard the wind picking up outside. It was beginning to rattle the windows. I chuckled as I thought about the irony that Banner being shot put him in a warm and dry place tonight. Was it possible that the weird turn of events actually benefited him from being shot? I'd say yes. At a minimum, he would be off the streets for a while and would be living in a nice hotel until I figured out what to do with him. He also would be having one of his better paydays in quite some time from me.

All in all, not too shabby for him. He was allowed some good fortune. I heard the front door rattling, looked up at the monitor as I switched it back to the front door view, and saw nothing other than a solid sheet of rain.

I tried putting the ring on. It wouldn't get it over my knuckle. This wasn't too surprising given the fact I saw a small figure fleeing the scene of the crime. I took the ring off and placed it in my safe.

The phone rang. I looked at the number appearing on my caller ID. I knew it was from Joseph Chen. Right now, it was one of the few phone calls I would bother to answer. I picked up the phone. "The Bishop Agency, Miller Rixey speaking."

"This is Joseph Chen. I hate to bother you at this hour. Do you have a few minutes, Mr. Rixey? I have a matter of great importance to discuss with you."

"Mr. Chen. I always have time to talk to you. I realize if you are calling me, it's going to be very important."

Another huge explosion from the thunder rocked the building. When I looked at my monitor, the lightning was making it look like it was daylight. The lights flickered in my office and I was sure grateful I was smart enough to invest in an excellent power surge protector. I looked out my window and noticed the street lights were out. Mr. Chen began to speak.

Chapter Twelve

"Once you eliminate the impossible, whatever remains, no matter how improbable, must be the truth." Said by Sherlock Holmes in The Sign of the Four *by Sir Arthur Conan Doyle.*

"I have a problem needing an unofficial solution. I am hoping you will be able to help me. I would consider this a personal favor if you are able to help."

"Mr. Chen, I would be glad to help you if I can. What's your problem?"

"A few days ago, a major robbery occurred in Hong Kong. Two paintings worth a combined value of close to five hundred million dollars were stolen from one of our museums. They were *The Card Players* by Paul Cézanne and *Number 17A* by Jackson Pollock. The unusual thing about the robbery was they left behind another two hundred million dollars of paintings."

"Most unusual," I agreed. "Wouldn't this be a matter better suited for your police department? I do not get involved in ongoing police investigations. How is it this crime never made it to the news?"

I began attempting to calculate what my recovery fee would be from this case. Fifty million was a nice number.

I heard a chuckle over the phone. "I'm sure you realize we can control the media much easier than it's controlled in your country. For political reasons, there can be no official or unofficial government agencies. It's unfortunate, it is the political reality. We cannot officially rebuke North Korea. To do so would be counter-revolutionary and we cannot permit such a thing to happen."

"I understand completely, Mr. Chen. Any idea where the paintings are or where they are being hidden? I mean if it's Hong Kong, not much I can do to help."

"We already recovered the paintings. The problem we have is during the robbery a son of a prominent Party member was killed. We can't allow this particular insult to go unrevenged."

I grimaced as I saw my finder's fee heading south.

"Without breaking any client confidences, I can tell you there have been a dozen or so robberies following the same modus operandi in the United States. They are what I label high-line robberies. It looks like these robberies are being committed to fulfilling specific requests for items. I don't know how many have occurred overseas. When you say political reasons, you're telling me you have reason to believe North Korea is somehow involved?"

"Mr. Rixey, why would you say the Democratic People's Republic of Korea is involved?"

"Mr. Chen, I know you are MSS. I figured it out when you were able to get me out of Hong Kong with so much ease during my vacation. I also know your agency is not afraid of taking matters such as revenge in hand. When you called me about this problem, the logical conclusion is, since you are North Korea's most powerful ally, you cannot officially retaliate. A scandal of such large magnitude would cause North Korea to lose face, as well as causing your country extreme embarrassment for having an ally who is reviled around the world, taking advantage of your country's generous support by robbing one of your museums. Please feel free to tell me if there is anything I missed in my level of analysis."

I heard a chuckle from the other side of the phone.

"You are even more perceptive than I thought, Mr. Rixey. You have some familiarity with the *Dae Song*."

"Some."

"Are you familiar with the captain of the ship, Pong Jon-Ho?"

"You mean Colonel Pong of the North Korean RGB?"

"Might I be so bold as to inquire how you knew about the colonel?" Mr. Chen asked with a tone of surprise in his voice.

"Mr. Chen, I am a successful private investigator. I'm paid to know things others don't. How I learn them isn't important."

I heard a chuckle over the phone. "You are indeed very knowledgeable about the nuances of the political scenes. Well done. Your level of analysis is the hallmark of a great detective, Mr. Rixey."

"I realize you work for one of the most effective intelligence agencies in the world. I also realize nothing gets past your agency or you. I know you were aware of the high-line robberies the North Koreans were committing. My theory of the case is with all the embargoes and sanctions against North Korea, they have a hard time putting together any large amounts of hard currencies. For some reason, they needed a lot of hard currency. Oh, and before I forget, the head of this crew is Colonel Pong and right now no one has any idea where he is. How am I doing?"

"You have my undivided attention, Mr. Rixey."

"Your country turned a blind eye toward their activities until they inconvenienced your country. Once they killed the child of a prominent party member, you now have to retaliate. This is what we would call in America being between a rock and a hard place. I don't envy your position at all."

I reached for a cigar, stuck it in my mouth unlit, and poured myself a cup of coffee. I heard repeated peals of thunder, the crackle of lightning, and the steady pounding of rain against my office windows. This was going to be the worst storm in Carbondale since the derecho in 2009.

Finally, after a long pause, Mr. Chen responded. "I am embarrassed to say, your analysis is once again, correct. We cannot find Colonel Pong. I raised objections to sanctioning their criminal activities. The problem is Pong has powerful support in my government. I am not sure if the support was bought or if they believed these acts were somehow helping the government. In any event, those who supported the crime spree have been dealt with, but we cannot officially and publicly condemn their acts. We have non-government people looking for Colonel Pong, with no success. I have a feeling you will meet the colonel at some point, and I wish you to do two things for me. I will be eternally grateful if you can."

"Always willing to do a favor for a friend. What did you have in mind, Mr. Chen? Nothing illegal, I hope?"

There was another long pause. "Two things. First when you find Colonel Pong, please kill him. Think of it as being a sword of justice. After all, he is a murderer and a traitor. Before you kill him, tell him I said goodbye."

Chapter Thirteen

"Collecting facts is important. Knowledge is important. But if you don't have an imagination to use the knowledge, civilization is nowhere." Ray Bradbury.

The plane ride to Mexico City gave me some time to think about what had happened in the past few days. Banner had recovered from his gunshot wound and was living large on my dime. He told the police the story of his shooting, and as I asked him, didn't mention the ring he wrested away from the attacker. As a reward, he was staying at one of the best hotels in Chicago for a few weeks while I sorted out what exactly was going on. It was costing me a lot of cash for the room as well as the babysitter I assigned to him. It was worth it to me. He tried to protect my property, discovered an important clue, and got himself shot in the process. I owed him. I wanted him off the streets in Carbondale and protected. The babysitter, Travis Newton, was a friend of Willard's who worked as a Fed for twenty years in WITSEC. Banner was in good hands. I was pretty sure the man who was messing around with my SUV wasn't still around Carbondale but couldn't be sure. In any event, there was no way this guy would be finding Banner.

As for finding the Chalice of Power, between my research, what I discovered in working the Hen's Egg case and the Zogg case, and most importantly my conversation with Mr. Chen, I had an ironclad link between these high-line robberies and the North Korean RGB. *Well, I thought, it did at least The problem remains, The Hermit Kingdom, as North Korea is sometimes called, has always faced difficulty obtaining hard currency. What caused the sudden need for large amounts of hard currency?*

The answer to the question seemed obvious. After my discussion with Mr. Chen and the favor he asked of me, it was apparent to me he expected me to see Colonel Pong soon. He referred Andrew Stuart to me and, with the research of one of the best intelligence agencies in the world, even if Stuart didn't tell him what his problem was, Mr. Chen would have known it dealt with recovery of the Chalice of Power. He would naturally know about the meeting of the OTO that was held every November 2nd in Mexico City. He most certainly knew because of Stuart's case, I was going to be in Mexico City around the time of their scheduled meeting, working on another matter. The Hermit Kingdom was paying lots of money either for access to or purchase of the Chalice of Power. It all made sense to me now. They were committing these robberies on contract. The Hen's Egg, the coins, and the paintings would be much too well known ever to be shown in public. Their clients were wealthy people who just wanted to have those objects to look at and admire, alone. I've been told the difference between being eccentric and crazy is the size of your billfold.

I felt the plane beginning to circle and heard the standard deplaning instructions. I felt the wheels hit the surface of the runaway and was jolted back in my seat. The plane slowly rolled to the passenger terminal and then came to a stop. I let the other passengers deplane before I did. I really wasn't in any hurry to get to where I was going. Finally, I stood up, thanked the flight attendant, and headed toward baggage claim.

31 October 20xx (All Souls Eve), Mexico City

For Mexico, it was a bit on the chilly side. I saw a digital display announcing the temperature was fifty degrees Fahrenheit. I grabbed my carry on and my laptop bag and headed toward the baggage carousel. I picked up my checked bag and headed toward customs. There was a pretty long line ahead of me. Finally, I was up. I took out my passport and showed it to the man at passport control. He was tall and dark-skinned with a full head of black hair. He was dressed in a paramilitary-type uniform with the name of Torres displayed on a nametag located next to his badge.

Torres studied my diplomatic passport carefully. "Señor Miller Rixey. Are you here for business or pleasure?" He barely glanced at my bags as he put an X on them with the piece of chalk he held.

"Yes, sir, I'm Miller Rixey. I'm here for your festival, the Day of the Dead, so it would be a pleasure." I smiled. "At least I hope so."

He nodded knowingly. "How long do you plan to be in the country, Señor Rixey?"

I shrugged. "A few days, maybe a week at the most."

He stamped my passport. "Very good, Señor. Please have a wonderful time here. The parade on the Day of the Dead is something to behold."

I nodded. "Thank you, sir." I headed toward the storage lockers.

As I left, I casually scanned the terminal. I didn't see anyone I saw before. I wasn't sure how many people were aware of my mission. Being paranoid comes with the job. I found the locker number to the key Stuart sent me. I opened the locker and found a brown briefcase inside. I took it out of the locker and headed toward the cab stand where I hailed a cab. Fifteen minutes later I was standing outside my hotel. I paid the driver, grabbed my bags, and got out of the cab. I knew I wouldn't have long to wait at a hotel as nice as this one seemed to be.

It was still two days before the parade, and the streets were already teeming with people. I imagined how crowded things would be on November 2nd. I saw a doorman heading my direction pushing a luggage cart. I smiled and nodded at him.

"Señor, do you need some assistance?"

"Yes, thanks." I placed my laptop bag, my carryon bag, and my suitcase on the cart, I decided to hang on to the briefcase. Once my things were put on the cart, I followed him to the lobby. The person behind the check-in desk was a very tall and willowy woman. She was dark-skinned and wore a day coat with the name Alejandra Cruz as well as the title General Manager. I handed her my passport.

"Señor Rixey, we have you arriving today and checking out November 3. Correct, Señor?

I nodded. "Yes, Ma'am."

She handed me a registration card. "Please fill this out, Señor."

I filled out the card. She quickly scanned the card and made a photocopy of my passport. She handed me the key to the room.

"Room 327, Señor. It's a two-bedroom suite. Even though you arrived here before our check-in time, the room is available for you now. I hope you find it to your liking. Please contact me personally if there are any problems with the room. We probably will not be able to move you due to the influx of people for the Day of the Dead festivities, but we will do the best we can to accommodate you."

"Thank you. How do I get to the elevator?"

She pointed. "The bellman will guide you there."

As I followed the bellman to the elevator and eventually my room, my phone began to ring. I fished it out of my jacket pocket and looked at the caller ID. It read Kaplan Cleaning Company. I let the phone call go to voicemail. I didn't think an elevator or hallway in a hotel was the place to take the call.

"Here we are, Señor. Room 327," said the bellman, as he opened the door and placed my bags on the bed in one of the bedrooms. "If you need anything else, please don't hesitate to call me." His English was broken and heavily accented, but it was still better than my Spanish.

I peered at his nametag as I handed him a tip. "Rivera, is it? I will certainly keep you in mind."

"Yes, Señor."

I saw his eyes light up as he looked at the tip. He handed me my key and left.

After the bellman left, I opened my suitcase and pulled out a wand to detect if there were listening devices in the room and turned it on. I walked from room to room studying the meter and found the room was bug-free. Once I made sure the place was secure, I turned off the wand and pulled out my phone.

I listened to the voicemail. It requested I call back and gave me an access code for the call.

I dialed the number I had just seen on the screen. The phone was answered after the first ring.

"Kaplan Cleaning Company, how may we assist you?"

"Miller Rixey, Plissken 1997."

"Let me transfer you, Mr. Rixey."

I waited for a minute and heard another voice come online. "Mr. Rixey, I must apologize to you. There was something we overlooked in our research and your assistant, Ms. Nickels, told us where you would be and about what time you would be off the plane. At last, we were able to get a hold of you."

I heard some clicking over the phone from a keyboard.

I took a seat on the couch in the living room. "You have my undivided attention. What was it you forgot to include in your research? I must admit, I am surprised. Usually your company does such fine work. I know it's important what you omitted, or you would be using other methods to communicate with me other than calling me," I growled.

Kaplan usually does excellent work. For the fees I pay them, they'd better. Anything less than excellent is not acceptable, I thought.

"We apologize, sir. Mistakes do happen from time to time. I am sure you understand. You're correct. We are contacting you with crucial newly-discovered information. Mr. Rixey, are you familiar with the term electromagnetic pulse, or EMP?"

Chapter Fourteen

"Surprise is the greatest gift which life can grant us." Boris Pasternak.

"Yes, between school and my reading of science fiction. It's typically used to refer to a form of attack destroying most electrical things and all computers unless they are protected in a special casing. I know it would render most modern cars useless due to the use of computers in cars. Meanwhile, property and the population would not be affected. It would be a disaster to the side on the wrong end of such an attack."

"Very good, Mr. Rixey. What we failed to include in our reports was, in addition to disruptions in the timeline continuum and the huge power drains that appear to coincide with the use of the Chalice of Power, there have been reports in the areas of massive failures of automobiles, computers, and other electrical devices. The affected areas reporting these occurrences seem to grow even larger with each use of the Chalice."

"Send me a copy of your report via email. We don't have the time for the usual courier service."

"Yes, Mr. Rixey. It is being sent even as we speak."

"Thanks for bringing this to my attention." I clicked off.

I dropped my phone and saw it bounce twice on the carpet before it came to a stop. I didn't think it was possible. I mean lunatics with the ability to time travel were bad enough. Now there seemed to be a link between the Chalice and potential EMP attacks which was just as bad if not worse. No way did I want to return to the 1400s.

I needed to think some deep thoughts about what I just learned from Kaplan. Two things always greatly aid this process, a good cigar and a good stiff drink. I reached into my jacket pocket and took out my pocket humidor. I removed a cigar and squeezed it. Perfection, not even a small crackle. I took out my cigar cutter and cut off the end. I flicked my lighter and ran it over the back of the end for a few moments, and then stuck it in my mouth. I lit it and saw a cloud of fragrant smoke rise over my head.

I then walked to the minibar and inspected it. My brain cells would need a good oiling and nothing works better than a good stiff drink. I didn't find my usual tipple, but the minibar offered some available substitutes. I poured myself four fingers of an adequate whiskey. Now armed with my thinking tools, I took a seat in the living room in a very comfortable lounger.

I wasn't totally convinced about the time travel capabilities of the Chalice when Stuart and I first talked. I began thinking there was a good chance it was right when I received information from Kaplan verifying what Stuart showed me about the interruptions of the time-space continuum. The frightening thought was people were unaware of how dangerous time travel can be in the current world. I began thinking about how the preventing of one major event would totally change the world.

As I sipped my drink and smoked my cigar, I decided to focus on only one event. It would serve as a good model for any of the potential disasters irresponsible time travel would do to the world.

If somehow, a person was in Dallas on November 22, 1963, and stopped the assassination of President Kennedy, quite a bit would have been changed. First of all, chances are good Lyndon Baines Johnson would have ended up in prison for the various crimes he committed throughout his political career. At a minimum, if Kennedy hadn't been assassinated, Johnson would have been out of power as Kennedy had already decided to dump Johnson from the national ticket.

I heard my phone buzzing. I checked my pockets, no luck. I saw it flashing on the hotel room floor where I dropped it. I got up and walked over to the phone and saw the name of Andrew Stuart on the caller ID. I picked up the phone and pressed answer.

"What can I do for you, Mr. Stuart?"

"Have you made any progress? Was the bag where it was supposed to be?"

"I just landed about two hours ago. Hopefully, I will be making progress tomorrow and the bag was in the locker as we discussed. Thank you."

I debated on telling Stuart about the EMP occurrences I just learned about. As honest as I like to be with clients, I couldn't help having a sinking feeling he was holding things back from me about the Chalice. Turnabout is fair play, isn't it?

"Please call me and let me know when you make progress, Mr. Rixey."

"Mr. Stuart, as soon as I discover something, you will be my first call."

I saw the call waiting feature indicating Mr. Zogg was calling. "I need to go, Mr. Stuart. I will be in touch." I clicked off.

"Yes, Mr. Zogg. What can I do for you?"

"Just checking in. I assume if there were anything to report, you would be calling me?"

"You're right. I am pretty sure I have a hot lead on at least the ringleader of the group who stole your coins."

"Mr. Rixey, while the coins hold a great sentimental value to me, they can be replaced. What cannot be replaced is my reputation. I cannot afford to have people thinking I am some kind of mark."

"Mr. Zogg, I doubt anyone who would matter would consider you a mark or a patsy."

"The world I survive in is a brutal one. One show of weakness and the people I deal with will be on me like a pack of wolves. I need to send a strong message about what happens to people who screw with me. Do we understand each other?"

I gulped for a moment and looked at my phone. I knew the call was not being recorded. He was genuinely angry and not trying to set me up as a fall guy. "The Bishop Agency does its best to make sure the client is taken care of and is satisfied with their results."

Seeming somewhat mollified Zogg responded. "Very good, Mr. Rixey. All I was asking for was your best. I have another call coming in and must take it. Good luck."

I heard him hang up. I was somewhat relieved. I got away with making a vague statement and not agreeing to kill anyone over the phone. I felt myself being caught in a very nasty situation with some very powerful men and with little old me in the middle. I didn't relish the idea of being in the middle of some power play from two powerful men. I tossed the phone on the couch and went back to the lounger, stopping first at the mini-bar to grab an iced coffee. I didn't need any more alcohol in me at this time of day with what I needed to do. Iced coffee secured, I began to think again about the implications of time travel.

I remember a professor telling me one time the effects of time travel, if it ever became possible, would be like a stone being thrown into a lake. The heavier the stone, the more violent the ripples, and a small stone would create almost no ripples at all. There was no appreciable way to figure out what changes would occur, but certainly stopping an event like an assassination would be a big stone. The only thing I was sure of was that the importance of the event being changed was of paramount importance. The more important the event, the more significant the change of history.

I decided, enough with the thinking, and now time to check my gear. I went to my suitcase and opened it up, removing my shaving kit. I then picked up the bag left for me at the airport. I opened the bag first and found it contained exactly what I told Stuart to put in the bag. I closed it. I opened up my shaving kit and pulled out two bars of soap. I stood up and walked to the kitchen area and found a knife and began cutting the bars of soap open Inside were three listening devices, wrapped in special plastic to protect them from the effects of the soap. These items would never show up on any TSA or Customs scan. They were pricey. It was the client's money not mine, so I wasn't too concerned. The devices presented unique problems for those attempting to detect their presence. They were able to be turned on as needed and then turned off by remote control. A small black box in the shaving kit with six tiny red buttons was the controller. After I unwrapped the listening devices, I tested them a few times and they worked fine and also turned off and on as they were supposed to. The ability to be able to turn them off and on remotely was their selling point. Now all I needed to do was somehow get in the building next door and plant them.

Before I went out to dinner, I decided to give Morgan a call and firm up what time she was going to be arriving. I dialed her cell.

"Miller, so great to hear from you. I've got an awesome gown and mask to wear for the festival," she gushed.

"Very cool. I have a rather smart-looking outfit to wear also."

"I couldn't get an early flight, so I won't be there until about ten P.M., Mexico City time. Is this going to cause any problems?"

"Not at all. It's fine. I have something to do tomorrow night and with any luck, I'll be done by ten."

"You coming to get me or should I cab it?"

"Cab it, we are in Room 327."

"See you then."

Chapter Fifteen

"To catch the bad guys, you've got to think like a bad guy—and that's why all the best detectives have a dark side..." David Videcette. The Theseus Paradox.

I sat on the couch reviewing all I learned. If my theory about the reason behind the North Korea's sudden need for a lot of hard currency was correct, and I was sure it was, maybe Pong was bringing the coins taken in the Zogg robbery with him as final payment for the Chalice of Power. It hadn't been long since the Zogg robbery, so chances were good Zogg's coins were still with them. The final payment to OTO wasn't made yet.

I took out my cellphone and, once I got a secured line, I dialed 212-555-2368. The phone rang a few times and was finally answered. "Hello?" The accent was pure New York.

"Fingers?"

"This is Julian Malone. Who am I speaking to?"

"Miller Rixey. I need you for a job in Mexico City."

"Oh hi, Mr. Rixey. Umm, I am a little busy right now. What did you require of me?"

"Hopefully, a simple snatch and run. I think I'm going to need you to grab a briefcase and run like hell. There is some danger involved. The job pays twenty-five thousand for you just to be here and if you grab the briefcase and get away, you get another twenty-five thousand. Are we less busy?"

"Umm, sure thing, Mr. Rixey. Problem is I don't have a passport or the money for a plane ticket. You know Fingers Malone always travels first-class. When did you need me down there?"

"November 1. If I can arrange the passport and ticket, can you be here then?"

"Sure, Mr. Rixey. I know I owe you big time and the money would come in handy."

"Stay by your phone, someone will be contacting you shortly." I clicked off.

I next dialed the number for Lothar Zogg. "Miller Rixey calling for Mr. Zogg. Is he available?"

"Certainly, Mr. Rixey."

"Lothar Zogg. Mr. Rixey, have you found my coins or the bastard who stole them?"

"I need to bring an operative down here. Two problems, first he does not have a passport and secondly, he does not have enough money for a plane ticket."

"Where is he?"

"New York City."

"Have him report to my office. I have enough clout to get him a passport very quickly. As for the plane ticket, I will have him flown down to Mexico on one of my jets. When do you need him down there and what's his name? I'll make sure my staff knows he is coming and is to see me immediately."

"His name is Julian Malone and I need him down here sometime on November 1. Can you take care of this?"

"Not a problem, Mr. Rixey. We will have him down there November 1."

I called Fingers back.

"Fingers, you need to get to Zogg Industries' offices as soon as you can. Everything will be taken care of. I am in Room 327 at the El Grande. Show up any time after ten P.M. I'll make sure I'll be back by then."

"I got it Mr. Rixey. See you then."

I dialed the front desk.

"St. Regis, how may I be of assistance?" a lovely feminine voice asked.

"This is Miller Rixey from Room 327. I have a cousin who decided to come down and see the Day of the Dead Parade and doesn't have a reservation. He would be arriving November 1, late, and be leaving sometime on November 2. Any chance you can help me out?"

"You're in luck, Señor Rixey. A cancellation just occurred. I will need a credit card number to hold the room though. It's a very nice room, not as nice as yours. You are fortunate to get any type of room here during the festival."

"Use my credit card number and most acceptable. I'm just glad you happened to have a cancellation."

"Your cousin's name and nationality?"

"Julian Malone and American."

"The reservation has been confirmed, Señor Rixey."

"Thank you again." I clicked off.

After putting Morgan's gear and my extra ammunition and most of my cash in the room safe, I checked my pistol one more time. I screwed the suppressor on and pulled back the slide to put a round in the chamber. I then slid the gun into my shoulder holster, put on my leather jacket, and finally my fedora. I was ready for a night out in Mexico City, the largest megalopolis in the world, with a population of about thirty million.

I left my room, waited for the door to click shut and then headed to the elevator. Once inside, I pressed the lobby key and down I went. My plans for the evening were simple enough: a good meal in a good restaurant and I needed to change some of my dollars for pesos. I would check out tomorrow's target, the building where the OTO would be holding their meeting on November 2. First things first, though, I needed to go to the Concierge Desk to try to change my money and find a good place to eat.

When the elevator door opened, the number of people and the level of noise was a bit overwhelming. I knew the parade would attract a lot of people, but I expected them to arrive sometime tomorrow.

I spotted the Concierge Desk and slowly began to work my way toward it. I got lucky as no one was ahead of me and I took a seat. The concierge, whose nameplate identified him as Raul Sanchez, was a balding man who looked like he was in his fifties. He was of fairly light complexion and sported a Van Dyke beard, turning silver. He was undoubtedly a distinguished-looking man.

"How can I be of assistance, Señor?" he asked amicably.

"Señor Sanchez, this is my first time in Mexico City. I need two things. First, can you suggest a good restaurant, and I also need about two hundred dollars U.S. changed into pesos."

He handed me a pamphlet for local restaurants and said. "These are the top restaurants in Mexico City. They list their price range and the types of food they sell. This will be easier for both of us and get you on your way quicker than me explaining the ins and outs of the local restaurants."

He paused. "As for your second problem, since I know you are a guest in our hotel, we can help you there, too. How much did you say you needed to be changed?"

"Two hundred dollars."

"Very good." He picked up the phone and said something in Spanish I did not understand. An attendant came by the desk with thirty-five hundred Mexican pesos in one-hundred-peso notes. I handed him my money, he nodded, looked to Sanchez, and left.

Sanchez coughed, then apologetically said, "We take a minimal fee for this service, Señor."

I nodded as I put the pesos in my money clip. "I understand completely. After all, business is business, isn't it? Thanks for your help," I said gesturing with the pamphlet as I stood.

"Not at all, Señor Rixey. Oh yes, in the guide I just gave you, in addition to describing the types of food offered, it also indicates restaurants that speak English. In fact, most places in this area do have staff who speak English."

"You know who I am?"

He smiled. "Not too hard to know. I was here when you checked in. Please enjoy your night, Señor."

I read the dining guide and by the time I reached the outside door of the hotel, I made my decision. I found a steakhouse about four blocks from the hotel. The doorman opened the door for me and I nodded my thanks.

"May I get you a cab, Señor.?"

"No thanks. It's a nice night for a walk."

The weather was cool, yet comfortable. One of the more critical lessons Willard taught me was always to be aware of my surroundings, especially when I am working on a case. I stretched as I stood outside the hotel. I used the opportunity to casually glance around as I looked for individuals who were standing nearby. This information is valuable because, if a person keeps popping up, it's either a coincidence or the person is following you. I don't believe in coincidences. It's a practice and a belief to make sure I will still be working when I reach Willard's age. Once done looking, I headed off to the steakhouse. The street traffic was heavy. This wasn't really a surprise given what I saw in the lobby. I wandered down the street to the restaurant I'd picked out of the brochure and was enjoying taking in the sights and sounds of Mexico City.

Adding to the crowds on the street where a proliferation of street vendors. They were selling anything and everything. You want a Rolex to turn your wrist green in about a week? This is the spot. I suppose it did add to the local color.

I stopped at a jewelry store and pretended to window shop. One person, who I hadn't seen at the hotel, stopped at the same time and was doing his best to look uninvolved and uninterested. I couldn't make out his age. He was dressed in an overcoat and racing cap. He looked tall and thin. Whatever the guy was wearing, whether it was aftershave lotion, cologne, or perfume, it was strong enough to smell the scent even a block away. I smiled to myself. This guy had zero shadowing skills.

I resumed my walk to the steakhouse and, on cue, my shadow began to follow me again. I made it a point to stop two more times and look at store windows. My shadow did the same thing each time. He stopped about a block or so from me and pretended to do the same. Like I said before, I don't believe in coincidences. The odds were in the neighborhood of one hundred percent he was attempting to shadow me. I knew he wasn't the brains of the operation, so I needed to know who he was working for. Was he working for Chen, Stuart, Zogg, OTO, or perhaps a new player in the game? It was paramount to my survival to know all of the players in this case.

I entered the steakhouse and noticed my shadow didn't follow me inside. I had a leisurely dinner and about an hour after I entered, I paid my bill and left. The first thing I noticed once I hit the street was that my shadow was nowhere to be found. I knew where I would see him. It was a mortal certainty he would be waiting for me in the hotel lobby. I surmised he reported to his superior and was given new orders.

While my shadow posed no immediate threat to me, I couldn't

afford to have him following me and making a nuisance of himself. There was work to do later and I didn't need any distractions while I surveilled the building I was going to be breaking into or, as a criminal friend of mine, Fingers Malone, likes to say, casing the joint. I needed to make sure my shadow was otherwise occupied. I thought of a plan to case the joint, nodding at my brilliance.

I returned to the hotel and it didn't take me too long to find my shadow. He was sitting in a plush chair, legs crossed, attempting to read a newspaper. I still smelled his overpowering aftershave or whatever it was. He looked like he was in his twenties. His overcoat and racing cap were neatly placed on a table on his right. He was dressed in a black suit, black shirt, and red tie. He needed to invest in a different cut of his jacket. It did nothing to hide the bulge under his right arm.

"Anything I can help you with, sonny?" I asked in a mocking tone of voice.

He ignored me. I saw him fold the paper over and continue reading. He reached into his pocket for a cigarette.

I slapped the paper out of his hand. "Hey, I'm talking to you."

When I slapped the paper out of his hand, his pack of cigarettes went flying.

He looked me over and spoke in his nasal and high-pitched voice. "Keep screwing with me and you're going to get hurt. I ain't gonna warn you a second time. You understand me, old man? No second warning."

"Who's going to hurt me, sonny? Certainly not you."

"Keep it up. You'll be picking lead out of your liver," he said with a sneer.

I laughed. "The cheaper the hood, the gaudier the patter. Tell whoever you're working for, I'll meet him tomorrow. Now, sonny, you need to run along."

"I'll leave when I want to," he sneered.

I heard some footsteps coming up behind me. I turned around and saw Sanchez, the concierge and a huge and very rough-looking man dressed in a hotel security officer's uniform.

I saw the concierge looking unhappy. "Mr. Rixey, is there a problem here?"

"Sure is. I thought you guys ran a nice hotel. It turns out you let grifters and hoods, like this born loser, hang out here with their guns bulging under their jackets. What gives?" I jerked an angry thumb at my shadow.

Sanchez looked concerned. "Excuse me, sir, are you a guest of this hotel?"

"I'm waiting for someone."

"Unless you are a guest of the hotel, I suggest you wait for your friend outside. We cannot have our guests being threatened. Before you leave, I will need to see some form of ID."

He took his passport out of his jacket pocket. "Wilmer Cook," Sanchez said after reading the man's passport.

"Rixey, you just made the biggest mistake of your life. I'll get you for this," Cook screamed.

Sanchez clucked. "Mr. Cook, I cannot have this type of behavior in my hotel. You are barred from here and any other properties owned by Hotel Ventures, Inc. Your picture will be sent to all facilities. If you are found in one of them again, you will be arrested." He turned to the guard. "Pedro, please allow Mr. Cook a moment to collect his things then escort him off the premises."

Pedro waited for a moment and when Cook moved a little slow for his likes, grabbed his arm roughly.

Sanchez smiled. "Gently, please. Mr. Cook, have a good evening."

We stood there watching the two leaving the hotel.

He turned to me. "Mr. Rixey, the next time you see Mr. Chen, tell him I give him my very best." He smiled at me, turned on his heels and headed back toward his desk."

I stood there, mouth open and totally surprised. I shook my head. *Mr. Chen does it again*, I thought. *He's a guy with some long-reaching tentacles. I sure wouldn't want to be on his wrong side.*

There was work to do and time was of the essence. I walked to the elevator bank, got in one, and pushed three. As I rode up the elevator, I was thinking about what an exciting trip this had already been. Being followed told me there was more than likely another player who was trying to get involved with the Chalice. I mean, the Chalice was the only reason I was down here to begin with. There was only one reason for me being followed.

Chapter Sixteen

"You can't live forever, but you can die tryin'." Maddie Banks.

1 November 20xx (All Souls Day), Mexico City

I stopped outside my room, weapon drawn and listened for any signs of movement in the room. Hearing none, I slid the keycard into the slot, watched it turn green, and pushed the door open. I reached into my pocket and opened up the carrying case for the wand I carry with me to help me detect the presence of listening devices. I turned the device on and went from room to room. I didn't detect any.

I went to the room safe, opened it, and removed my laptop computer. I never leave my laptop out when I am in a strange place, like a hotel room. It is too easy to tamper with it. I put it on the table in my living room and turned it on. I was on the sign-on page. The computer made a series of very annoying beeps. I pulled my keys from my pocket and quickly found what I was looking for. It seemed like an ordinary key ring medallion from Illinois State University. There was one crucial difference between this device and a regular key ring medallion. It was a transmitting device a friend of Willard's invented a few years ago. It was keyed to my laptop. I squeezed it twice and it sent a code to my computer. The computer flashed twice and I ended up on another page. I entered a password and after a few seconds to process the password, was on my regular computer page. I connected to the internet and quickly checked my email.

Nothing of any consequence was in my email. There was an offer from a Nigerian Finance Minister informing me, due to an odd occurrence of events, I was entitled to ten million dollars. All I had to do to collect my windfall was contact them with my bank information, my social security number, and my mother's maiden name. I decided to pass on this generous offer and sent the email to spam. There were notices about coin auctions I stored in a folder for holding such information. A couple of requests for my services that looked very mundane. I forwarded them to Ms. Nickels to deal with. What I was looking for wasn't there. No emails from Stuart, Zogg, or even Mr. Chen. I logged off and returned the computer to the room safe.

I decided rather than merely checking out the building the OTO was going to be meeting in on November 2, I would go ahead and plant the listening devices now. I knew I would have to meet with Wilmer Cook's employer later today and Morgan would be arriving about ten P.M. I wanted to have the vital task out of the way. I didn't like the idea of leaving them in the building early. It did give them more of a chance to be discovered, as I was betting they wouldn't be found. Failure to plant those listening devices would be disastrous.

I knew there was a way to get to the building from the hotel. On the map, it looked like a simple walk, about one hundred yards from my room. There was supposed to be a barrier that would protect us from being seen from the building. I thought if the street facing the building and the hotel were vacant, I'd merely lower myself down a rope to the street.

I went to my room and dressed totally in black, including a ski mask. I thought about bringing a weapon with me and finally decided against it. It would be bad enough to be caught breaking into a building in a foreign country. I did not want to complicate things by being found with a pistol. I wasn't sure if my diplomatic passport would allow me to carry or not. I figured I was probably okay as long as I wasn't caught committing a felony. In any event, the last thing I needed was to get in a gunfight. If I were confronted at any point, I would just do my best to escape.

I packed a doctor's bag I carry for just these situations. In the bag, I placed the listening devices, my binoculars, a rappelling rope, my lockpick set, my night vision goggles (NVGs), and my mini-computer I used to open digital locks. I grabbed my flashlight and I was set. I walked out the window of my room and was soon on a ledge. No real danger here unless I did something incredibly stupid. The ledge was six feet wide. I set the beam to low and narrow. I carefully made my way down the ramp. I'd heard the noise of the pedestrians and the honking of horns from the automobiles below. I was glad of the light because every thirty feet or so there was a small drop-off. The drop hadn't been indicated on my map. I would have to talk to Kaplan about this oversight when I got back home. The drop-off wasn't a problem unless you didn't realize it was there and then it was a three-story drop to the street.

I finally made it to the end of the ledge. The area opened into a courtyard of sorts. I doubted this area saw much use anymore. No chairs or tables out. The area was littered with liquor bottles, crumpled cigarette packages, and broken glass. A small wall directly ahead of me, as shown on the map, would shelter Morgan and me from observation from the meeting site. On the third floor were three windows. I nodded in satisfaction as the map Kaplan gave me was accurate about the window locations.

I took out my binoculars and set them to night vision as I scanned the windows. All three windows were connected to one large room containing twenty-one chairs and a long conference table. Bookshelves were stuffed full of books. I focused back on the conference table. I was hoping to find paperwork lying on the table. No such luck. Nothing is ever so easy. I looked down at the street and saw no foot traffic in this section of the street. I checked up and down the street and soon discovered why there was no foot traffic. The section was fenced in. Not good. The good news was there were locked gates at either end of the fencing. There were also guard shacks located at each entrance. I looked down at the building, scanning the ground level with my binoculars. I saw a door with an electronic keypad glowing back at me. No doubt during the day, this was the employee and delivery entrance. That was a concern. Were the building owners really this slack on defense or did they want to make it look like there was no defense? Nothing is ever this easy.

I put on my NVGs and flipped the selection to infrared. I looked at the street and now saw a ruby-red light running from one guard shack to the other. I nodded to myself. This was nothing short of brilliant. The light looked like it was about two feet off the ground. Just the right height to catch someone unaware who decided to cross the street to the building. The truly inspired part was whoever set up security here realized while, for inside security setup, more lights would be a better idea, the only thing more lights on an outside trap would generate would be a lot of false alarms. Birds, rats, and even swirling garbage would keep setting off the alarms. It would take someone such as myself who carried sophisticated tools to avoid the trap and also to be able to unlock the numeric keypad. Just like a boy scout, I am always prepared.

I attached the hook of my rappelling rope to a thin portion of the ledge in front of me. I tugged on it a few times and, finally satisfied the line was secure, I grabbed my bag and began to lower myself down the rope. I made good time coming down. I landed smoothly and quickly checked both gated sides of the fence. The streets were streaming with people. None of them even looked my way.

Once on the ground, I'd make an accurate measurement of the light beam. It was about eighteen inches off the ground. It wouldn't be much of a challenge to crawl under. I took the opportunity to examine the door from the ground level. The keypad glowed back at me. I saw a small red light on the top of the panel, ten spaces to enter numbers and the numeric pad. The door did not have a lock or a handle on it. *To each his own,* I thought. Seemed an odd way to have an employee entrance or delivery door set up. What did I know?

I got on my stomach and crawled until I was right in front of the door. I stood up dusted myself off and checked both sides of the fence. People were still walking by and no one noticed me yet. I opened my bag and pulled out the microprocessor I had used in Mr. Zogg's office, turned it on, and attached it to the keypad. I pressed start and looked at the panel. Within about twenty seconds, all ten numbers appeared in the ten panels and I heard a satisfying click. I removed the microprocessor from the keypad and returned it to my bag. A few seconds after the click, I heard a whirring sound and suddenly the solid door was no longer solid. I saw a panel slide down the door and a lock appeared. Another challenge. I took out my set of graphene lockpicks and went to work on the lock. I am very good at lock-picking, having learned from one of the best. If I cannot get into a lock, then no one can. This one was tougher than most. I heard the tumblers fall into place about a minute after I began. There was no handle on the door, so I used the lockpicks to pull the door open. I looked at my watch. It was one A.M. and things were going according to plan. With any luck, I would be out of here shortly and back enjoying a few drinks in my hotel room.

Holding the door open with one hand, I carefully removed my lockpicks from the key and put them back in my bag. I glanced around the entrance area. I breathed a sigh of relief when I didn't see any lights similar to what I saw outside. I guess the building owners were convinced the light beam was invisible to the naked eye and was sufficient protection. I saw an elevator straight ahead of me and a set of stairs to the right. Two things made me opt for the stairs. First, some places log when an elevator is used. I didn't want to leave indications of a trip being taken to the third floor and then back down at one A.M. Second, while unlikely, there was always the chance of a power failure would leave me trapped in the elevator until the people who worked in the building or the police found me.

I took out my flashlight, turned it on, and aimed it at the floor so as not to conflict with my NVGs. I moved deliberately and slowly up the stairs. I couldn't hear a sound other than my breathing. I sure didn't want to run into any security officers or hard-working employees working late. I thought about checking out some other offices to see if it was possible to find some information on the OTO. I quickly dismissed the idea as being a long shot at best. I was in great danger every moment I was in the building. I had one task to do and decided to focus on the task at hand. It's imperative to keep the focus on your primary assignment. It's too easy to lose focus on side issues and end up bungling the job you were sent to do.

I finally arrived on the third floor. I stood by the door, listening for any sounds. I heard some voices speaking in Spanish. I froze. *Security guards perhaps,* I thought. I looked under the door and saw no light. I heard the elevator door open and shut and the whir of the elevator as it headed back down to wherever the passengers were taking it. I waited another few moments and, hearing no voices, I was satisfied with the owners of the voices I heard left the floor, and I slowly opened the door. The hall was dark with only some glowing emergency lights showing the indicated exits.

My target, the conference room, was only a few feet away from the door. Once in front of the room, I tried the door handle. It wasn't locked. I wasn't too surprised. I was sure there was really nothing worth protecting in the room and rooms like this are used all the time by different groups of people. There was no reason to restrict access to the office. I slowly turned the handle and entered the room. I didn't see anything new in the place I hadn't already observed from my perch in the hotel courtyard.

I quickly went to work. I first removed my NVGs, and I removed three listening devices from my bag as well as the control pad. I hid the listening devices behind the books I saw shelved in the room. I used the control panel to test the devices, turning them off and on a few times. I made a mental note of where I placed them. The first one I set would cover the area of the conference table. The others would cover the rest of this very large room. Satisfied they worked, I put my NVGs back on, and, no longer needing my flashlight, put it back in my bag. I snapped the bag shut and prepared to make my escape. One more thing to check. It would be embarrassing if I decided to shoot Pong and the glass was bulletproof. I tested the glass on the three windows and it seemed to be made of just regular glass. I double-checked everything to make sure nothing was disturbed during my work and I tested the listening devices one more time. Satisfied everything was working as it was supposed to and satisfied nothing was disturbed, I left.

I worked my way down the stairs until I came to the first floor. I listened carefully and, hearing nothing, slowly pushed the door open. I heard the same voices I had heard earlier above me and heard their footsteps getting closer and closer. *Shit, they must have been on the second floor, doing rounds or something.* Once back in the main entrance area, I made sure to close the door as softly as possible. I heard the door close with a click. Walking quickly toward the exit door, I gently pushed on the bar releasing the door and stepped out into the cool evening. I hadn't realized I was totally soaked in sweat. I eyed the light beam and once again dropped to my stomach to crawl under it. Once I was clear, I cannot tell you how thrilled I was to see my rappelling rope was right where I left it. I quickly scaled it, making sure to pull the rope up behind me. I removed my NVGs and placed them along with my rope back in my bag. I took the flashlight out to make sure I didn't miss any of the openings on the ledge. A few minutes later, I was safely back in my room.

I stripped and showered. The hot shower was wonderful. Quickly dressing and now feeling totally revived once again, I poured myself a generous drink from the minibar. As I enjoyed my drink, I noticed the message light on my room phone was flashing. I picked it up.

"This is Señor Rixey, Room 327. I saw there were some messages for me?"

"Yes, Señor Rixey. We have a package from World Wide Exports and a letter left for you. Would you like us to deliver these to your room, or will you come down and pick them up yourself?" a husky female voice asked.

"Give me a few minutes and I'll come down and pick them up myself. Thanks."

I finished my drink and headed toward the elevators. I stepped in and pressed the lobby key. I was soon back in the lobby. The lobby was still full of people, no doubt getting a head start on celebrating what would be happening the next few days.

I walked to the front desk and caught the eye of a very comely young lady with blonde hair. "Señor Rixey, Room 327." I stole a glance at her nametag. "I believe you said you were holding a package and a letter for me, Señorita O'Toole?" I said with a tone of surprise as I saw her name.

She smiled. "I am an American college student who is majoring in Hotel Management and am working down here for this semester on an internship. Yes, sir. I have the packages for you. If you would be so good as to sign for them?"

I took her pen and scribbled my name on the receipt. She handed me the package and the letter. "Enjoy the rest of your day and visit, Señor," she said with a chuckle. "Oh yes, if there is anything, anything at all I can do for you, Señor, please let me know," she added.

I nodded and checked out what I received. The package was from Hong Kong and the letter was from a Hanover Fiste. I assumed Fiste was the brains behind Wilmer Cook. Once back in the relative security of my room, I would check both. I headed back to the elevator and was soon on my way back to my room.

Chapter Seventeen

"To be prepared is half the victory." *Miguel de Cervantes.*

Once I was back in my room, I laid the package and the envelope on the table in front of my couch. I went to the minibar and, as much as I wanted a drink, coffee seemed more appropriate. I poured myself a cup, lit a cigar, and sat down to read the letter from H. Fiste.

Sir:

I must apologize for the conduct of my underling, Wilmer Cook. His job was to contact you and arrange a meeting between you and me. I am most anxious to discuss with you a business proposal which would be most beneficial to both of us. If you would be so kind as to meet with me at La Cantina at three this afternoon, you will find the meeting to be well worth your time.

I look forward to meeting you.

Hanover Fiste

I felt the texture of the paper. It was indeed a very high quality. Perhaps vellum? It contained a watermark and the name of Hanover Fiste was printed in gold at the top of the page. Looked like someone wasn't hurting for money. I was pretty sure I would be able to find Mr. Fiste on the internet easily. I set the letter off to the side and began to open the package I received from World Wide Imports. With a Hong Kong address, I was pretty sure I knew who sent it. Once the box was open, I saw a small carrying case. I flipped the latches on the case and saw inside the case was a rifle. Naturally, it was broken down.

A pamphlet came with the rifle identifying it as the DRD Paratus P762 Gen-2. The country of origin was the United States. Despite the fact it was a semi-automatic weapon, it was considered one of the best sniper rifles in the world. Ammunition was easy to find, too, NATO 7.62 x 51 mm. I checked the magazine and found it loaded to my specifications. It usually held twenty rounds. This magazine only contained nineteen rounds. I smiled. Someone I knew me pretty well to do this. I smiled, even more, when I saw the rifle came with a strap and suppressor. The weapon still had the new-gun smell indicating the original oil was still on it.

I took the rifle out of the case and put it together as quickly as possible. It took me about sixty seconds. Not too bad considering I had never laid eyes on this weapon before. When I looked down at the hotel carpet, I noticed a white envelope lying beside the couch. I picked it up and opened it. The note was short and to the point. It was from Mr. Chen.

Miller:

I hope this note finds you well. Best of luck and happy hunting.
Joseph

I repacked the weapon in its case and went to the room safe. I took out my laptop and put the gun case in it and then locked it. While I was waiting for the computer to warm up and go through its various protocols, I began thinking.

I was really feeling the squeeze. Here I am, a small-town shamus and once again, I'm in the middle of an international powerplay. There was Eldor Jamieson Crypt, Hanover Fiste, Alfred Zogg, Andrew Stuart, and last but not least, Joseph Chen. Then we can consider the United States State Department. They were still mad at me over what went down in Argentina. I can only imagine their reaction when they find out an American citizen, carrying a diplomatic passport, killed a North Korean spy in Mexico. I winced thinking about what a mess I'd find myself in. It hardly seemed fair. No one has ever been able to convince me life is fair. I doubt they ever will.

As bad as things looked right now, would I change a single aspect of my life? Not a chance. I couldn't imagine living any other way now. My practice had already taken me to foreign countries, allowed me to meet very important people, and most importantly, allowed me to meet Morgan.

The annoying beeps my computer likes to make woke me out of my reverie. I reached into my pocket, pulled out my key ring, and pressed twice on the device. It would send a signal to the computer it was indeed me or someone who with access to my key ring which was attempting to access the laptop. When I did a search for Hanover Fiste, he lit up my search engine like a rash. I now saw why I hadn't heard of him before. No one had seen him in public for the past ten years. He lived in a well-guarded compound just outside of England. He was a Howard Hughes type, without the germ phobia. He was only your typical multi-billionaire who shunned publicity at all costs.

He was born in England. According to the information I found, Mr. Fiste was fifty-five. His family was very well off. He was educated in some of the finest private schools in the world. He got his Bachelor's degree from Harvard and also received his MBA from the same school. He returned to England after completing his college work and began working in the family business. The family owned a dozen banks, most of them in Europe, two located in the United States. Nothing in my information indicated the banks and the family business weren't run in a lawful manner. His parents died in a car accident twenty years ago. Once the life-changing tragedy occurred, Fiste, an only child, assumed control of his parents' holdings.

In addition to being a banker, he ran a sizeable import-export business, Fiste Ltd. No one was quite sure what exactly his company imported and exported. He was under investigation in a dozen countries for supposedly illegally contributing to various political campaigns. He was also suspected of allegedly funding multiple terrorist networks. Some of the articles said he reportedly made hundreds of millions of dollars by having the foresight to short airline stocks the day before September 11, 2001. With the staff of attorneys he kept on retainer, it sounded like allegedly and supposedly was about as close as any government was going to get to him. He didn't seem like a very nice guy. I would have to be extra careful in my dealings with him. I found a 'recent' picture of Fiste. It was eleven years old. In his file picture, he was very tall, obese, and very bald. I had my doubts as to how much he might have changed over the past eleven years. He would be easy to spot at the restaurant.

I looked at my watch and saw it was four A.M. There was still a full day ahead of me today. I went back to the minibar, poured myself a drink and lit another cigarette. My work done, I logged off, put the laptop back in the room safe and decided it was time for me to go to bed.

Chapter Eighteen

"There is something intoxicating about ending a life, about wiping bad people off the face of the earth. But it's also a dark and deadly pull. After all, who am I to decide who lives or dies?" Paula Stokes, Ferocious.

I heard a buzzing sound seemingly growing louder and more insistent by the minute. I barely opened my eyes and saw the clock next to my bed. It read one thirty P.M. I staggered to my feet and by two thirty was on the elevator and on my way down to the lobby.

The lobby was noisy and congested. Tourists were arriving all day for the Day of the Dead parade and various rituals. I worked my way to the front desk and saw Ms. O'Toole was working.

"Good afternoon, Ms. O'Toole. Can you tell me where La Cantina is?"

She smiled warmly. "Please call me Lindsey, Mr. Rixey." She looked off into the distance and wrinkled her nose as she thought. "The simplest way to get there is to head out of the hotel and take a left. Go four blocks and then take a right for two blocks. It is located on the right side of the street." She paused. "I'd recommend you walk there. The weather is nice and the traffic is horrible out there."

I doffed my hat. "Thank you so much, Lindsey, for the directions and advice. I will heed both." I headed for the hotel exit.

The doorman asked. "Cab, Señor?"

"No thanks. I'll walk."

I looked at the streets. It was just as Lindsey described it. It was a good day for a walk through. The weather was cool and crisp. I didn't notice anyone following me, though with this many people on the streets unless my shadow was as incompetent as Wilmer was last night, it would be virtually impossible to tell if I were being tailed. I did check back a few times though and saw nothing out of the ordinary. I made it to La Cantina a few minutes before three and saw Wilmer Cook standing at the entrance.

He was still as pungent as last night. He was dressed the same way I saw him in the hotel except for a pink tie. He glowered at me. "You got me in a lot of trouble with Mr. Fiste."

I laughed. "Your problem, sonny. Now be a good boy and step away. I have an appointment with your boss."

Still laughing, I walked inside the restaurant. Wilmer came up behind me. "Step into the cloakroom. Mr. Fiste wanted me to make sure you weren't carrying anything dangerous."

I went inside the cloakroom. It was empty. I decided once and for all, I was going to have to show Wilmer how the world worked. I wouldn't be attracting any undue attention giving Wilmer his lesson away from prying eyes.

"Okay, turn around slowly. I'm going to frisk you. I want your hands behind your head," Wilmer said in with a touch of menace in his voice.

I needed to make a snap decision. Would I allow a lowlife gunsel like Wilmer to frisk me? I quickly weighed the pros and cons of letting him do this to me.

Decision made, I turned around to face Wilmer. There are times in one's life when one has to make a stand. If word ever got out I stood for a frisk from a two-bit punk like Wilmer Cook, my reputation would suffer greatly.

Wilmer made a mistake, he thought I was cowed and wasn't prepared when I attacked him. I twisted one of his arms behind him and he let out a howl. I took his pistol from him. He used some pretty choice words. It was nothing I hadn't heard before.

"Come on, asshole, this will really impress your boss. Who knows, maybe he will give you a raise and a promotion," I said as I frog-walked him to the maître'd's desk.

"Miller Rixey and a friend to see Mr. Fiste. We are expected."

He was an older swarthy-looking man. Gray hair, medium build and wore the look of a man who been doing this job his entire life and seen everything. He led me to Mr. Fiste's table, which was located in a private room. Fiste was as I expected from the picture. He looked six foot five and probably tipped the scales at three hundred fifty. I shoved Wilmer into a wall and tossed Willard's pistol on the table. Both hands free, I turned to the maître'd and gave him three hundred pesos and thanked him for his assistance. Once he left, I spoke to Mr. Hanover Fiste.

I pointed at Wilmer. "A crippled street vendor took his gun away from him. I made her give it back."

Fiste roared with laughter. "Wilmer, please leave. It's time for the men to talk."

If looks could kill, the one Wilmer gave me as he slunk out of the room would have planted me.

Fiste continued. "You are as my reports on you have indicated. You are truly a rare breed, Mr. Rixey. Wild, tough, and intelligent is a rare find in today's society."

I brushed away the compliments. "Why did you want to meet me, Mr. Fiste?"

"Straight to the point, I like your attitude in a man. Let me get to the point. What do you know about the Chalice of Power? Don't play dumb with me Mr. Rixey, my reports indicate you are in Mexico City to attempt to recover the Chalice."

I shrugged. "I know about the history of the artifact and I also know something of the powers it's supposed to have."

Fiste's head bobbed. "Who are you attempting to recover it for, Mr. Rixey?"

I shook my head. "You know I can't tell you, Mr. Fiste. I would be violating a trust."

"I would expect nothing less from you, Mr. Rixey. I was just seeing how far you would go. What would you say if I told you I was prepared to pay you twenty-five million dollars if you happened to find it and would give it to me?"

"What about the person who originally hired me?"

Fiste waved one of his huge hands dismissively. "They are giving you nothing for your task. They are cheating you. I am giving you a fair share of what the item is worth."

"Why do you want The Chalice? Now it's time for you to be honest with me isn't it, Mr. Fiste?"

"A fair question. I am a collector of artifacts. It's one of the few pleasures I still enjoy. The Chalice would be a wonderful addition to my collection. Once I have the Chalice, I'd invite you to my estate to view my collection. I promise you, you will be impressed."

Though I would sooner cut off one of my arms before I would betray the trust of a client, I decided there was no reason not to play along and see where Fiste's involvement would lead me. "You made a generous offer, Mr. Fiste. While I, if I accepted your offer, I would be unable to ever work as a private investigator again. I must admit though, twenty-five million dollars would go a long way in overcoming any problems. Give me a day or so to think your offer over? Fair enough?"

Fiste nodded. "I can see you are a man who knows, in the long run, he has to look out for himself first and foremost. Shall we meet in a few days?"

"Sounds good." I paused. "One thing. I don't want to keep seeing your cheap gunsels following me. For that matter, anyone in your employ following me. I'm pretty quick on picking up on tails. I'll kill the next one you send after me. Do you understand?"

Fiste roared with laughter again. "You are coming in loud and clear, Mr. Rixey. As wild as you are, I don't have the slightest doubt you would do exactly what you promised."

I stood. "Good day. You will be hearing from me." I couldn't help but crack a smile as I left.

I didn't see Wilmer in the restaurant nor did I see him following me. It turned out to be a productive meeting. I knew for sure Fiste interjected himself into the Chalice derby, though I didn't believe the reason he wanted it was what he told me. I headed back to the hotel and decided it was time to take a nap. This had been a long day and I still needed to meet with Morgan and Fingers in about five or six hours.

Chapter Nineteen

"But sometimes when you are getting nowhere, you have to give the wasps' nest a wallop." Benjamin Black.

It felt like my head had just hit the pillow when I heard the annoying ringing of the room phone. I glanced at the clock on the table by my bed and saw it was eight thirty P.M. I'd been asleep for four hours. I groaned. I was going to have to be getting up to greet Morgan and Fingers. I reached for the phone, fumbled and dropped it, picked it up and tried to sound as coherent as my sleepy brain would permit.

"Yes?"

"Señor Rixey, this is Señora Valdez at the front desk. I have two packages from *La Compañía de Vestuario*. They are a costume company in Mexico City. Would you like us to deliver them to your room or would you prefer to come down to the lobby to pick them up?"

It was an easy decision. "Please have someone bring the packages up."

"Very good, Señor. Say, ten minutes?"

"Fine." I heard her click off.

I was somewhat presentable when I heard a knock on my door ten minutes later. "Room service."

I walked to the door, opened it, and saw the same bellman who initially checked me into the room. I pointed to the table. "Set them there." I fumbled in my pockets and came up with a fifty peso note and handed it to him.

Nodding gratefully, he said. "Thank you, Señor. Is there anything else I can do for you?"

"I'm good. Thanks for bringing up the packages." I watched him leave the room.

The packages represented something I overlooked initially. If you aren't dressed the right way for the Day of the Dead parade, you will stick out like a sore thumb. Naturally, the day before the biggest festival in Mexico there was not a costume to be found anywhere. Luckily, Señor Sanchez came through big time. He was able to find a couple of outfits for Fingers and me. After I mentioned to him Mr. Chen was interested in my project, he went to work.

I opened the first box. It contained a black top hat, a set of tails with a skeleton outline on the back and front, a pair of black pants with a similar design, a horrible-looking ruffled purple shirt, a lavender tie tastefully adorned with white skulls, a white skull mask and a white cane with a zombie head on top. I checked out the shirt and saw it was my size, so the other package was going to be Fingers. I couldn't resist the urge to try on the costume. I admired myself in front of a mirror. I thought I looked quite dapper. I took off the costume and put it back in the box. I looked at my watch. It was nine thirty P.M. I went to the minibar, poured myself a cup of coffee, and lit up a cigarette. I put my legs up on the table as I sat on the couch. I reached for the remote and finally found a station where English was spoken. I knew I wouldn't have long to wait.

Chapter Twenty

"Things fall apart and happen out of stupidity and carelessness." John Sandford.

About ten, I heard a knock on the door, followed by a clicking sound and I heard the door being pushed open.

"Miller?"

I got up when I heard the feminine voice. "Hey Morgan. How are things going? How was the trip?"

I walked over and we embraced. She dropped her suitcase and garment bag as we hugged. She hadn't changed a bit since the time we spent together after our adventures in Argentina and our wonderful vacation in D.C. She is the perfect field agent. She just looks like another pretty face and seems to be as deadly as a kitten. One thing I learned about her from our visit to Argentina was you misjudged her at your own risk.

"The worst part of the trip was the cab ride. Did you know traffic sucks?"

I laughed. "So I've been told."

I pointed to the bedroom with a closed door. "Your digs for our duration down here. What's in the garment bag?"

She smiled coyly. "Oh, just a little something to wear tomorrow." She unzipped the bag and revealed a long, black, and very lacy dress. She pulled a mask off one of the hangers. It was your basic white with some blue coloring around the eyes and attached to the mask were some flowers. She reached into the bottom of the bag and pulled out a box. When she opened it and took it out, I saw she had brought a long black wig with her. She was set. She walked into her bedroom and was back shortly.

"I presume you have some sort of plan for this adventure?"

I nodded. "Yeah. I'm waiting for the final part of our team to show, then I'll tell you both at once. Grab yourself a drink."

She walked to the minibar and grabbed a couple of the airline-size bottles of whiskey. She unscrewed the top of the first one and gulped it. She quickly followed suit with the second bottle. "Damn, I needed a stiff drink after suffering through the cab ride."

I went to the room safe, opened it, and pulled out a small carrying case. I closed the room safe and heard it lock. I stood up and handed it to her. "Your brand, I believe?" I went back to the couch and flopped down on it. I picked up my coffee cup and lit another cigarette. Now I was just waiting for Fingers.

"Oh, Miller. You remembered. You really do love me," she cooed as she tested the Sig Sauer P 229-Legion. She took the case and went back into her room. When she came back out, she put the Sig in a shoulder holster. She headed to the minibar for some coffee. "I don't want to get too lit right now. We'll have time enough later."

I heard a knock on the door. "Mr. Rixey?"

I stood up and walked to the door. "Ah, the third member of our crew." I opened the door and there stood Fingers Malone. "Good to see you again, Fingers."

He frowned. "Julian, if you please. People might get the wrong idea about me. I have a reputation to maintain."

I handed him a card key. "Here is your room. It's 463. You can go there once we discuss what we are going to be doing tomorrow. Oh, yeah, before I forget, here is your costume for tomorrow," I said, handing him his package.

I pulled a map of the area out of my pocket. "Now pay attention." I pointed to the map. "We are here," I said pointing to the hotel. "We need to be at this intersection which runs parallel to the meeting place and the hotel by nine A.M. Here's where you come in, Fingers, I mean, Julian. If a snatch is going to happen, it's got to happen in this intersection. Once you are out of gun range, you should be golden. Lots of people will be in the street and another person dressed in a costume isn't going to be noticed. Take the briefcase back to your room and stay there. If all goes well, Morgan and I will be there after we get done surveilling the OTO meeting. We will arrive separately and, after the snatch, Morgan and I will head back to our room, change, and monitor the OTO meeting. I'm sure it will be a lively one if Julian pulls off the snatch. Colonel Pong is going to have to explain why he is thirty million or so short on the agreed price for the Chalice. Any questions?"

Fingers spoke up. "Yeah, how will I know who to go after? I can't be grabbing every briefcase I see out there?"

I nodded. "Good question. The briefcase carrier is North Korean, very short and very thin, very deadly, and will be accompanied by a man who is six foot seven, weighs over three hundred pounds, and has olive skin. The man I'm talking about is Eldor Jamieson Crypt. He is the chairman of OTO. He is always dressed in a style impossible to miss. White suit, black shirt, red tie, and a white fedora." I took out a picture of Crypt and Pong and laid them on the table. "These are the people involved in our snatch. Crypt will stand out like a sore thumb."

Fingers first picked up the picture of Crypt, then Pong. He nodded. "You're right, Mr. Rixey, both these birds will be hard to miss." He shifted his feet nervously. "Look, Mr. Rixey, I know I owe you big time and I also know you wouldn't be paying me this well unless the job was dangerous. What's in the case or supposed to be in the case?"

"The client's name is Lothar Zogg. Normally I wouldn't be able to tell you. I'm sure Julian has already figured it out. There are some very valuable coins in there. At least I am pretty sure there are. They are the proceeds from a robbery staged by a group of North Korean operatives. It's important to this client the coins be recovered and his name is kept out of the news. He's afraid if word got out he has been robbed, it would cause him to lose face."

Fingers nodded and yawned. "I need some sleep. If you don't need me anymore, I'm going to head to my room. I'll be outside in costume at nine A.M. I have a feeling you and your lady friend have a few other things to discuss that are way beyond my paygrade." We shook hands, then he bowed, grabbed his costume package, and headed out of the room.

"Good night, Julian," Morgan called after him.

"Thank you, ma'am."

I waited until I heard the door click closed before turning my attention to Morgan.

Morgan took a seat on the couch and patted a spot next to her for me to sit. "So, what favor did you do for Julian? It must have been a big one."

I nodded. "He was accused of murdering some lowlife. I'd been working on a case involving a jewel theft. I was able to prove at the time witnesses said the lowlife was shot that Fingers was busily engaged blowing the safe. He got five years and did two." I smiled. "Not a bad deal when you're looking at forty-five years minimum and you have to do one hundred percent of the time. I use him on jobs from time to time."

Morgan nodded. "Wow, crazy. Now, why do I have a sinking feeling you are holding back some information you're dying to tell me?"

I chuckled. "Because you are one of the smartest people I know. Oh, there is more and, I promise you, if the State Department ever finds out what I have planned for Colonel Pong, they are going to be really unhappy with me as well as anyone involved with me."

I shrugged helplessly with a what-can-I-do look on my face. I knew I was in way over my head and didn't like the feeling.

I got up, lit a cigar, and walked back over to the minibar. I poured myself a cup of coffee then returned to the couch shaking my head. I took a seat and put my legs on the table. "You read the information I sent you?"

Morgan nodded.

"The time travel ability of the Chalice was a big-enough threat.

Since then I've been convinced of the existence of another power The Chalice has the ability to generate an EMP attack. It's been pretty well documented. Every time the Chalice is used, there are reports of cars no longer working, computers frying out, and other things that normally quit working after an EMP attack. The areas are small but getting larger with each use of the Chalice. I figure it's just a matter of time before the power of the Chalice becomes big enough to take out whole cities and maybe even entire countries. Can you imagine what an EMP attack on New York City would do?"

Morgan shivered.

"North Korea got interested for the obvious reasons. If the United States were disabled, their leaders would be free to do whatever came to their sick minds. I have a feeling they would like to put the rest of the world in the sixteenth century while keeping their current position. North Korea would be in the catbird's seat. They'd be in a position to do something they have been unable to do. They will make demands on the world and the world would be forced to listen."

"Sounds really bad."

"Oh, I have some good news. You know who Hanover Fiste is?"

"Everyone knows who he is. Fiste is a British billionaire banker or some such. I wouldn't be much of an intel officer if I didn't."

I turned red. "He offered me twenty-five-million dollars for the Chalice. He claims he wants it for his artifact collection. I'm not buying it."

Morgan nodded. "Agreed. The only question is what he wants the Chalice for. Is it for time travel or to use it for an EMP attack, or maybe even both?"

"Right. Assuming he wants the Chalice for either purpose, it's not good. No one, not even a rich guy, would offer me twenty-five million to betray my client's trust and eventually turn over the Chalice simply for his own collection."

"You know who Joseph Chen is, I'm guessing?"

"You're talking about the head of Red Chinese intelligence in Hong Kong?"

"One and the same. It seems in the commission of these high-line robberies the son of a Party official was killed. He knows, as I do, that Pong was the head of the ring and wants him taken care of. He has groups looking for him all over the world. Officially, they cannot be seen doing anything that might be construed as rebuking anything North Korea does. He did me a big favor when I was in Hong Kong. He and your Gramps are longtime friends. Anyway, he wants me to kill Pong if I get the opportunity. He even sent me a sniper rifle to move the process along."

Morgan put her hand over her mouth. "Miller, what are you going to do? You can't go around bumping people off."

"Normally I'd agree with you. It's not my first run around with this guy. He is really bad news and needs to be put down."

"So, you're going to try tomorrow at the meeting?"

"If the opportunity presents itself. I hate getting involved like this, but I don't feel like I have any choice. I don't feel helpless very often. In this case, I know I am really up against it."

She took my hand and looked deeply into my eyes. "You know I'll back any play you make and support you one-hundred percent. I am also smart enough to realize you really don't have a good choice here."

I nodded. "I was counting on your support." I looked at a clock on the wall. "Time for some sleep. We have a full day tomorrow."

Morgan nodded and we both got up and retired to her bedroom.

Chapter Twenty-one

"Hell is empty and all the devils are here." William Shakespeare, The Tempest.

2 November 20xx, Día de Muertos (The Day of the Dead), Mexico City

Our day started early. Fingers came back to my hotel room and I gave him and Morgan earpieces so we would be able to hear each other over the noise being generated from the parade and the parade spectators. I stepped out on my ledge and looked down. Even at eight A.M., the streets were full of people.

We made it to our stations by the agreed-to nine A.M. time. There was a light rain falling and the skies showed only signs of continued rain. The rain didn't seem to have an effect on either the participants in the parade or the spectators. The crowds were boisterous. You were able to hear strains of music coming from Mariachi bands. Everyone seemed to be in a very festive mood. Morgan, Fingers, and I stood at the intersecting street of the El Grande and the OTO meeting site. I was happy I made the last-minute decision to insist on earpieces. I was afraid we wouldn't be able to communicate due to the noise. Even though it was still relatively early in the day, already a fair amount of action was going on in the streets. Vendors were peddling their wares and people were selling programs listing the parade order.

It was my first time attending the Day of the Dead parade and what a parade it was! Balloons similar in size to the kind you would expect to see in the Rose Bowl parade or perhaps Macy's Thanksgiving Day parade were all either tastefully adorned with skulls or made into skull shapes. One balloon caught my attention. It was a skull wearing a top hat with a half-smoked cigar sticking out of its skeletal mouth. The floats were too numerous to count, all adorned with skeletons or other symbols representing the Day of the Dead. Some of the floats contained one to three people mounted on swings and making good use of them. Marching bands would also pass blaring their music in an attempt to be heard over the crowd noise. What an experience the parade was.

I wanted to give the earpieces one final check to make sure we would hear what was going on in the room over the din of the parade. We checked them in the room and they worked there. Now we were under what I like to call game conditions.

I bit down a transmitter located in my mouth. "People, check in."

I heard Morgan and Fingers check in and I relaxed for a moment. At least the first part of my plan was working.

I spotted Eldor Jamieson Crypt walking with a man who I was sure was Colonel Pong. Crypt was dressed in his signature outfit of a white suit, black shirt, white fedora, and red tie, just like my intelligence report indicated. Even though he was wearing a mask, with his size and outfit, he would be hard to miss. The man he was walking with also wore a mask and had the same physical characteristics of Colonel Pong I read about and carried a metallic-looking briefcase. I couldn't tell if he'd somehow attached the briefcase to his wrist or not. I was too far away. I didn't believe it had been attached. If it that were the case, it was going to make the snatch almost impossible under the circumstances.

I bit down on the transmitting device. "Fingers, your target is about one hundred feet from you and closing. They are to the right of you. It looks like they have the briefcase with them."

"Copy that. I have him in sight and the case does not appear to be handcuffed to the carrier. What amateurs," he sneered.

"Morgan, come on over and stand by me. We may need to help Fingers get away."

She glided over to me and took my hand. At this point, all we were able to do is wait and see if we were going to be needed.

There didn't seem to be any security for Crypt or Pong. I guess because Crypt was used to the area, coming here for so long and never running into any problems, he was getting a little sloppy. Overconfidence will get you every time.

I saw Fingers pull a long thin blade from somewhere and stick the knife in Pong's arm. Pong dropped the briefcase in reaction to being stabbed and saw Fingers field it on the first bounce. Pong's mouth fluttered open in a scream of pain. He and Crypt were temporarily paralyzed by the savagery and speed of the attack. Before they were able to recover their senses, Fingers was gone, vanishing in confusion and using a large number of people watching the parade to aid his escape. I saw Pong, using his right arm, pull a pistol, and saw Crypt shake his head no. Pong put the pistol back in its holster.

Seeing Fingers' mission was a success, Morgan and I needed to complete our part of the mission to make the day a total success. We walked hand in hand back to our hotel and, when we entered the crowded lobby, no one paid any attention to us. We were soon back in our room.

Chapter Twenty-two

"We are all ready to be savage in some cause. The difference between a good man and a bad one is the choice of the cause." William James.

We quickly changed out of our costumes and prepared for the next stage of our mission. After we were changed and enjoyed a celebratory drink, my cellphone rang. I recognized the number as one of Finger's. I clicked on. "Miller Rixey."

"Julian here. I'm back in my room. There were no problems once I got away. My concern is the briefcase is booby-trapped. I've seen this type of briefcase before. They are often trapped with something designed to kill the opener, not to destroy the contents of the case, if the opener uses the wrong sequence to open it. With a safeguard like what they have, no reason to use handcuffs to secure it." He paused and then chuckled. "I'd recommend you get someone down here with a clue on how to open this damn thing."

"Thanks for the update, Fingers. Just stay put and maybe enjoy some room service. You earned it. Oh yeah, send me a picture of the briefcase. I have something requiring my immediate attention. I will be in touch with you when I get back."

I clicked off and thought for a moment. I decided to call Zogg and tell him it looked like we recovered his coins and explain the problem with the briefcase to him. Chances were good that with his resources, he would have an employee or consultant who would be knowledgeable about the bag.

I dialed Zogg's number. This time his direct line.

"Mr. Rixey, I trust you are calling me with some good news?"

"Yes and no, Mr. Zogg. It looks like we probably recovered your coins. Fingers seems to think there is a good chance the bag is booby-trapped. I am sending you a picture of the briefcase even as we speak. Can you send someone down to look at it?"

"Yes. I'll send down Christopher Manny. You will know him by sight. There will be no need for any passwords or countersigns. He will be down there in about five hours. Thank you for finding my coins."

"Fine, I will be done with my other work by then. Tell him Room 327 at the El Grande. If things don't go according to plan, I'm going to be on the run. One last thing, Mr. Zogg. Do you still want Colonel Pong taught the lesson that he made a mistake when he chose to rob you?"

"If you would be so good as to perform my simple request, I will be forever in your debt, Mr. Rixey."

"Outstanding, Mr. Zogg. I will do my best to impart the lesson to him," I said stiffly. I clicked off.

I glanced at my watch. Time to leave and learn about the Chalice and what was happening to it.

I went to the safe and pulled out the gun case. I quickly assembled the rifle and slapped the magazine in place. I pulled my shoulder holster on and double-checked my pistol. I was ready to go.

Morgan came out of her bedroom carrying her laptop under her arm and the listening device control in her free hand. She wore an earpiece. "There's not even anyone in the room as of yet. I wonder if they decided to cancel the meeting?" She placed the laptop in the safe and closed the door. We both heard it click.

I shook my head. "Delayed it. The meeting is too important for OTO to cancel. Groups like OTO thrive on tradition." I put my earpiece in and, like Morgan, heard nothing.

"Let's get this over with," Morgan said grimly.

I nodded and we both stepped out on the ledge.

Chapter Twenty-three

"Never underestimate the power of human stupidity." Robert A. Heinlein.

Nothing much changed weather-wise from the time we entered our room to the time we stepped out on the ledge. It was still misting. I carried my sniper rifle on my right-hand side to make it harder for someone looking up at us or looking from across the street to see I was carrying it.

We made better progress toward the courtyard area than I did last night. There was no chance of falling down one of the gaps in the ledge due to not seeing it. I wasn't too concerned about the likelihood of someone seeing Morgan and me on the ledge. People on the street would be focused on the parade and probably no one was in the office buildings across the street. If anyone saw us, they would probably mistake us for enthusiastic parade spectators trying to get a better view. When we made it to the courtyard area, it looked as forlorn and abandoned as it seemed last night.

I rested the rifle on the partition I discovered last night. It gave me a clear view of the three rooms at the top of the building. I wouldn't be seen from here and shortly I would be ending the miserable life of Colonel Pong. The world would be better off without him. His robbery ring made the world a more dangerous place. We would be better off without him. I kept telling myself those facts, hoping I'd believe it eventually.

I sighted the rifle and worked the scope until I was satisfied. With a weapon this powerful and a scope this good, the one hundred or so yards from my perch to the office window would be an easy shot. Satisfied all was in order, I leaned the rifle against the partition, removed my earpiece, and took a seat next to it.

"This your first trip to Mexico City?"

Morgan shook her head. "No. I played in some qualifying rounds in a Girls' Seventeen and Under basketball tournament the last time I was down here. I was a senior in high school. We won the tournament and qualified for the World Games, where we also won."

"Very impressive. I didn't realize I knew a World Champion."

She laughed.

"I bet you didn't have as much fun or excitement on your basketball trip as you are having on this trip, did you?"

Morgan giggled. "This trip has been kind of boring, though I am expecting a change fairly soon."

I nodded.

Morgan put her hand to her ear. "I just heard the door open and I'm hearing a bunch of voices and the sounds of people filling the room. Too much movement and too much chatter to make out what exactly is being said."

I got up, put my earpiece back in, and began watching the room through the sight of my rifle. I saw Colonel Pong with his arm in a sling and an outraged look on his face. Various members of the OTO board were coming up to Crypt and bowing as they shook hands with him. Crypt mumbled something and the multiple members took their seats.

He called the meeting to order and began to speak. "A regrettable incident occurred on our way to the meeting." He pointed to Pong. "The good Colonel was bringing the final payment of fifty million dollars to pay for the rental of our most prized artifact, the Chalice of Power. I have people looking all over Mexico City for the thief. Quite frankly, I am not optimistic. There was clearly a leak from someplace. We will deal with the leak later. For now, I am asking we give Colonel Pong and his group one week to come up with the remainder of the funds. He has assured me he will be able to come up with the funds in a short period. Keep in mind his group has already paid the Order four hundred and fifty million dollars. I so move."

Every hand at the table was raised. I couldn't believe what I saw. Crypt just cracked a twisted smile. He nodded slowly.

"We will be meeting in Denver at the usual place in one week," Crypt concluded.

"Before we move on to new business, do we have any questions?" Crypt asked. He noticed a hand in the air. "Yes, Number One."

"I was looking forward to another demonstration of the Chalice. Am I to assume the attack on you and Colonel Pong made you decide to keep the Chalice away from this site?"

Crypt nodded. "Correct, Number One. The Chalice of Power is our most powerful artifact and I have concerns concerning the security of this building and am concerned about potential leaks."

"Mr. Chairman?"

"Yes, Number Two."

"If the Colonel's group fails to make the payment in one week, will default be declared and the Chalice will be made available to another group?"

Crypt smiled with no warmth. "As I said earlier, his group has already paid The Order four hundred and fifty million dollars. They have more than shown their good faith. I think there is no hurry on this matter. One week or two weeks, it's all the same as far as I am concerned. Now if there are no other questions, on to new business." He pressed a buzzer on the table and the door of the room swung open.

A bald-headed man walked into the room. He was at least six foot six and looked like there wasn't an ounce of body fat on him. He nodded to Crypt and took a standing position behind one of the board members.

Crypt began to speak. "Number Four, can you explain the ten-million-dollar wire transfer from a Hanover Fiste to your daughter's checking account? Did you really believe we were stupid?"

I saw the enormous bald guy lift the person Crypt referred to as Number Four out of his seat. He turned the startled man around.

"No. I did nothing to betray the Order. You have to believe me," Number Four screamed.

The bald man forced both of his thumbs into the eyes of Number Four, or should I say what used to be Number Four. The man's body buckled and he slumped to the floor.

Crypt buzzed again and again the door swung open and two men entered. Crypt made a gesture and the two men picked up the dead body and took it from the room. The bald man stopped them for a moment and wiped his hands on the dead man's jacket. Once he was satisfied that his hands were blood-free, he gestured to the men.

Everyone in the room was focused on the horrible scene they just witnessed.

I decided I'd seen enough, heard enough, and the timing would be perfect. Pong was lined up in my sights. I took a deep breath and squeezed off two rounds. I heard the tinkle of the glass as the bullets crashed through the windows on their way to their target. I saw his body spin around from the force of the two rounds striking him in the head before it slowly dropped to the floor. There was little left of his head. I heard the screams of panic coming through my earpiece loud and clear. Morgan was already moving, heading back to our hotel suite when she saw me squeeze the trigger. I heard a lot of cursing and swearing in languages I didn't understand. I could tell from the tone and what. I knew they weren't kind words. It took us longer to make it back to the room as on the return trip we were both on our hands and knees. We wanted to make sure we couldn't be seen by anyone looking out the window. We were about fifty feet away from our room and all I heard over my earpiece was silence. They cleared the room. I didn't blame them. I wouldn't want to be found in a place with a dead body in it. We both crawled into our room. I stood up, closed the outside window and pulled the drapes. I lay on the carpet, totally spent.

Morgan pulled me up and walked me over to the couch. She went back to her bedroom and came out with a bottle of Macallan, my favorite tipple. Morgan went to the minibar, grabbed a couple of glasses, and joined me on the couch. She poured a generous amount in each glass and handed me one.

She smiled at me. "Thought I would bring you a little present. I was saving it for a special occasion and this seems like the time to bring it out."

I gratefully accepted the glass. "Morgan, what would I do without you?"

Chapter Twenty-four

"Time is the coin of your life. It is the only coin you have, and only you can determine how it will be spent. Be careful lest you let other people spend it for you." Carl Sandburg.

I enjoyed my drink for a few minutes. Then it was back to work. "Listen, Morgan, these OTO people are much more dangerous than I thought. To make things even worse, they apparently have a ton of cash."

Morgan nodded. "No kidding. They sounded batshit crazy. What the hell went on in there? All I got was the audio. I was afraid to stand up because someone in the room might see me. I didn't want to expose our position or get us shot. No good would come from either thing happening.

"I agree. You heard the part where Crypt blamed the robbery on a security leak?"

"Yes."

"He accused one of the members of the board, the one he called Number Four, of being the leaker. He claimed our old friend, Hanover Fiste, wired ten million dollars to Number Four's daughter's account."

She nodded.

"Crypt summoned a man, who turned out to be an assassin and more than likely is now the new Number Four. The man Crypt accused of leaking the information got his eyes gouged out by the assassin. The assassin was huge. He was bald, didn't look like he had an ounce of body fat on him, and I'd never seen such big hands. Once he went to work on Number Four, the room situation became very chaotic. It seemed like the best time to shoot Pong. I wanted to make sure Pong didn't leave the room alive, so it seemed like the right time to do it." I shrugged.

"Agreed. The only problem I see is the shooting may cause OTO to change their plans for their Denver meeting."

"I doubt it. They blamed the robbery, and I suspect OTO will blame the shooting, too, on Number Four. With him out of the way, they will feel secure again. I'm also positive they did not discover the listening devices in the room. They were pretty well hidden, so why change your plans if no one is listening?"

"Oh yeah, thanks for reminding me. I turned off the bugs as we were heading back to our room. I didn't want some police investigation stumbling over them."

"Good idea, the police won't be investigating anything. I saw them drag out Number Four's body and I suspect Pong's body is long gone and the room will be sanitized. By tomorrow, no one, other than the OTO board members, will know what went on in the room."

I stood up, fortified by my drink. "Now I have some phone calls to make. Let's get something to eat once I'm done."

Morgan smiled. "Sounds good. We just need to make sure we are back so you can meet the guy from Zogg."

She stood up and went into her bedroom. I went to the room safe and pulled my phone and laptop out. I also took the gun case out and broke down the rifle, placing it back in the case. I slid the case back in the room safe and heard the door shut.

First things first, time to call Fingers, Stuart, Zogg, and Chen. I would check my email later. I glanced at the room phone and saw the message light flickering. I shrugged, time for messages then.

"Fingers, Rixey here. How are things going?"

"Fine. Do you know how expensive a room service steak is? Man."

I laughed. "Don't worry about it. It's on my dime. With any luck, the man from Zogg will be here in a few hours. If our plan succeeds, you will be home, and spending your hard-earned money by the end of the day. I will have instructed Zogg to pay you fifty thousand dollars in cash once you bring the briefcase to his office. You won't have any problems. Manny will be with you all the way to Zogg's office."

"Okay. I don't mind telling you I'm nervous about this. I'm sure they have people looking for me all over the city."

"Just keep your head down and you will be fine. One thing, they claimed Pong was bringing fifty million dollars to the OTO. Zogg's coins are worth between thirty and thirty-five million. This means there were more than Zogg's coins in the briefcase." I thought for a moment. "Just turn over the whole briefcase to Zogg and I'll deal with him later."

"Gotcha."

My next call was to Andrew Stuart, the man responsible for me being here.

"This is Andrew Stuart."

"Miller Rixey here. The OTO didn't have the Chalice with them. Some security issue caused Crypt not to have it brought to the Mexico City meeting. They plan to have the Chalice at a meeting in Denver in a week. There was a reference to the usual place. I need you to find out where the usual place is." I figured he didn't need to know I created the security issue. The less he knew about who stole the briefcase, the better.

"I'll get on it right away. We both know they have never used the Chalice in Denver."

Even though he couldn't see me, I nodded. "Yes. I gathered from the reports you gave me. We don't have a lot of time to figure out where the usual place is. Oh yeah, thought I would mention this to you. I prefer you heard it from me first. Hanover Fiste has offered me twenty-five million to give him the Chalice when I find it. I told him I'm thinking about it." I heard a gasp on the other side of the phone. I laughed. "Don't worry, you're my client and I never betray a client. Besides, I'm not sure I'd live long enough to enjoy the money."

"When did he offer it to you?"

"I met with him yesterday in a restaurant in Mexico City and, before you ask, I am positive it was him. I suggest you get some field agents you can trust on him, fast. If he wants the Chalice, it can't be any good for the world."

"Thanks for telling me. I will. Keep me informed."

"I will." I clicked off.

It was time to call Lothar Zogg.

"Lothar Zogg. You have good news for me, Mr. Rixey?"

"Nothing has changed since we last spoke. We are waiting for your man to show up. One thing I didn't mention earlier was I doubt Colonel Pong will be causing you or anyone else any more problems or embarrassments."

Zogg would never know why I really killed Pong There was no reason he should. My purpose behind even telling him was excellent customer service. After all, at the Bishop Agency, we pride ourselves on giving the clients what they want, within reason. It would make him happy and perhaps he would give me a recommendation to another friend of his or he may wish to retain me for another case.

"Excellent, Mr. Rixey."

"Just so we're clear, Mr. Zogg. I am not an assassin, I'm a private investigator. I don't have a problem working for you on cases. If your future employment requires an assassin, I suggest you look elsewhere. I hope I made myself clear."

I knew a man like Zogg wasn't used to be talked to in the manner I was talking to him. I wanted to learn how he reacted.

Zogg's stammering voice came back over the phone. "You have made yourself very clear, Mr. Rixey. I understand very clearly. I do want to thank you for your assistance though."

"One more thing. Julian Malone will be coming back with Mr. Manny, hopefully with your coins. I expect there will be something extra in the briefcase as Pong was supposedly carrying fifty million dollars' worth of items."

"Yes, Mr. Rixey. What do you want to be done with the extra

items?"

I paused for a moment, giving what I wanted to be done some serious thought.

"If the items that aren't yours are liquid, please dispose of them and split the proceeds between the Breast Cancer Research Fund, Susan G. Komen Foundation, Living Through Breast Cancer, National Breast Cancer Foundation, Inc., and Breast Cancer Network of Strength. Those are the groups I typically donate to as they are the most likely to spend the donations on research. Make the donations anonymous. I'm sure you know how to make anonymous donations. I don't want to explain to the police how I came across the extra seventeen million."

"Consider it done. Anything else?"

"Mr. Malone will require fifty thousand in cash when he gives you the briefcase. Go ahead and pay him and take it out of my finder's fee."

"Very good."

"I'll see you when I see you, Mr. Zogg." I clicked off.

My final call was to Joseph Chen.

"Good to hear from you, Miller. My sources told me about your successful hunt."

I scratched my head. "You already know?"

"Yes, we have been monitoring various police bands and news services. It turns out a man resembling the Colonel was found in a very bad section of Mexico City. He seemed to be missing most of his head. They were able to identify him through his dental records. You must not be watching the news?"

"No, I've been busy on the phone since I returned."

"It's all over the news. North Korea is outraged and demanding a complete investigation of how a counselor officer would have a thing this outrageous happen to him."

I gulped. "So where does this leave me?"

"Unless you decide to confess or are caught with the weapon, nothing. I suggest you ask Colonel Burke to help you destroy the barrel. Once the weapon is destroyed, the investigation will reveal nothing. I look forward to seeing you on your next trip to Hong Kong. I also look forward to meeting Colonel Burke. You did well, Miller. Now, I need to go."

"One more thing of interest to you, Mr. Chen."

"Yes, Miller?"

"Hanover Fiste has entered the fray for the same item the North Koreans want and the U.S. Government has contracted with me to find."

"Why exactly would Mr. Fiste's location be of interest to me, Miller?"

"The item I am charged with finding is supposed to have the ability to create a dimension allowing for time travel. I don't know if the item really is capable of performing such a feat. What I do know is it does have the ability to cause an EMP attack in limited areas. Fiste offered me twenty-five million for the item. He gave me a reason I don't believe for wanting it. It was along the lines of completing his collection. Whatever his plans, whether it involves time travel or EMP attacks, it cannot be good for either of our countries."

"What did you tell him?"

"I told him I would think about it. You should know I would never betray a client. Right now, he is waiting for my response. I told Andrew

Stuart about the offer and he seems very concerned."

"You two met in Mexico City, I take it?"

"You take it correctly."

"Keep meeting with him. Don't worry about him, he has a fatal accident in his future, or perhaps a suicide. This is nothing you need concern yourself about. Thank you for confiding in me, Miller. We will speak again soon."

I heard him click off.

I went to the safe and took out the gun case. "Morgan, got a minute?"

Morgan came out of her bedroom dressed only in a robe and a towel wrapped around her head. "Whatcha need?"

I handed her the case. "Chen says the body of the good colonel has been discovered."

"Not at the building where you killed him?"

I shook my head. "Nope. His body was found a good distance away. Chen says it's all over the news and North Korea is going bonkers. He thinks it would be a great idea to destroy the barrel. I also think it's a great idea. After you take care of the barrel, wipe the gun. We get rid of it like we got rid of our weapons in Argentina. You know how messy things can get when you get caught with a murder weapon. I imagine it gets twice as messy if it happens to you in a foreign country."

Morgan held out her hands. "Not a problem. Give me ten minutes and the barrel will be untraceable and I will have wiped the gun clean."

She walked back into her room.

I logged onto my laptop and, after going through the tedious but necessary steps, found myself back on the internet. Only spam was in my email. I shrugged and logged off. As I went back to the safe to put my laptop away, I noticed again a red light flashing on the room phone indicating a message still awaited me.

I pressed the button and heard the mechanical voice of the hotel's messaging system. "You have a message from Hanover Fiste. Please press one to listen to this message. Please press two to save this message for later. Please press three to delete this message."

"Hey, Morgan. Get out here. Something interesting just came up."

"Out in a minute."

Morgan came out of the room, wearing surgical gloves and brandishing the gun case. "Mission accomplished." She set the case on the table in front of the couch. She frowned. "So, what's so important my immediate presence is needed?"

"You'll never guess who called. I'm pretty sure you wouldn't have been too happy if I hadn't called you."

Morgan looked confused.

I put the phone on speaker and pressed number 1.

The message began to play.

Chapter Twenty-five

"You have to be careful of people who like to talk a big game but can't back it up." Ray Lewis.

"The voice you are about to hear is the man who wishes to become my new partner for the Chalice of Power, Hanover Fiske."

"Please meet with me at La Cantina at seven. I will be in the same room as I was during our last meeting. Something necessitates meeting earlier than either of us planned."

"I've never been there before. Is it a fancy place?"

I made a gesture with my hand. "Kind of, nothing too elegant is needed. Use your always-good judgment."

I looked at my watch. "In the meantime, we aren't going anywhere until Zogg's guy shows."

It seemed like we had a few more hours to wait. Morgan decided to do some things in her bedroom and I decided to take a snooze on the couch. I knew I'd hear Manny knocking on the door from the couch.

The knock came in about ninety minutes.

I stood up and called out. "Yes?"

"Miller, Chris."

I went to the door and took a quick peek through the viewer. I saw Chris Manny standing outside. I opened it.

When I opened the door, I saw Chris was accompanied by four very rough looking men. We shook hands. I looked at him quizzically.

"Part of the group is going to escort Mr. Malone back to Mr. Zogg's office. I have two more men waiting in an SUV and once we get the briefcase open, off we go," he answered.

I nodded. "Room 463 for Mr. Malone and do you see any problems opening the briefcase?"

Chris shook his head. "Nah. You sent a good picture. We have the make and model. The bag is no doubt booby-trapped, but it's not a very complicated model. I should have it open in about five minutes."

"Let me call Malone and tell him you're coming. He is armed and I don't want a shootout occurring here."

Chris nodded.

I dialed Fingers. "Your escort and someone who can open the briefcase without killing or maiming anyone will be at your room in less than five minutes. Two knocks, a pause, one knock, a pause, and followed by two knocks. Got it?"

"Sure thing. I got it. I'll see you when you get back."

"Keep yourself available. I may require your skills shortly. Good luck."

"Yes, Mr. Rixey. I sure will. Thanks again for bringing me in on such an easy score. I really needed the cash."

I turned back to Chris and shook hands. "Have a safe trip back. You caught what I told Malone?"

Chris nodded. He barked an order to his men and I saw them heading for the stairway as I closed the door. About ten minutes later, my phone rang. I recognized the number and pressed answer.

"Bag is open and disarmed. We are heading out. Best of luck on the rest of your mission," Manny's voice came over the phone. I heard him click off.

Chapter Twenty-six

"Death is the solution to all problems. No man—no problem." Joseph Stalin.

We left the hotel room at about six thirty. Morgan was dressed in an adorable long dress, with a slit up one of the sides, some medium height-heels, and a very fashionable clutch purse. I was guessing her pistol was in the purse. I chose not to ask.

"Cab, Señor?" the doorman greeted us as we left the El Grande.

I shook my head no. It had stopped raining. This wasn't a surprise as Mexico City doesn't usually get much in the way of rain, especially in November. The streets were still crowded, but since the parade had ended and some people were planning on leaving, the numbers were about half of what they were during the parade. I took my usual precautions on being followed and nodded to myself, satisfied we were probably not being tailed. It looked like Fiste may have gotten the message and was taking me seriously.

As we neared La Cantina, I smelled a very unpleasant odor. I immediately knew who the source of the sickly perfume smell was. It had to be Wilmer. I spotted him. He was standing with some young-looking, wiry man, with ashen skin and black hair. He was dressed as garishly as Wilmer as he was dressed in a green shirt, yellow tie, and a flaming red suit. I'll give him the fact he didn't smell as bad as Wilmer. I eyed Wilmer closely: red shirt, green tie, and a white Panama suit. Naturally, he was wearing his black racing cap. I smiled to myself. Maybe after I retire from the detective business, I'd be able to open a school to teach minions how to dress for success? It seemed like a needed calling.

"Who's your boyfriend, gunsel?" I growled.

"Keep riding me, shamus, and you're going to find out."

Morgan began to laugh in her melodic way. "Miller, where do you find these guys? Shamus? If this guy knew how to read, I would say he read one too many Damon Runyon stories." She wrinkled her nose. "Someone or something smells really bad."

Wilmer's escort stepped up. "If it should matter to either of you, my name is Alfie Foley." You didn't have to a linguist to realize his accent was pretty clearly British. He eyed Morgan wolfishly. "I'm going to enjoy strip-searching you," he rasped.

"Not very polite, what's a girl to do?" Morgan pointed to the checkroom. "In there I suppose?"

Foley smiled, revealing a terrible set of teeth. I sensed they would look even worse when Morgan was finished with him. "Good choice, slitch." He nudged her toward the checkroom. He turned to Wilmer. "See, if you are a good persuader, people will do as you ask." He turned his attention back to Morgan. "In with you now, and I'll have none of your lip."

Morgan studied him carefully. "You sure you want to do this? Mr. Fiste will be really unhappy with you. He needs us to help in one of his schemes."

"You're testing my patience, slitch. Off with you now," Foley roared.

Morgan shrugged and said cryptically. "Remember, you asked for this."

"After my boy Alfie is done with your girlfriend, he's going to search you. What do you think of me taking charge, shamus?"

"I'll let you know in a minute or so."

I heard a scream from behind the closed door. The voice was male and was high pitched. The door exploded open and Alfie staggered out, blood gushing from his nose.

"Fugging slitch sucker punched me. I'm gonna kill her for this," Foley whined.

"Maybe you should tend to your broken nose before you begin trying to kill people," I offered in an attempt to be helpful.

Morgan appeared a few moments later. She was smiling. "I guess inspection is done. Now Wilmer, let's go see your boss."

Wilmer ground his teeth and made some threatening noises. He pointed Foley to the men's room and very reluctantly led us to the room where Hanover Fiste was seated. As we entered, I observed him, he looked like he had just finished a many-course meal and was now enjoying a glass of wine. He looked up as we entered.

"Forgive me for not getting up. Good to see you, Mr. Rixey, and this must be Colonel Morgan Burke, late of the OAR?"

She nodded.

He made a sweeping gesture. "Please, the both of you, take a seat and help me enjoy this wine." He rang a bell and three waiters showed up instantly. "Please clear the table leaving the wine and bring some glasses for my guests." He looked at us. "Do either of you need anything to eat? The menu here is really quite good."

We took our seats as we both shook our heads no. Fiste nodded.

"Did you see Wilmer and Alfie when you came in? They were supposed to meet you and bring you here."

I smiled wanly. "Alfie suffered an accident and it seems Wilmer is tending to him. They are going to be a while."

Fiste nodded. "Mexico City can be a dangerous place. I'm correct about Mexico City and danger, aren't I, Colonel Burke?" He smiled at her.

"Very dangerous indeed," Morgan concurred.

Fiste turned his attention to the waiters. "Hurry up and get this table cleared. We are all very busy people."

Once the waiters left and Morgan and I were drinking our wine, Fiste leaned forward. "Events are happening and my plans are changing. I need to know if you, Mr. Rixey, are going to cooperate with me and help me in my venture to acquire the Chalice or not?"

Chapter Twenty-seven

"Of mankind, we may say in general they are fickle, hypocritical, and greedy of gain." Niccolo Machiavelli.

"Time for me to lay my cards on the table. I have a man who was on the inside of the OTO. He was actually a board member. He missed his check-in call about an hour ago and I am concerned."

I thought, *First time for everything.* "Well, Mr. Fiste, perhaps something came up? There might be any number of reasons."

I saw no reason to give Fiste any of my knowledge of what happened at the OTO meeting and inform him his inside source would never be calling him.

Fiste cleared his throat. "Young man, when you work with Hanover Fiste, you are never too busy to keep an appointment with him. He never missed a check-in call or any type of appointment with me before. There was no reason for him to start now."

Morgan sipped her wine. "This wine is splendid. I must remember its name for future reference."

She picked up the bottle and studied the label for a moment and then put it back on the table.

Fist looked at her beaming. "I'm so happy you are pleased, my dear. It's from my private stock."

Morgan nodded and looked thoughtful. "As you said earlier, Mr. Fiste, Mexico City can be a hazardous place to be. Maybe your inside man, as you call him, met a fate similar to the North Korean diplomat whose murder has been all over the news. The North Korean was killed not far from this restaurant." She smiled. "I'm sure he would have known better than to miss an appointment with someone as important as you simply."

Fiste nodded. "I fear you are right, my dear." He smiled at her again.

Morgan seems to have a certain effect on people. People who wouldn't give me the time of day are somehow enwrapped by her personality.

"Please, call me Hanover. Mr. Fiste is so formal."

I heard a series of loud and rapid knocks on the dining room door. Fiste looked annoyed at being disturbed. "Enter and you better have a good reason for disturbing me."

The door slowly opened and Wilmer stuck his head inside. "We just need a couple of minutes of your time, sir." He glared at Morgan.

Fiste waved him in impatiently. He saw Wilmer and Alfie enter the room heads lowered like they endured a bad time. Alfie looked much worse for wear. One of his eyes was swollen shut and his nose was covered with a bandage. At least, the bleeding had stopped.

Fiste leaned back in his chair, his enormous girth causing the chair to creak. "Alfie, what happened to you?"

He pointed at Morgan. "The little slitch sucker-punched me. I'm going to get her. No way she would be able to break my nose in a fair fight."

My laughter didn't seem to help the scene at all. It did get me a glare from Alfie.

Fiste tut-tutted. "Alfie, you must learn to have more respect for your betters. I doubt Colonel Burke has ever sucker-punched anyone in her life. You're lucky you are still alive." He turned to Morgan again. "Am I right, my dear?"

Morgan smiled. "Right on both counts, Hanover. The only reason he isn't dead was I knew he worked for you. I wanted to show you some respect. All bets are off should we tangle again."

Fiste looked up at his two gunsels. "Now if you idiots think you can stand guard outside the restaurant, I suggest you follow my orders right now. I'm not too happy with you."

Alfie began to say something, but quickly decided against it when he saw the look on Fiste's face. "Yes sir," he said meekly.

They both left the room to assume their guard positions.

"I'll be contacting you in a few days to see what decision you have made regarding working with me. In the meantime, any information you can come up about my missing man will be well compensated."

He turned his chair back away from Morgan and me signaling the meeting was over. We stood and left.

We saw Wilmer and Alfie hanging out in front of the restaurant.

They glowered at us, saying nothing. Morgan took my arm and we headed back to the hotel.

"A valuable meeting," I said.

Morgan looked at me quizzically. "How so?"

"First, we know for sure Number Four was working for Fiste. Second, we know Fiste has no idea what we know. He really no longer has any type of source regarding the Chalice."

Morgan nodded. "Good points. You're going to have to tell Fiste something, eventually, about you working for him. You know you can't. It would be the end of your career as well as your relationship with Gramps and me. I don't envy your situation. What exactly are you going to tell him?"

"I'll put him off for as long as I can. I think he knows I am going to refuse him. That makes both of us nervous. I'm nervous because he is one of the most powerful men in the world and can reach out and touch me. He's nervous because I'm the wildcard in his quest. I can easily make sure he never gets it or even comes close to getting it. All I would have to do is contact Crypt. As for betraying clients, we both know it'll never happen."

Morgan gave me a peck on my cheek. "I know, Miller. I'm sorry I made the crack about ending our relationship."

I waved off her comment. "I know exactly what you mean."

I felt a vibration in my jacket pocket. I had set my phone to vibrate for our meeting with Fiste. I pulled it out and saw the call was from Lothar Zogg. I let it go to voicemail.

Chapter Twenty-eight

"Well done is better than well said." Benjamin Franklin.

Even though the crowds diminished dramatically since the end of the parade, there was plenty of local color going on. Roving Mariachi bands and street vendors were all trying to make last-minute pitches while tourists were still about.

The doorman greeted us with a tip of his cap as he opened the door for Morgan and me. I slipped him a crumpled peso note. I didn't check what it was. It was probably too much as the doorman gave me a broad smile.

Once in the lobby, I looked around and saw Señor Sanchez busy at his Concierge Desk and Ms. O'Toole working behind the front desk. I waved to both of them. Morgan and I headed toward the elevator bank and once the door opened and we entered, I pressed three.

"Who's the voice message from?" Morgan asked.

"Mr. Zogg. I hope it's good news."

"How can it be bad news? You killed the Colonel and recovered his coins."

"True enough. Hey, you mind checking the room when we get there? I do want to play the message. I just didn't want to listen to it on the street."

"Sure thing. I promise you, it will be good news."

We stopped outside the door, once again listening outside the room. When we heard no noises, I slid the keycard in the light flashed green, I pushed the door open and went inside. I handed Morgan my wand and she went to work. I flopped down on the couch, took out my phone, and chose the option to hear my voicemails.

"Congratulations on a successful recovery and resolution to my case. Your fee has already been wired to your account per your contract. Also, per our agreement, the extra items found in the briefcase will be disposed of to the beneficiaries as you asked. Once again, I wish to thank you for your competent and discreet handling of my case. I will keep your firm in mind for future cases."

By the time I finished listening to the voicemail, Morgan was done sweeping the hotel room. By her smile, it was apparent she found nothing. She joined me on the couch.

"What time does your flight leave?" I asked.

"Nine A.M. It's a straight shot to D.C. What about yours?"

"Ten A.M. Goes straight to St. Louis, then I have about an hour wait, and then will fly to Marion." I shook my head. "I hate the idea of wasting the rifle Chen sent to me. It seemed like such a fine weapon."

Morgan laughed in her melodic tone. "Then don't waste it. The barrel I have destroyed is the only thing linking you to the shooting if you were ever under suspicion. Put the gun in the briefcase with our other weapons and leave them in the locker Stuart provided. I'll see both the pistol and the rifle are returned to you. As for the barrel, drop it down a garbage chute here. It will be buried by tons of garbage by the time we leave."

"Good thinking. I kept the locker Stuart used. I'll just join you when you head off for your flight, make the drop-off, and give you the key to give to him."

"Great, now first things first, I saw a garbage chute just down the hall from us. Go get rid of the barrel. I'll pack everything else up." She yawned. "Once the barrel is disposed of, we're done, we won't have anything to do until morning."

I nodded and stood up, handing her my pistol. "I'm sure you will think of something, you're pretty resourceful."

Morgan was already at the room safe opening it up and removing the briefcase and the gun case. She started packing the case before I left the room. I hid the barrel under my jacket and went to look for the garbage chute.

Morning came all too soon as it usually does when you're either operating on little sleep or have been in a stressful situation. In my case, I was two for two. I stopped at the Concierge Desk with some envelopes. Each envelope contained a one-hundred-dollar bill. The staff did a fine job and I wanted to reward them. I was low on pesos and didn't want to waste time screwing around converting more money. I knew they would be happy with the generous tip.

Morgan was dressed in her Class A's. Her silver eagles glinted in the early morning sunlight. She figured she would get through customs quicker wearing it. I wore my usual fedora, bomber jacket, button-down shirt, and jeans. *She put me to shame!* As we left the hotel, the doorman asked us if we wanted a cab and help with our luggage. I agreed to both and we were soon on our way to the airport.

I stopped at the locker Stuart and I used as a drop, slid my key in to open it, and deposited our weapons in it. I relocked it and gave the key to Morgan. She would see Stuart before I would. Morgan and I easily and quickly cleared both customs and airport security. We exchanged good-byes and I watched her board her flight and watched her plane take off. I glanced at an airport clock and saw it would be an hour before my flight would depart.

I looked for a kiosk that sold coffee and soon found one. I ordered a cup and took it to the dining area where I began sipping it. It looked like I had picked up an admirer. I first noticed him when I watched Morgan board. I didn't think anything of it until I saw him again. He wasn't very good. In fact, he was much too obvious. When he saw me glance at him, he quickly looked away. *Stupid amateur. Why not wear a button saying I'm following you and aren't very bright?* I arrived at another absurd possibility. *Maybe it's just a coincidence he is here? I quit believing in coincidences shortly after I found out Santa Claus didn't exist. Yet another childhood illusion shattered.*

He looked like he might be formidable. He was about my height, maybe ten to fifteen pounds heavier, white, and seemed to be in good shape. He was my age, so I took his bald head to mean he shaved it. He was dressed pretty casually, wearing a tee shirt proclaiming the virtues of a beer I've never heard of and a pair of torn jeans. I don't believe in fair fights and was not about to change my beliefs anytime soon. I activated the prongs on my phone. They were harmless until I pressed another key. Then they would become very harmful.

It was about thirty minutes before I needed to board, which was more than enough time to test my coincidence theory. Chances were good if he followed me into the bathroom, all bets were off. I got up from my seat, tossed my now-empty coffee cup in a trash bin, and headed to a men's room I saw earlier when I was looking for the coffee kiosk. Once there, I spent my time standing in front of a sink with the water running, washing my hands and admiring myself in the mirror. My newest admirer followed me in a few minutes later. I dried my hands.

"Mr. Miller Rixey?"

"Depends who's asking," I smarmed.

"I've been sent by a Mr. Hanover Fiste. He has concerns about your commitment to a joint project the two of you are working on. He asked me to illustrate the importance of your compliance."

I saw him draw a silenced small-caliber pistol. How the hell did he get a piece past security? He gestured with the pistol. "If you please, empty your pockets on the counter and then walk over to me."

When I didn't immediately respond to his command, I saw in the mirror he was walking closer to me. His weapon gave him a false sense of security. Stupid amateur. Why would he allow me to get within arms range of him when he held a weapon on me? You would think with the money Fiste was worth, he would get some real talent. I hadn't been too impressed with what I saw so far.

"I'm not telling you a second time, Rixey." He jabbed the gun in my back for extra emphasis. I slowly began emptying my pockets.

Chapter Twenty-nine

"I don't even call it violence when it's in self-defense; I call it intelligence." Malcolm X.

My wallet, money clip, passport, keyring, cigarette lighter, a pack of cigarettes, pocket humidor, and cash, a mix of Mexican pesos and American dollars were on the sink.

He jabbed the pistol in my back. "Your phone. I need to see your phone on the counter now." He smacked me in the back of my head.

I reached for the phone, thumbing the key activating the prongs at the bottom of the phone. I spun quickly and jabbed the prongs into his neck. He let out a shriek and fired a round into the ceiling. He dropped to the floor, his body twitching from the first fifty thousand volts he received when I first stuck him. It continued to pulse through him at twelve hundred and fifty volts, still enough to make an impression. I savagely kicked him in the head as he was crumpled on the floor. His gun went flying.

Once the prongs lost contact with him, he staggered to his feet and assumed a boxing position. I knew I was in big trouble. The volts and the kick in the head would keep an average person on the floor for quite a while. I came after him, the phone still in my hand and he backed away. I saw him spot his pistol on the floor and dive for it. I was on top of him in a flash, punching him in the back of his head and back as savagely as I was able to. He struggled to get back to his feet, I gained the advantage of being on top of him. He was finally able to shake me off his back and get to his feet. I stuck him again with my phone. He went down again. Then taking advantage of the situation, I put him in, I picked him up and sent him flying head first into a urinal. He crashed into the urinal and I heard a sickening crunch as he made contact. The urinal fell to the floor and cracked in two, sending a cascade of water flowing in the bathroom. I quickly felt his neck for a pulse. There was none.

I quickly searched his body and not to my surprise found no ID on him. I went back to the counter and collected my things and promptly stuffed them in my pockets. I took a deep breath and, now feeling more composed, left the bathroom and headed for my flight home. I was fortunate no one came into the room to witness my handiwork. I headed down to the gate from which I would be taking my flight. I kept telling myself not to run, just walk. I felt like everyone was looking at me. I realized I was being silly. At least, I hoped I was. They had just started allowing passengers to board when I arrived at the gate. I quickly glanced around. No one was following me and, even better, no alarms were raised.

I was physically and mentally drained. I was looking forward to some sleep once I made it onboard. The ticket taker, a young and very comely blonde, smiled at me as I gave her my ticket. "Mr. Rixey, first-class seating is immediately to your left once you board. I hope you enjoyed your visit to Mexico. My name is Ms. Branham and I will be your flight attendant for this flight. If there is anything you need, please let me know."

I smiled back at her. "Thank you. It was an exciting trip to say the least. The Day of The Dead festivities were something to behold."

I walked up the jetway and found my seat. My carry-on bag was already being stored in a compartment above me. I was really hoping the plane would be taking off before an alarm was raised about the dead man in the bathroom. The plane began to taxi to its takeoff point and I breathed a sigh of relief. My relief was short-lived though. I felt the plane turning around. No matter the reason, I knew it couldn't be good for me.

I heard an announcement first in Spanish and then in English. "This is your captain. We regret to inform you we must head back to the terminal. We ask all passengers to deplane once we have returned to the jet gate. We hope the delay won't be too long."

The plane finally came to a stop and after about five minutes, the door opened. About a dozen men, dressed in various uniforms ranging from Air Port Security, the Federales, and Mexico City police entered. There wasn't a smiling face among them. They parted ways and made way for a tall, very thin, and hawk-faced man as he stepped aboard and cleared his voice.

"Please deplane this plane at once. Leave your bags in the storage facilities. They will be quite safe. Hopefully, you will be on your way soon."

Chapter Thirty

"Better to remain silent and be thought a fool than to speak out and remove all doubt." Abraham Lincoln.

Expecting the worst, hoping for the best, I left the plane. I really had no choice. The number of authorities on the flight left no options to remain on board. I began thinking of how I was going to explain what happened in the bathroom. Self-defense should work. Who knows what will work?

As I walked off the jetway, two very well-dressed and middle-aged men approached me. I knew they were some form of a cop even before they flashed their creds at me.

The taller of the two men said, "Señor if you would be so good as to follow us to the security office? We have a few questions to ask you."

"Can you tell me what this is about? I mean, I'm still trying to figure out why the flight was interrupted."

The shorter of the two men said, "It would be better to discuss this in our office.

Seeing I had no choice, I shrugged resignedly. "Lead the way."

As we headed to the office, I heard a series of piercing screams. I saw a lot of activity by the men's room where my fight occurred. Someone had finally discovered my handiwork. Finally, some good news for me. I realized they hadn't stopped the plane because of the stiff in the bathroom. He wasn't even discovered at the time of the deplaning message.

I heard various announcements I was sure was code for we got a dead guy in the bathroom. I saw some EMTs on the bounce enter the bathroom.

We soon arrived at a door marked *Seguridad del Aeropuerto*. Even I figured out the sign meant airport security. The taller of the two men unlocked the door and politely ushered me in.

It wasn't bad as offices of this type go. A Mexican flag stood behind two large desks. Three portraits hung on the wall. I assumed they were the Mexican President, the head of three Mexican equivalents of Homeland Security, and probably some airport honcho. The desks looked almost as good as the one in my office. Both desks were outfitted with computers. Each desk bore an ornate nameplate. One said *Director de Seguridad*. The name under it said Diego Gomez. The other nameplate read *Subdirector de Seguridad*. The name on the bottom of the nameplate read Angelo Cabrera. Gomez assumed his seat behind his desk and Cabrera took a seat on the edge of his desk.

"Why am I here? One minute I am heading home and the next minute I find myself being interviewed by I'm guessing number one and number two of people who are supposed to be Airport Security."

Gomez flashed a smile showing a perfect set of the whitest teeth I ever saw. Smack in the middle of them was one very bright gold tooth. "Please, Señor Rixey, we know who you are. You are Miller Rixey, an American detective, who just so happens to carry a Diplomatic Passport. Your reputation for your work has preceded you. I was hoping to meet you someday and here we are."

I rolled my eyes. "I realized you knew who I was from about five seconds into our initial meeting. You never asked for any ID. I also noticed there were over one hundred other people on my flight. Why single me out for questioning?"

Both men roared with laughter.

Cabrera spoke up. "Don't worry, Señor. The others are being questioned. We felt it would be better for the two of us to question you." He shrugged. "Call it a form of professional courtesy." He looked at Gomez and then gestured to me. "Please feel free to smoke. Would you like a cup of coffee?"

"Thanks, and yes." I took out my pocket humidor and removed a cigar. I offered cigars to my questioners. They both nodded and accepted.

After accepting my offer of a cigar, Cabrera stood up and walked the coffee machine returning with a cup of coffee for me.

As we all puffed away, Gomez spoke up. "Do you have any idea why you are here?"

I sipped my coffee and shook my head no.

"A message was written in lipstick in a bathroom in coach claiming there was a bomb placed in the airplane. Naturally, this caused great concern."

"Naturally."

"Why were you in Mexico City? Were you working on a case? I ask because we are trying to figure out why someone would either want to bomb the plane or cause confusion by simply writing a note."

"My girlfriend and I came down for the Day of the Dead Parade. Neither of us saw it before. It was quite an event. I'm glad we got to witness it. I have no idea about the message. I cannot imagine it involved me. I mean who would want to blow up a simple country private investigator?"

The grimace I got from both of them told me they didn't believe me. I sensed their frustration. They just knew I was somehow involved in the message being written. They weren't sure exactly how. They had to believe me. As far as they knew, I hadn't violated any Mexican laws and, more importantly, they couldn't prove my story false.

Cabrera said with a headshake, "Señor Rixey, despite your act, we all realize you are more than a simple small-town private investigator. We are well aware of the work the Bishop Agency does." He paused. "Shall we say, you are well known to most of the police forces throughout the world? Your fame and reputation have spread oh so rapidly."

"What am I? Required reading?"

Gomez nodded. "You have become required reading for our more advanced policing classes."

"Señor Rixey, I guess your story will have to do for now."

I heard the phone ring. Gomez picked it up. He said a few words I didn't understand then hung up. He stood up. "Señor Rixey, you are free to go. Your flight will be cleared in about one hour. No bomb has been detected. I wish you the very best of luck in your endeavors." He extended his hand, as did Cabrera.

When I left the office, the men's room was blocked off. I saw the area surrounded by police tape. Six uniformed officers, some lab techs, and an undetermined number of plainclothes officers milled about the crime scene. I decided the best place for me to wait was to go straight to the passenger lounge, located right across from where I would be boarding. Very convenient.

I pushed the lounge door open, heard a chime announcing my presence and walked in. I saw the blue haze of cigarette smoke hanging like a shroud over the room. I looked around the lounge. There was a bar, and a menu hung behind the bar in English and Spanish. Maybe a dozen people were seated at the bar. I motioned to the bartender.

"A double of Macallan, if you please."

"Right away, Señor." She found a bottle and poured me a double and returned with the glass. "Señor, enjoy."

"How much do I owe you?"

She made a dismissive gesture. "Drinks are complimentary for all first-class passengers who have been delayed by the plane having to return to the airport."

I reached into my pocket and placed a few peso notes on the counter. "Thank you. This is for you."

"Thank you, Señor."

I sat sipping my drink. According to the electronic board over the bar, my flight would be ready for boarding in about forty-five minutes. *There are worse ways to wait for a plane,* I thought. I took a puff on my cigar. I knew as soon as I got back home, I needed to contact Morgan, Stuart, and Chen. It didn't feel right to try to reach them now. I finished my first drink and debated the virtues of ordering a second one. I knew I'd be able to sleep on the flight and went ahead and ordered.

I heard the ringing of a chime and turned toward the door. An olive-skinned man entered. He displayed a mop of jet-black hair, was of medium build, and was very well dressed. I looked away and began working on my second drink. I felt a tap on my shoulder.

"Excuse me, sir. My name is Carlo Borgia," the olive-skinned man said. "I have a proposition which will be of great financial interest to both of us. May I have a few minutes of your time?" His English was excellent, his accent was pure Sicilian.

Chapter Thirty-one

"No man has a good enough memory to be a successful liar." Abraham Lincoln.

I was about to tell Mr. Borgia to hit the bricks when he slid a white envelope in front of me. The envelope was about a half inch thick and was transparent enough for me to see it contained my favorite papers, portraits of Ben Franklin. I picked up the envelope and put it in an inside jacket pocket.

"Okay, Mr. Borgia, you just purchased ten minutes of my time. My flight leaves shortly."

Borgia coughed and made sweeping gestures as if those acts would drive my cigar smoke away. "Mr. Rixey, you are a tough person to get ahold of. My organization was forced to go to extreme lengths to contact you before you left Mexico City."

I rolled my eyes. "You can look me up in the phone book, stop by my office, or even check out the Bishop Agency website. It's really not very difficult."

"You misunderstand, we needed to contact you immediately."

"I hope you aren't the assholes who left the bombing message on the mirror," I growled.

Borgia coughed nervously. "I'm afraid so. We wanted to meet with you at the coffee shop. You left before we got there. You really left us with no other choice."

I looked at my watch and gruffly said, "You have five minutes, Mr. Borgia. You need to get to the point of this meeting."

Acting very indignant, Borgia replied. "I represent an influential group who wishes to gain the artifact you are currently charged with finding. We are prepared to reward you substantially if you turn it over to us once you find it."

I roared with laughter, drawing the attention of the people standing around the bar. "All I need to do is betray a client? Sorry, not happening."

He looked at me red-faced. "Mr. Rixey, you are causing an unneeded and unwarranted scene. My sources have told me you are fast and loose with the rules and laws. If we are asking you to betray a client, what's the big deal for someone of your dubious reputation?"

"Don't believe everything you read about me being dishonest. Sometimes a bad reputation works for my benefit or the benefit of my clients. Now I need to leave."

"You'll regret having shown me such little respect. You'll rue the day you treated me in such a poor manner," Borgia sputtered.

As I pushed the lounge door open, I turned toward Borgia. "I'm already regretting it."

I headed for the gate, I noticed Gomez and Cabrera were doing a much too obvious job of following me. It was more a case of making sure I got on the plane and became someone else's problem.

The plane took off on schedule and there were no unscheduled stops or delays. Once arriving in St. Louis, I quickly cleared customs. The customs clerk didn't even open my bags once he saw my diplomatic passport. He scribbled an illegible mark on each of my bags in chalk and sent me on my way.

St. Louis was experiencing its first snow of the year. It was a light dusting, still snow none the less. I knew a bunch of things faced me at the office, but there would be plenty of time tomorrow to get things done. All I wanted tonight was a good steak and a good night's sleep.

I took a cab back to the hotel where I parked my SUV. I dropped one of my bags off in my SUV and reclaimed my pistol and holster. I always believed in walking around armed before I became a PI and, since becoming one, I consider it mandatory. Not many people were in the lobby so it was a pretty quick process of checking in and getting my keycard. It was a nice change of pace from the crowds in Mexico City.

I looked out the front window and saw the snow, what little there was of it, finally stopped.

I refused the help of an overeager staff member to carry my bags. Feeling poorly for the employee, I still tipped her five dollars. I like to do my share to encourage people who want to work. I found the elevator, pushed the button, and made it to my room, dropped my bags just inside the door, raided the minibar for a drink, and after finishing the drink, laid down for a nap. The events of the day caught up with me. I was asleep before my head hit the pillow.

I woke up an hour later and decided it was time to turn my phone back on. I checked the room with my detection wand and turned up nothing. I looked at my phone and saw a voicemail from Morgan with a high-priority tag on it.

Chapter Thirty-two

"Accept the challenges so that you can feel the exhilaration of victory."
George S. Patton.

I made it to the voicemail retrieval system and pressed play. "This is M. I need you to come to D.C. as soon as possible. Tomorrow would be great. I informed Stuart about the OTO meeting and all the events that went on there. He was surprised to hear about Pong attending the meeting and being murdered in Mexico City. Apparently, his knowledge of what was going on with the North Koreans was badly lacking in comparison to yours. I told him I'd continue to monitor the investigation. I also told him not to expect much of anything in the way of resolution. Call me with your flight details and I'll arrange to pick you up. Oh, yeah, see if Julian is available for the meeting also. We may require his services."

No rest for the wicked it seemed. I pulled out my laptop and set it on the room desk. Once I made it to the internet, I first sent an email to Ms. Nickels informing her I was going to be out of the office for another few days.

I checked my emails and forwarded those requesting my services to Ms. Nickels. She knew who to use and not use for referrals. It was important to me that, even if I didn't have time to handle a case, the person received excellent service.

I booked my flight and sent emails to Stuart and Morgan telling them to expect me at two P.M. Eastern. One more thing to do before going out and enjoying some drinks and a steak dinner.

I knew Morgan was right. There was a good chance Fingers would be of value on the next leg of this case, the recovery of the Chalice. He did a great job in Mexico City and wouldn't turn down the chance to possibly work again. One thing about Fingers was the only thing he loved more than stealing was living the high life on someone else's dime. Not too terrible of a worst-case scenario, a few days at a five-star hotel in D.C.

I dialed his number and he picked it up on the fifth ring. "Julian Malone. How can I be of service to you?"

"Quit screwing around, Fingers. You know this is Mr. Rixey. I need you to get on a plane and fly to D.C. I'll send you my flight and hotel information. Make sure you tell Colonel Burke when your flight is expected to land."

"Very short notice, Mr. Rixey. Let me consult my calendar and see if I am available."

I heard a short pause.

"You're in luck. It just so happens I'm available. I take it there is some work for me?"

"Good chance of it. We will know more tomorrow. Wear something nice as we will be meeting with some big shots. In the meantime, you're booked into the Jefferson for three days, on my dime, naturally. Just make sure you get on a flight and make it in tomorrow. I'll see you then." I clicked off.

I stretched for a moment and then grabbed my hat and jacket and left in search of a great steak.

Chapter Thirty-three

"Notice that the stiffest tree is most easily cracked, while the bamboo or willow survives by bending with the wind." Bruce Lee.

I arrived in D.C. at about two as expected. I went outside the terminal and saw Morgan waiting for me and, much to my surprise, she also brought along Fingers. I got into the black SUV and she greeted me with a kiss.

"Glad to see your plane was on time. This case has some people pretty worked up. Our meeting is set for three thirty at OAR Headquarters."

I yawned. "Good. Maybe they will finally have the government do its job and let me go back to being a small-town PI."

As Morgan began to drive, she laughed. "Not a chance in hell. It seems they think there is a renewed sense of urgency to recover the Chalice. The powers that be seem to think they want you and me to continue on the recovery."

I nodded. "Plausible deniability when this thing blows up in our faces."

I turned around to talk to Fingers. "Looking good, Fingers, how was your flight?"

He sniffed. "It's Julian and my flight was fine. Thank you for showing me you really care," he added with a grin.

Traffic wasn't too bad and we made pretty good time. We pulled into a secured lot. Morgan was stopped by an armed guard. She flashed her cred pack at him. He nodded, saluted and pointed where she needed to park. After she parked, both Morgan and Fingers started to get out of the car. I stopped them.

"Look, we still have about forty minutes before the meeting and there have been some alarming developments, I want to fill you two in on." They both nodded.

She turned the SUV back on. "The vehicle is secure. Go ahead, Miller."

"Fiste sent someone to convince me on the merits of working for him in the recovery of the Chalice. Somehow, the guy was able to get a silenced handgun through airport security."

"So, what happened, Mr. Rixey?" Fingers asked.

"What happened is he died badly and is now resting on a slab in the Mexico City Coroner's office. Fiste is no fool. When this guy doesn't report back, he's going to figure out what happened. He will know I'm not on his team. What this all means, your guess is as good as mine. What this does do is further complicate things."

I took out a cigarette and lit it. I wasn't too concerned about rules concerning smoking in government vehicles. I knew there were more significant problems in dealing with this caper. "Now if things weren't messed up enough, you both heard about the jet being delayed in Mexico City due to a bomb threat?"

Morgan and Fingers both replied in unison. "Yes."

"I was on the flight. The threat was precisely that, a threat. It turned out another group, which I suspect is the Mafia, wanted to talk to me about turning over the Chalice to them. I met their guy in the passenger lounge while I was waiting to get back on the plane."

Morgan giggled. "Why, Miller, you seem to have become very popular."

"Too popular."

Morgan, Fingers, and I waited outside the Sensitive Compartmented Information Facility (SCIF) located at OAR Headquarters for Andrew Stuart and Arch Stanton, the Director of National Security. The room was locked and even Morgan didn't have access to it.

Morgan asked. "Have you or Julian ever been in one of these rooms before? There aren't a lot of them to be found. They are very expensive to build."

Julian and I both shook our heads no.

"While rooms may differ as to what is inside them, some similarities are found in all of them. The room is lit from strips of LEDs attached to the ceiling. The first thing you will notice is the silence. It's really kind of creepy. The method of air delivery makes sure there can be no attack involving any types of gasses. Cell phones don't work in these rooms for obvious security reasons."

Julian looked curious. "What's to stop someone from tampering with the compressors and introducing something into the air system?"

Morgan smiled. "I suppose anything is possible. It takes either a key from the Director of National Intelligence or, in his absence, one of his two Deputy Directors who are the only people allowed entry to the room. Retina scan, a state-of-the-art voice recognition system, and finally a digital pad requiring the correct twenty-number sequence on the first attempt. Failure at any of these stages locks the room for twenty-four hours." She shrugged. "An attack on the room with the compressor would require an act of treason by one of those three men. Hasn't happened yet and not too likely to ever happen."

"Who's the guy with Stuart?" I asked Morgan.

"Arch Stanton. He's the Director of National Intelligence. He's the main reason you and Julian are here."

"What got him interested in the case?"

"He believes the recent events in Mexico City require his attention. This has gone beyond a simple OAR case. Since we last talked, North Korea is threatening retaliation for the death of their diplomat."

"Diplomat? The guy was a criminal," I scoffed.

Stanton was short, balding, and walked with the use of a cane. He was dressed in an expensive blue-serge suit with silver threads running through it. He also wore a costly tie I couldn't place and wore what I was sure was a highly-polished and expensive pair of shoes. When he closed to arm's length, I saw the tie was a Charvet Tonal-Stripe Silk Tie. I have a few of them hanging in my closet. They are hard to mistake for anything else once you know what they look like. When Stanton stretched out his hand to shake, I noticed a very expensive Rolex on his wrist. *The government must be paying pretty well these days,* I thought.

We shook hands and Morgan made the necessary introductions.

Stanton looked at Fingers. "Don't I know you from someplace? I never forget a face."

Fingers smarmed, "I'm sure if I met someone as important as you are, I would have remembered. You must have me confused with someone else."

Stanton, unconvinced, shook his head. "It'll come to me sooner or later. Anyway, let's get this meeting going. I'm a busy man and the President wants a full report."

He slid a keycard into a slot on the door handle and the door sprung open.

Stanton turned to Stuart. "You sure both these guys are cleared for this level of meeting?"

"Yes, sir. Both Mr. Rixey and Mr. Malone are government contractors who have been working on this case since its onset."

"Just remember, Stuart, if either of these guys screws the pooch, heads are going to roll, and I don't intend for my head to be one of them. Are we clear?"

"I'm clear, Mr. Stanton."

Morgan was right. The room was absolutely quiet, dead quiet. I strained to at least hear the sound of the compressors pumping air into the room, nothing. Even Morgan's heels didn't click as the room was carpeted. There was a conference table looking like it was made from the same type of wood as my office desk. Ten chairs and ten work stations surrounded the table. On the far wall hung four widescreen monitors.

Stanton sat at the head of the table and took the keycard out of his pocket and inserted it into a slot on the desk. The door whooshed closed. "Now this room is one-hundred-percent secure. Take your seats and we will begin," Stanton announced.

Chapter Thirty-four

"To live is to suffer, to survive is to find some meaning in the suffering."
Friedrich Nietzsche.

"Does anyone know what the term Cat's Paw means?" Stanton asked as he glanced around the conference table.

Fingers blurted out. "Like the *Star Trek* episode called Catspaw?"

Stanton glared at him angrily, causing a few chuckles. "No, Mr. Malone. This has nothing to do with an ancient TV show," he sputtered.

I thought he was going to have a heart attack on the spot. His face turned beet red and the veins in his neck were throbbing.

"Does anyone have anything intelligent to contribute? If not, let me help you out. A Cat's Paw is a person or an organization used either unwillingly or unwittily to accomplish another's goals or purpose. I am convinced Eldor Jamieson Crypt and his group are someone or some group's Cat's Paw. God knows who the group or person is who is doing the manipulation."

"What do you know about the OTO, or better yet, what do you

think you know about them?" I asked.

"They are a charitable organization that researches and preserves various artifacts from throughout the world. They do great work. I mean everyone knows of their work. You don't seem to agree with me. Why not?" He turned to Stuart. "Where did you find this guy?"

Stuart stammered something I wasn't able to make out.

I snorted in disbelief. How did this guy get to be the Director of National Security? He didn't have a clue. "How many OTO board meetings have you attended? I'm guessing somewhere between zero and one and closer to zero."

Stanton flew into a rage. "You're a young idiot. You know those meetings are always closed to the public. I imagine you've been to some OTO board meetings?" he said with sarcasm dripping from his voice.

I nodded, leaned back, and looked askance at Stanton. "Yes. Both Colonel Burke and I have attended one, in a manner of speaking."

Morgan nodded in agreement.

"Preposterous!"

"What did you say?" I snarled.

"I said preposterous. Was that too big of a word for you, Mr. Rixey?"

Morgan stood and said in a calm voice, "Gentlemen, let's have less testosterone and more cooperation. We are supposed to be on the same team. Let's try to remember we are working together." She scowled. "Both of you have been acting like children and it's very counterproductive."

Somewhat mollified, Stanton said, "Very well, Colonel Burke."

He turned his chair toward me. "Okay, Mr. Rixey, can you explain how you and Colonel Burke attended an OTO board meeting?"

"It really wasn't tough. As Mr. Stuart will tell you, my firm was retained by OAR to recover the Chalice of Power. Through some intelligence work and analysis of the facts, I was with Colonel Burke and Mr. Rixey in Mexico City."

Stuart nodded. "What he says is true. We did retain him and he was in Mexico City during the latest OTO meeting."

I held up an SD chip. "If one of you can figure out how to install this chip, it will give you the forty-five minutes of audio I was able to record of the Board meeting. I got in the meeting room the night before and planted some listening devices."

Morgan took the chip from me and inserted it into her work station. She punched a few buttons and the meeting began playing. It was the first time Fingers, Stuart, or Stanton heard all of what occurred during the meeting.

Stanton turned ashen and gulped. "Mr. Rixey, I owe you, Colonel Burke, and Mr. Malone an apology. I don't know how I was so wrong about OTO. At the end of the meeting, I heard some glass break, some screams, and it sounded like the room was cleared out. Were you in a position to see what happened?"

"An assassin shot Colonel Pong. The people in the room decided it was time to scatter. They obviously moved the body as it was later discovered in a different location. If I were to hazard a guess, I would say OTO considers it likely Hanover Fiste hired the assassin."

What I said was true and would have passed any lie detector test.

I saw nothing to be gained by revealing my role in the death of the Colonel. I knew both Zogg and Chen knew of it. There was really no reason for anyone else to know. The only witness to my act, Morgan, would never reveal what really happened.

I let what I said sink in before I spoke again. "Two other things should be brought up while we are on this topic." I paused for dramatic effect. "As you gathered from the OTO meeting, North Korea is interested in the Chalice. My guess is the interest comes from the apparent ability to cause the effects of an EMP attack in the area it's used. Also, Hanover Fiste wanted me to betray my client, which in this case is OAR. He offered me twenty-five million to give the Chalice to him when I recovered it. When I put him off, he sent someone after me to persuade me to change sides."

"What happened?" Stuart asked breathlessly.

"The person he sent died badly. Sooner or later Fiste will figure out what happened to his messenger and is very likely going to be coming for me and perhaps Colonel Burke."

"Finally, and I admit I can't be positive, I have a pretty good idea someone from either La Cosa Nostra or the Mafia has more than a passing interest in the Chalice."

"What makes you think either LCN or the Italian Mafia is involved?" Stanton demanded.

"A number of things. First, they committed a terrorist act by writing a message on the mirror of one of the plane's washrooms about a bomb being on board. The act was done so the plane would have to be cleared and someone from their organization would be able to meet with me. I have no doubt, as he admitted his group wrote the message. The person I met identified himself as a Carlo Borgia and had an accent that had to be Sicilian." I shrugged. "There, you have my theory of the case for what it's worth."

"Very interesting, Mr. Rixey." Stanton looked at Stuart. "What do you think, Andrew? Do we continue with the Bishop Agency or do we turn it over to a governmental agency?"

Chapter Thirty-five

"It is always darkest just before the day dawneth." Thomas Fuller,
English Historian and Theologian (1608-1661).

Stuart riffled through his notes, strummed his fingers on the conference table, and began to speak in halting tones. "The combination of the security problems leading us to go outside the government to begin with and the unlikelihood of being able to bring a government agent up to speed in time on this case lead me to an obvious conclusion, Director Stanton."

In an impatient tone, Stanton said. "While we are all still young, Mr. Stuart."

"We have no choice available to us except to keep using Miller Rixey and the Bishop Agency, Director."

Stanton nodded. I could tell he wasn't very pleased. "Well, if we must, we must. I don't like the idea of using non-governmental actors in this situation. We have no way to discipline them if something goes wrong. On the other hand, we do have plausible deniability and plausible deniability is always good. Be aware, Mr. Stuart, if this plan goes haywire, heads will roll and the heads won't be mine or any of my staff, I promise you that."

"We will put Colonel Burke in charge of this project, at least paperwork-wise. If the mission fails, she would be available to be the fall guy."

The Director nodded sagely. "Good thinking, Mr. Stuart.

"What do you think of that idea, Colonel Burke?"

"I think it sucks."

Stanton made a dismissive gesture. "That was a rhetorical question. No one really cares what you think. I've read your record. On the surface, it's quite distinguished. Beneath your record, I see all the signs of you being an assassin. There is nothing I can do about that now. You are clearly being fast-tracked for something. Maybe Joint Chiefs or perhaps a director of an intelligence agency." He leaned forward. "Should this mission go south, you won't be asked to resign. You will wish you bailed out of this case. You will be assigned to a post so remote and so backward when you ask them what a time machine is, they will answer a wristwatch. I fully expect my orders to be carried out. I cannot accept any failure in this project. Are we clear, Colonel Burke?" he asked pointedly.

Morgan sighed. "Quite clear, Director."

"As for you, Mr. Rixey, you will continue to be in charge of this project. If it goes south, there isn't a lot I can do to you other than to make sure you never work as a contractor for the government again. Are we clear?"

"Couldn't be clearer, Arch baby," I sneered.

Stanton rubbed his hands together, ignoring my disrespectful comment toward him. "Excellent. We are all on the same page. Do we have a list of likely places capable of being the next OTO meeting site?"

Stuart removed a sheet of paper from a folder in front of him. "We programmed for possible meeting places. We included proximity to Denver International Airport, a place where it would be easy for their security purposes and would have rooms large enough to hold a meeting of twenty or so people in one room. We have a place scoring one hundred percent using those variables. We came up with the Westin Denver International Airport. It's only about a tenth of a mile away from the airport. A group of twenty or so wouldn't be noticed and, if you needed to, it was an easy walk to there."

"Excellent, Mr. Stuart. I suggest you, Colonel Burke, and Mr. Malone get to work," Stanton said, pointing at me. "You don't have very much time."

What insane plan was I involving myself, Morgan, and Fingers in? It was apparent we were engaged in a mission with very little chance of success and was very dangerous to boot. How were we going to be able to capture the Chalice of Power in a public setting? I shook my head. "When you're right, you are right, Archie."

I saw him grimace. He was clearly used to people fawning and doing everything he commanded. Miller Rixey grovels for no one.

Chapter Thirty-six

"The journey of a thousand miles begins with one step." Lao Tzu.

7 November 20xx, Reagan National Airport, Two P.M. EST

In this case, the step was to a black Cadillac Escalade with the mandatory heavily-tinted windows and, just in case there was any doubt it was a government vehicle, one only needed to look at the license plate.

The drive was mainly in silence. The driver introduced himself as Daniel Stephens. He told me he worked for Mr. Stanton, as he called him, in some capacity he was not at liberty to discuss. I tried to be social with him, being rebuffed with a series of grunts and a very pointed silence. You didn't have to be a world-class detective to realize Mr. Jones was not up for any chit-chat. He drove with the same grim look on his face he wore when we first met. He must have shown an impressive cred pack when we passed the two security screening stations as we were waved through with no questions and no hesitations. When we arrived at the airplane, I silently grabbed my bag and started to get out of the SUV.

"Thanks for the ride, Mr. Stephenson. Your department needs

some training in being a little politer. After all, I am a taxpayer." I shrugged. "I know being a taxpayer means nothing anymore."

"Mr. Rixey, I hope you don't think I was being rude. I'm sorry I wasn't more talkative. Mr. Stanton gave me a stringent protocol to follow with you. I don't think he likes you one little bit. I don't want to know what he has you doing. It's well beyond my paygrade. Let me wish you good luck." He extended his hand.

I chuckled as I accepted his hand. "Two things, one I don't think he likes me at all and two, I have a sinking feeling I'm going to need every bit of good luck. Thanks."

I saw Morgan standing at the entryway to the jet. She had created a different look. Her hair was dyed black and, even though I knew her vision was 20/15, she was wearing a nerdy-looking pair of black horn-rim glasses.

"What's with the new look?" I asked as I gave her a peck on the cheek.

"You like?"

"Maybe. I need some time to think about it."

"It's my disguise for Denver." She flashed an FBI cred pack at me with her new picture and the name Meagan Reeves.

"Someone a fan of Numb3rs?"

"Yeah, it's one of my favorite shows."

I smiled.

Morgan pressed on the intercom button. "Mr. Rixey is aboard. You may leave when ready. We will be taking our seats and strapping in." She turned to me. "Miller, time to have a seat and buckle up. Oh yeah,

Julian will meet us in Denver International."

"Why didn't he fly out to Denver with us?"

"Something about a project in New York City. He said Zogg assigned a high priority to it."

I nodded and took my seat. What the hell could be more important than saving the world? The plane soon lifted off. Once we were airborne, Morgan handed me a large manila envelope. "This is your ID for Denver. Make sure you put your real things in the envelope and leave them here."

I held the envelope on my lap and began thinking out loud. "Looks like Archie is going to a lot of trouble to recover the Chalice. It also looks like, if this mission gets screwed up, you will be counting penguins in Antarctica and I'll get to go back to being a small-town PI. Heads are going to roll and it won't be his, just like he said. I've seen people like him before."

I opened the envelope and saw two items inside. First was an FBI cred pack. It contained my picture and the name of Richard Deckard. I appreciated the Blade Runner reference. I also found a wallet containing some credit cards and an Illinois driver's license. I took my wallet and Bishop Agency cred pack and slid it in the envelope and handed it back to Morgan. "Very impressive. I sense Arch Stanton's hand in this?"

"Nope. It was all my idea and he went along. Even if they run our credentials through whatever device they want, they will come back legitimate. No one is going to challenge an FBI agent."

"Good point. What makes you think we would even pass through any type of security checkpoint though? I mean I know OTO has a lot of clout and a lot of money, I doubt even they can force a hotel to set up security or, better yet, make the hotel allow them to set up their own security checkpoints."

"I don't know how much you keep up on the news, but the World Bank is meeting at the same hotel the OTO is meeting. There will be all sorts of crazies out protesting and picketing. They won't give a second thought to two FBI agents who are armed and a consultant."

I smiled wanly. "Somewhat. I was aware of the meeting. I might have been one of the protesters out there for my assignment. I'm not a big fan of the World Bank. I take it Fingers is the consultant?"

I gripped the seat as I felt the plane begin to descend at a rapid pace. The fasten seatbelt light flashed on. I felt the blood rushing from my head.

Morgan clicked on the intercom. "What's going on out there?" All we heard was static over the speaker. The plane was continuing its rapid descent. Morgan pressed the button. She pushed the button again. I couldn't understand what she was saying. The last thing I remembered was the oxygen masks dropping out the ceiling. I passed out.

Chapter Thirty-seven

"When it is obvious that the goals cannot be reached, don't adjust the goals, adjust the action steps." Confucius.

7 November 20xx, Denver International Airport, Six P.M. MST

"Are you okay, Agent Deckard?"

Still a little dizzy and totally disoriented, I made a snappy reply. "Huh?"

"Rick, this is Doctor Kiser and he wants to know how you're feeling," Morgan said.

I was still trying to clear my head. It wasn't working. I was still disoriented. I finally realized Agent Deckard and Rick referred to me. Rick Deckard, FBI agent. "Feeling much better, Doctor Kiser. I'll soon be as good as new, thanks to you."

Kiser snorted. "Nonsense, young man. I just ran a few tests to make sure you weren't going to die on us. Your pulse was still a little high as was your blood pressure. I'm sure your job as an FBI agent is stressful. Putting those two factors together combined with what I was told happened on the jet, it's not surprising. My diagnosis of you is to take a few days off and you will be fine."

I looked at his kindly face. "Well, thanks anyway."

Morgan said, "Dr. Kiser, here is your money for the work you did and they are currently holding your flight back to Omaha. A first-class ticket has your name on it. The driver will take you to the plane. Thanks for your help."

Doctor Kiser accepted the envelope and the plane ticket. "Thank you, young lady." He went to the exit, waved, and was gone.

I asked Morgan, rather pointedly. "What the hell happened?"

"First, the intercom went out. You probably heard the static when they tried to respond to me. Then something happened to the plane. Some part of it froze up. While you were out, we were experiencing one of the worst blizzards in history for this time of the year. We landed in Omaha, picked up Dr. Kiser to take a look at you, repaired the broken parts of the plane, and we left for Denver."

A driver came on board, collected our bags and headed back to the traditional black SUV with heavily-tinted windows that our government seems to love. I stepped onto the tarmac and was hit with a sudden blast of cold air. The wind blew the snow in such a manner it stung my face.

"It's about ten minutes to the hotel," the driver said.

I was pleased to see Fingers was already in the SUV when we arrived. He handed me an envelope. "I've been here since this morning. Zogg Airlines is for sure the way to go." He smiled. "I put my time out here to good use, as you'll see."

I nodded. "Always glad to hear good news, Fingers. Let's see what you have here." I opened the envelope. I saw a picture of the outside of the hotel. To say it looked a little unusual would be an understatement. It looked to me like it was designed as a ship and seemed to be leaning. I later found out it was supposed to represent a pair of wings. I guess the design made sense considering it was built in an airport. There was a picture of the conference room where the OTO would be holding their meeting. Most importantly, there was a keycard that would open the door to the room. It looked like things were finally shaping up.

"You been inside the conference room, I take it?"

Fingers nodded. "Yes. It's pretty nice. It's on the second floor as is their entire conference center. It's got a long table made of some nice highly polished dark wood. When I was there earlier today, the room was comprised of twenty chairs and twenty work stations. Ten tables on each side. At the head of the table, there is a speaker's dais and a series of buttons on a pad. The buttons control the doors and the microphones at each seat. The far wall is entirely made of glass and the adjacent wall is made of marble. The room is lit by incandescent lighting. It also has blue carpeting and the logo of the hotel on it. If you're going to plant a listening device, I'd recommend under the chair by the speaker's dais."

"What about when we get the Chalice, do we have a fast way out?" I asked Fingers.

"Yes. There is a transit system which will take us right to the airport. It's located on the third floor. There is also a commuter system located on the first floor to take us to downtown Denver."

I nodded. "Great work, Fingers."

I turned to Morgan. "Other than engaging in a major shootout, have any ideas on how we can get the Chalice away from Crypt?"

Morgan smiled. "Oh, I have a few ideas, Miller. I decided to have a special case shipped to the hotel. All sorts of interesting things are in the case. There are sonic screamers, devices emitting sounds which will induce a feeling of terror. The person who hears this is quite helpless. We will have the proper earplugs needed to counteract the screamers. The case also has flashbang grenades, tear gas, and smoke grenades. We will also have nose plugs so as not to be affected by the tear gas. With any luck, we should be out of there in sixty seconds max."

"Other than in sci-fi books, I've never heard of sonic screamers."

"Not too surprising. It's a top-secret project from DARPA. I guess Stanton thought the mission was vital enough to give them to us."

I grimaced. "What happens when someone finds one? Not too much of secret anymore, are they?"

"Here's the best part. Once activated, they emit their sounds for five minutes, then they self-destruct. No chance at recovery."

Before I continued, the SUV lurched to a stop. I saw a man in a bellhop's uniform making his way through the crowd, pushing a cart. We pushed our doors open and stepped into the ice storm. I heard the trunk pop. "Help you with your bags, sir?"

"Yes, they are in the trunk."

I heard Morgan's phone ringing. By now I knew her ringtone. She handed me the phone. "It's for you. Andrew and Arch are pretty upset. They said your phone was turned off and they needed to contact you ASAP."

I rolled my eyes. If they wanted to do the job, they should have sent themselves.

I couldn't think of anything more important than checking in and getting out the blizzard. I took the phone. "We're checking in right now. I'm sure this can wait. I'll call you back when I get a chance."

I heard some screaming on the other end and some very unchristian words as I clicked off. "Fuck 'em if they can't take a joke," I said to no one in particular. I was getting pretty sick of the two of them.

Chapter Thirty-eight

"Who controls the past controls the future. Who controls the present controls the past?" George Orwell.

7 November 20xx, The Westin Denver International Airport, Six Thirty P.M. MST

I eyed the bellhop's nameplate. It identified him as Scott Smith. Scott was twenty-something, white, clean-shaven, had a full head of black hair, and was tall and thin.

"Looks like things are getting pretty crazy around here, Scott?" I asked as I kept a watchful eye on the crowd of protesters engulfing the outside of the building.

Signs were displayed everywhere supporting the pro and anti-globalist positions on the World Bank.

"It's only going to get worse tomorrow when the World Bank meetings begin. Only the storm has kept the crowds down, somewhat," Scott agreed.

With Scott leading the way, pushing our luggage cart, we slowly worked our way through the masses of the protesters. The protesters were loud and enthusiastic and, so far, well behaved.

We made it to the door where we were greeted by a large white man, fully decked out in traditional doorman's garb. As he opened the door for us, he said, "Welcome to the Westin."

I smiled at him and slipped him a Hamilton. The bill vanished as quickly as I gave it to him. He smiled and doffed his cap as he held the door. "If there is anything you need, please contact me. I'm Ernie. I'm here a lot."

"Thanks, Ernie. I will keep you in mind."

Straight ahead of us was a slow-moving security checkpoint. When we got to the head of the line, we were through quickly as Morgan and I both flipped our FBI cred packs and indicated Fingers was a consultant working for the government. The man checking IDs looked harried and with good reason. More than twenty people were queued up behind us in the ten minutes or so we'd been in line. He waved us through, not even checking our bags. When Morgan's and my pistols set off the alarm, he quickly turned off the signal.

The lobby was crowded, but it was nothing like the teeming hordes we witnessed outside. I suppose the five-hundred-a-night price kept the protesters and anyone with any level of common sense staying elsewhere. I don't blame them. If I hadn't been on the job, I sure as hell wouldn't be staying here either.

Morgan made it to the front desk. "Reservation for Reeves. We have two adjoining suites."

The clerk, a young, tall, and a very athletic black woman with bright red hair nodded. "One moment." She typed something into a computer. "Very good, Agent Reeves. I need you to fill out this card, please. Do you need a parking sticker?"

Morgan shook her head as she filled out the registration card. "No vehicle. I'm expecting a package though. Has it arrived?"

As the clerk handed Morgan two keycards, she smiled. "Let me check. I do seem to recall a package arriving in the past couple of hours."

My attention was drawn to a brief disturbance taking place in the lobby. One of the protesters got through the security checkpoint. He was quickly subdued and led out.

The clerk returned a few minutes later carrying a package one foot long and a foot deep. She handed Morgan a pen. "If you will sign for this?" Morgan nodded and quickly signed. The clerk glanced at the signature and then asked. "Will there be anything else?"

Gathering up the package, Morgan said. "No thanks."

Scott guided us to the elevator banks. "What floor?"

Morgan said in a doubtful voice. "Fifteen. Odd, I thought this hotel was fourteen stories."

Scott laughed and pointed to the panel of buttons. There were no buttons for four, thirteen, or fourteen. "We get a lot of Chinese guests and in China, the numbers four and fourteen are very bad luck. Thirteen is eliminated for obvious reasons due to the rest of our guests."

Scott pushed the button and up we went. The Westin has some interesting twists to it not found in your average hotel. Guest rooms don't begin until the eighth floor. The first seven are given to shopping, dining, forms of transit, and a power plant. Our target, the conference room, was located on the second floor along with the rest of the various convention center amenities.

The door opened when we reached fifteen. As Scott pushed the luggage cart out of the elevator, he asked. "Room numbers?"

Morgan looked at the two envelopes with the keycards inside them. "1507 and 1509."

Morgan handed Fingers the key to 1507. Scott opened the door and put Fingers' suitcase on his bed. I saw Fingers give Scott a bill and heard him say, "If there is anything else needed, I will be here the rest of the night."

Scott led us to our room and put Morgan's bag in her bedroom and mine in the other. I handed Scott a Hamilton. He smiled and repeated what he said to Fingers. Once he left Morgan and me alone, I asked Morgan to get me a drink. I flopped down on the couch and pulled out my phone. It was time to face the music with Arch and Andrew.

Chapter Thirty-nine

"Better to be a dog in a peaceful time, than to be a human in a chaotic (warring) period." Feng Menglong. Stories to Awaken the World *(1627).*

November 7, 20xx, Westin Hotel Denver International Airport, Eight Thirty P.M. MST

"Tell me, Archie, what's so important it can't possibly wait?" I asked in a tired and aggravated tone.

I heard him sputter. "Why was your phone off?"

I yawned, I was becoming very bored very quickly. "Habit. I always turn my phone off when I fly. I noticed you didn't leave a voicemail," I said sweetly.

Ignoring my apparent dig, he continued, still in a very aggravated tone of voice. "Why did you hang up on me when we were talking? What gall."

"Did you really want me to discuss our business standing outside, in a snowstorm and surrounded by lots of protesters? I mean you're not being very security-minded."

"Well, I suppose you have a point there," Stanton conceded.

"So why did you call me? Run out of whipping boys to yell at or did you have a constructive reason?"

I looked over at Morgan who had just put my drink on the table and she was working hard not to laugh.

"I don't appreciate your tone of voice, Rixey. I just needed to know how things were going. Is that too much to ask?"

"Not at all. I'm going to be putting a listening device and an optical device in the meeting room later tonight. I don't think we will need it, though. If things go according to plans, we should be able to have the Chalice in Andrew Stuart's hot little hands by sometime on the ninth. And I might add, with a minimum of casualties. Fatalities, anyway."

"Low casualties? Seems like it would be a first for you, Mr. Rixey. People seem to die on cases you're involved in."

"Only the bad guys." I clicked off. I heard enough and told the client enough.

Morgan roared with laughter once she saw me click off. "I bet he turned purple the way you talked to him." She said somberly, "Be careful when you deal with him. I don't need to tell you he's very dangerous."

"I know, as you know, I have little tolerance for bullshit. So, what's in the package?"

Morgan took a seat next to me on the couch and began to open the package. I stole a glance at the mailing label and smiled. "Good old Willard. Well, let's see what he sent you."

She smiled wryly. "You aren't the only one who has special

friends."

She opened the package. It contained some surveillance tools, some listening devices, some optical devices, and a control pad. The listening devices were exact duplicates of the ones I used in Mexico City. She removed those devices and set them on the table. She then lifted a plastic cover to reveal three sonic screamers, three flashbangs, three smoke bombs, and three canisters of tear gas.

Morgan took one of the sonic screamers out the box and showed me how it worked. "Pull this cord, then roll it. It's pretty basic."

I checked the envelope Fingers gave me. "I see the OTO meeting is scheduled for nine A.M. in two days. There is another meeting scheduled tomorrow that caught my interest. It's listed as an Executive Committee meeting of the World Bank. I'll probably go in the room later tonight and plant the listening device. If there is a good spot, I'll also plant the optical device."

Morgan nodded.

"I want Fingers down in the lobby so we can know when the various players arrive. I don't think Hanover Fiste will be there. He will probably send Tweedledum and Tweedledee to observe the comings and goings of the OTO. Even with your disguise, Morgan, they are going to pick you up pretty easily. Carlo Borgia will know me, not you or Fingers. As for Mr. Crypt, we never met. I'm sure by now he knows who I am. Fingers is the only one who isn't known to all of the likely players."

"Good idea, Miller. I have a complete photo array of most of the suspects. Julian can commit those to memory."

I smiled as I arose from the couch to walk to Finger's suite door.

I knocked and a few seconds later the door opened. "What ya need, Mr. Rixey?"

"I need you to stake out the lobby beginning tomorrow morning. We need to know when the players, in this case, show up. It'll be boring, but Morgan and I are both known by most of the players. They don't know you. You met Eldor Crypt, but he won't know you as you were wearing a mask. I'm pretty sure Hanover Fiste won't be coming. Chances are good he will send his two henchmen, Alfie and Wilmer, to monitor the situation. They don't know you, but they know Morgan all too well. We are trying to keep our presence concealed. Morgan has a photo array with the various characters involved in this little play." I turned to Morgan as she handed me the array. "Here it is. The wild card is who North Korea will be sending to make the final payment for the Chalice." I stood there for a moment. "If you can take pictures of the OTO group of anyone you don't see on the array, at least it will give us some extra information. With any luck, we can have them run through a facial recognition program."

"Fair enough, Mr. Rixey. I'll be downstairs blending in by seven A.M. tomorrow."

I nodded and shut the door. I went back to the couch where Morgan still sat. Her face looked flushed. "They say they are closing Denver International Airport in the next hour or so."

Chapter Forty

"I can't change the direction of the wind, but I can adjust my sails to always reach my destination." Jimmy Dean.

November 7, 20xx, Westin Hotel Denver International Airport, Eight forty-five P.M. MST

I rang Arch Stanton. The phone was answered on the first ring. "Archibald Stanton."

"Miller Rixey calling with an update on our mission."

"I'm listening, Mr. Rixey."

"Denver International Airport is closing within the hour. As you and Mr. Stuart are the Agency's clients and there was no contingency plan in place, I'm calling to see how you want me to proceed."

Stanton's tone softened somewhat since our last chat. "Very good, Mr. Rixey. Perhaps I was too judgmental in our earlier dealings. Very professional."

"You will find the work at the Bishop Agency is always very professional," I said pointedly.

"Yes, quite right."

Even over the phone, I sensed Archie was feeling very uncomfortable. He didn't enjoy being forced to come to his senses about me and it would be much too painful to admit he was wrong. "Mr. Rixey, are you there? You seem to be fading in and out."

"Yes, I'm here."

"I have Mr. Stuart on speakerphone. He has been apprised of the situation."

"Very good."

"What would you recommend, Mr. Rixey?"

Just then I heard a commotion coming from Morgan's room. She charged out of her room. "The fucking internet has just crashed. I called down to the front desk and they claim they are investigating. They are hoping to have it back up by sometime tomorrow morning."

I rubbed my forehead. I felt like I was getting the mother of all headaches. I turned my attention back to Stuart and Stanton. "Did you guys hear what Morgan said? For whatever reason, the net is down in this is a five-hundred-dollar-a-night hotel."

"Yes, Mr. Rixey, we heard. Not a big deal. We can handle tracking and what other information is required for the successful completion of your mission," Stuart replied in a calm and evenhanded tone.

Both Stuart and Stanton could afford to be calm, cool, and collected. They were in a protected building thousands of miles away from where we were, ground zero.

The voices on the other end began fading in and out. This is never supposed to happen with my phone. I had a sinking feeling about what was happening.

I didn't like this. My ability to recognize potentially fatal situations have allowed me to survive for as long as I have in my line of work. "Morgan, try to dial out on your cell phone."

She took the phone out her pocket. "No need to dial. I have no service."

"I was afraid of that happening. Now go get Fingers and bring him here. See if his phone works."

Morgan returned with Fingers. She didn't look thrilled. She shook her head no. "Julian has zero bars also. What the hell is going on? You think maybe the hotel is under some sort of electronic attack?" Morgan walked back toward the hotel phone in the living room. She picked up the handset, punched a few numbers and hung up. "Room phone's out too."

"Okay here is the situation. The net is out. I don't think it has anything to do with the weather. Apparently, someone is using a cell phone blocker and for the cherry on top, our room phone doesn't work. The only reason we are still chatting is the person who designed my phone accounted for cell-blocking programs. We are under an electronic attack from someone and the Chalice is the reason. I'm sending one of my people out to check out the goings-on in Denver. My guess is the attack will be all through the Denver Metro area."

"What a fantastic idea, Mr. Rixey. How can you come to such a conclusion?" Stuart spluttered.

"Mr. Stuart, I'm a private investigator. I'm paid to know and reason things most people don't know or can't reason. Now you understand why people such as yourself hire people like me."

Stanton interjected, "You realize with the storm and the lack of communications, you are quite alone. What's the best way to proceed?"

"Let my group proceed as we originally planned before all these things began happening. I've got a good crew out here. Do I have your authority?"

Stanton and Stuart both responded, "Yes."

I clicked off.

I wasn't too surprised by the answer. I mean what the hell else were they going to do?

I eyed Fingers. He was looking quite dapper in his black beret, expensive sports coat, and cashmere scarf. "I don't suppose you carry a pistol, Fingers? I mean a convicted felon isn't supposed to."

Fingers made a dismissive gesture and grinned. "Don't worry about me, Mr. Rixey. Mr. Zogg said he would do something to allow me to carry concealed." He opened his jacket to reveal a black revolver. "Eight shots, almost no kick, made by Smith and Wesson."

I started to say something, but my attention was diverted to the door of our room by a loud pounding and an even louder, "Hotel Security."

Chapter Forty-one

"Sure, shit happens we can't control, but that's exactly what it is: shit you can't control. You can't control what it is, or sometimes what it does to you. But like I've told you before, you can control how you feel about it, how you deal with it." Bobby Adair, Torrent.

November 7, 20xx, Westin Hotel Denver International Airport, Nine Thirty P.M. MST

"Agent Reeves? We are checking room to room to make sure everyone is okay."

"Why wouldn't everyone be okay?" Morgan asked as she walked to the door to open it. Fingers and I were standing off to the side. Weapons were drawn, to be safe.

A very harried-looking managerial type, dressed in a Westin sports coat with the nametag announcing he was Jackson Chancey, the General Manager of the hotel, was being escorted by two beefy types dressed in hotel security uniforms. He was an older bald man, who wore a goatee, and was of average height and weight. When I saw him, I nodded to Fingers and we both put our weapons away and stepped out from where we

"We are having multiple problems. The internet is out until sometime tomorrow, the hotel phones are knocked out, and there seems to be a problem with cell phone reception. Also, if you are planning on traveling, the trains running through here are experiencing difficulties too. We aren't sure if these problems are weather-related or not. What I can tell you is the internet problem and the problems with the phones, both cell and landlines, is a Denver Metro area problem, not just restricted to the Westin. We will keep you informed. In the meantime, all the shops and restaurants are open in the hotel." Chancey laughed. "We have never seen weather like this before. I will be here for the duration and the concierge's desk will also be open. We will do our best to make you comfortable."

"Thanks for the update and the concern," Morgan said, smiling.

"Your suitemate, Mr. Malone, wasn't in his room when we knocked. Would you please update him?"

She pointed to Fingers. "Consider him notified. Thanks again, Mr. Chancey."

Chancey looked at his clipboard and no doubt marked off our two rooms as having been contacted. He said something to one of his escorts I was unable to make out, bowed, and left.

As I watched the door close behind Chancey, I furrowed my brow. "Now we know for sure the problem is area-wide, there's no need to send Fingers out in this weather." I laughed. "From the way Chancey was talking, Fingers probably couldn't even get a cab between the number of people here and the weather."

Finger scratched his head. "What you want me to do, Mr. Rixey?"

I smiled. "Fingers, go out and enjoy a nice meal, maybe have a couple of drinks, and be ready to sit in the lobby by seven A.M."

"If the phones are out, how do I communicate with you and Colonel Burke?"

Morgan cautioned him. "Remember, I'm Special Agent Reeves for this caper."

She reached into the package she received and pulled out an earplug and what looked like a lapel pin and handed them to him. "If you need to contact us, press on the lapel pin. It will activate the microphone in it. That way you'll be able to talk to either Agent Decker," pointing to me. "or me. This mike is super sensitive and we will hear everything you do. You can still take pictures with your phone so do so and when the net comes up, I can run the facial recognition program on the pictures you get." She paused. "It's imperative you address both of us by our cover names."

"Gotcha, Agent Reeves. I'll be more careful," Fingers said with a broad grin.

He pocketed the earplug, the lapel button, and waved goodbye as he left.

I glanced at my watch. It was a few minutes shy of eight thirty. "There shouldn't be anything or anyone roaming around the Convention Center. Hotel Security has too many other problems to be keeping too close an eye on the floor. If there's no one around, I can be in and out of the room in a few minutes. I'm not convinced the room even needs to be bugged as I'm hoping we can snatch the Chalice before the meeting. This is just in case."

"Understood." Morgan handed me an item identical to what she gave to Fingers.

"I'll be in touch." I put the lapel pin on and put the earpiece in my ear. It was small enough it wouldn't attract any notice. I picked up the key to the conference room and a flashlight. I headed for the elevator and punched two. Mercifully, the trip was a quick one, meaning I didn't have to suffer through too much Muzak resonating in the elevator. When the door opened, I headed to my right. I knew the conference room entrance was two doors down from the elevator. The lights were off everywhere on the floor.

I stopped outside the door to the conference room. I looked to my right and saw the key slot glowing red. I turned on my flashlight. I found what I was looking for. It was the schedule of the room for the week. No meetings were scheduled until the OTO meeting the day after tomorrow. It was planned from eight thirty A.M. to five P.M. Perfect. My work wouldn't be inadvertently disturbed before the meeting by people using the room and there would be no need for the custodial crew to come in and clean the room. I slid the keycard into the slot and the light turned green. I pushed the door open gently closed behind me hearing a click. I worked the flashlight around where the speaker's dais was and saw where I wanted to plant my listening device. I got down on my knees and crawled under the chair. I heard the door click and I turned off my flashlight and froze.

Chapter Forty-two

"Buy the ticket, take the ride." Hunter S. Thompson.

November 7, 20xx, Westin Hotel 2nd Floor Conference Room, Ten P.M. MST

I saw the lights flicker on and heard two voices. I hid under the table. I mean what choice did I have? I knew I would be discovered in any competent search. I was hoping the two voices were more lazy than qualified.

An older raspy voice said, "My, my, we seem to have a regular mystery here."

"There ain't no mystery," a younger voice with a Texas twang said.

"My supervisor's badge says there's a mystery. We have a code for unauthorized access to this room and the room is empty. I would call it a mystery." The older voice paused for effect. "We also have the fact someone in the past ten minutes stopped the elevator on this floor. Looks like a double mystery."

"Seriously, there ain't no mystery. With all the problems with electronics this place has tonight, the answer is electronic malfunctions. The hallway is dark. The valuable stuff from the conventions is locked up. Who the hell breaks into an empty conference room? The nice pizza we left in the guard shack is getting cold while we sit here debating this nonsense and investigating malfunctions," the younger voice whined.

"I suppose you're right. I am not too fond of cold pizza. I'll log it as a malfunction and we can go back to eating."

I saw the lights flicker off, heard the door close, and heard the patter of the guard's feet as they went back to wherever they came.

I waited for a few minutes to allow things to settle down and for my pulse to drop back to normal. I knew I still had work to do before I left here and I needed to get to it. I first rechecked the listening device. It was both hidden from prying eyes and securely placed. I finally decided to put the camera in a section of the curtain rods holding the drapes up. The section I chose was the section closest to the table and unlikely to be disturbed or discovered.

"Okay, Morgan, I'm turning off the device for a moment. What you'll hear is coming from the listening device."

"Copy that."

I counted to ten. Then I stood up where I was able to be hopefully viewed by the mini camera I'd installed.

I turned the device back on. "Everything working?"

"Yes. Time to get the hell out of there."

I stepped out of the conference room back into the more comfortable pitch black of the Westin Convention Center. At this point, if I got stopped, I would merely flash my FBI cred pack and mumble something about national security. I decided to walk to the third floor and take the elevator from there back to my room. As I opened the door to the third floor, all I heard were the noises coming from various machines such as compressors that run the hotel.

I made it to the elevator and punched fifteen. For some reason, no Muzak was playing, something I'll be forever grateful for. The door opened and I stepped out. I noticed Mr. Chancey was dealing with a hysterical customer who was threatening to sue the hotel as well as Mr. Chancey. *Better him than me*, I thought. We all have our crosses to bear. I sighed and shook my head in disgust.

I made it to my room and inserted the keycard into the slot and pushed the door open just in time to see Morgan finishing up a conversation with someone. Naturally, since as far as I knew I had the only working phone in the hotel, I'd left it with Morgan. She heard me enter and said, "Oh, Miller is right here. Let me put him on."

Chapter Forty-three

"Life is 10% what happens to you and 90% how you react to it."
Charles R. Swindoll.

I took the phone from Morgan and said, "Hello." You can imagine my relief when I heard the voice of the ever-faithful Ms. Nickels.

"Colonel Burke told me you two were having a real adventure out in Denver. I hope everything is going okay."

I chuckled. "Ms. Nickels, this trip has truly been an adventure. We experienced airplane problems on the way out there. We were in a bad storm during the flight. Umm, oh yes, the internet and house phones are out at this swanky hotel where we are staying. Oh yeah, I almost forgot, someone is running a cell phone blocking program in Denver."

"Good to see you haven't lost your humor, Mr. Rixey."

"Never let them see you sweat, Ms. Nickels. Anything from the office?"

"Yes. We got a divorce case and a suspected insurance fraud case. I hope the people I refer the cases to appreciate what you're doing for them. The big news is a potential client called about being swindled out of some very rare books. He's pretty confident the book restorer sent him back reproductions. He will know in about a month or so. He said if they are copies, you will be getting a call from him. He's a pretty big name in the book collecting business, Charles Hutchinson. He runs some billion-dollar communications conglomerate. He says he got your name from Luther Zogg."

"Hmm. This might be very interesting. Have you heard anything from or about Banner? Has he been staying out of trouble, I hope? I did assign a good man to babysit him. After what he did, it was the least I could do for him. He showed me what OTO was."

"Yes. Believe it or not, Banner is in a ninety-day rehab center in Hawaii. I hope he makes it this time. I was very pleasantly surprised when he called me and told me he was checking himself in."

"He will if he chooses to. I never thought he would do it. Looks like a good sign if he went in on his own. He's due for a break, I guess. You're in the office pretty late, aren't you?"

"I like working late at night. No phone calls and no off-the-street traffic."

"Terrific, Ms. Nickels. Keep in touch and remember this is the only way you can be certain to contact me. We probably won't have the internet for another day or so."

"Good night, sir. Wish Colonel Burke a good night, too."

"I will. You have a good night yourself." I clicked off. "Ms. Nickels said to have a good night."

Morgan nodded impatiently. "So, you ever going to tell me what happened down there? You should have been in and out of there in a couple of minutes tops."

"Should have been being the operative word. I seem to have set off an alarm when I used the keycard to open the door. I guess they weren't expecting anyone to be in there at this hour. They also log the trips on the elevators. Anyway, two members of the hotel's security team stopped by. They looked around the room, didn't see anything, and decided to get back to their pizza. Luckily for me, they didn't look under the table. I hope I never need to rely on those two clowns for anything. Don't get me wrong. I'm glad they were inept."

"Speaking of pizza. I'm starving. What say we check out the restaurants in this place?"

"I need some food, too. Let's go."

We got into the elevator and headed for the Plaza level. This was the level, according to the hotel guide, where the restaurants were located. As you might imagine, the place was packed. Under the circumstances, the majority of the guests had no other place to go. I was about to tell Morgan we needed to try later when we were approached by a short, long-haired, and swarthy individual.

"Signore Miller Rixey?" he asked in broken English.

I nodded.

He pointed to a large table with a couple of vacant seats. "Would you and the lady please join my padrone, Signore Carlo Borgia?"

I saw Borgia waving at me and gesturing to his table. I looked at Morgan and she shrugged in resignation. "Fine bit of help you are," I said with a wry smile. I turned back to the man. "Lead the way, sir."

Chapter Forty-four

"You have to walk to the fire. You have to embrace it." Ben Shapiro.

November 7, 20xx, Westin Hotel Restaurant, Eleven Thirty P.M. MST

Six men were seated at Carlo Borgia's table. They were of different heights and builds. One thing was for sure, they all wore the map of Sicily on their faces. They all stood as we neared the table. I figured the standing was for Morgan's benefit; something about her usually puts even the worst people in a very pleasant mood. No one ever stands for me unless I have a pistol on them.

Carlo was oozing graciousness from every pore. "Colonel Burke, I have heard so much about you. It's so nice to meet you finally."

Morgan smiled and gracefully extended her hand. Carlo took and kissed it. Waiters rushed to the table and pulled out Morgan's chair for her. She nodded approvingly as she sat down. I was left to my own devices of sitting down.

Morgan cooed at Borgia. "It was so very nice of you to allow us to join you for dinner." She pointed around the room. "Miller and I decided to make other plans before we received your generous offer as this place is packed. Thank you."

Borgia leaned over the table and smiled wolfishly at Morgan. "Please call me Carlo, and if I may be so bold as to call you Morgan?"

"Signore Borgia, I'd rather we stayed more formal until we know each other better."

Borgia never missed a beat. "Please pardon me for being so informal, Colonel. Please feel free to call me Carlo." He oozed his olive-oil charm. Still, I detected a troubling undercurrent of brutality. He was not used to being refused anything.

He motioned to the waiter who was hovering around our table. "Champagne for all," he said as he made a sweeping gesture. "Champagne is okay with you, Mr. Rixey? I know you love your Macallan, I believe, neat?"

I nodded. "It will be a nice change of pace."

If he was trying to shock me as to how much he knew about me, he was going to have to do better than knowing my favorite liquor.

Once the champagne was delivered and poured, our orders were taken. About five minutes later, Carlo called the waiter back over to our table and said something to him I didn't understand. Not surprising, with all the noise in the place. He turned to me. "Mr. Rixey, I find it best to discuss our business away from the table. Would you care to take a walk with me?"

I didn't have a choice. "Sure thing, Signore Borgia." I stood up and we walked to a more secluded area of the restaurant.

Chapter Forty-five

"For there to be betrayal, there would have to have been trust first."
Suzanne Collins, The Hunger Games.

The restaurant was packed, so we were going to have to have our chat outside of it. Borgia and I slowly worked through the teeming crowds on our way to one of the restaurant's exits.

Once we reached the exit and stopped outside, Borgia removed a small black device from his jacket pocket. I saw him press a button and put the machine back in his pocket. "This device emits soundwaves that will make any form of electronic surveillance impossible. I know you have used these in your line of work."

I nodded. "I'm familiar with the device. Now, why did you need to talk to me so badly? I mean in Mexico City you committed a terrorist act in an attempt to speak to me, and I don't believe your presence here is an accident, is it?"

He smiled, there was no sense of amusement or warmth in it. "You are very perceptive, Mr. Rixey. As for a reason, it should be obvious to you. It hasn't changed since Mexico City. My group needs the Chalice."

People were beginning to stare. "Let's keep moving," I said. "Neither of us wish to attract any undue attention." As we walked, I continued. "I don't like being pushed around. Mr. Fiste made me a very generous offer to give him the Chalice. I turned him down for two reasons. First, I doubt I would have lived long enough to spend the money and more importantly, I make it a rule never to betray a client. Perhaps if you or Mr. Fiste had contacted me first, we would be having a different conversation." I shrugged. "I would have thought you received the message in Mexico City. I guess not."

Borgia turned purple and gritted his teeth. "Everyone has a price, even the incorruptible Miller Rixey. I'm not one to be taken lightly or trifled with. Do you understand?"

I shook my head. "No price when it comes to client loyalty. As for me, you are aware of what happened to the messenger Hanover Fiste sent to try to convince me to work for him, aren't you? I'm not one to be taken lightly or trifled with either."

He gulped and turned pale as he began to reconsider his position. "Forgive me, Mr. Rixey, I seem to have lost my head during our discussion."

I wasn't buying what he was selling. His apparent change of attitude was just another dodge. This guy and his group were as dangerous as any group I had ever come up against. Rather than continuing to press his buttons, I asked, "So, what is your group's interest in the Chalice?"

"As you refuse to cooperate with us, our interest isn't your concern," Borgia answered pointedly.

"Fair enough."

"I would also appreciate you keeping our discussion to yourself."

"I always do. You are a potential client, looking to hire me for an assignment. I never discuss such meetings without the client's permission. How about we go back and rejoin our party?"

"Yes, an excellent idea."

We headed back to the restaurant and, while the crowd had thinned out some, it was still packed. I heard Morgan's laughter resonating from the room. Borgia's other friends seemed quite taken with her. When we got back to the table, a double shot of Macallan was sitting in a crystal glass where I was seated. *Borgia didn't miss much. I'll give him that,* I thought.

"Oh, Miller. Signore Borgia has the funniest companions. They kept me in stitches the whole time you were gone."

I smiled and nodded to Borgia as I sipped my drink. I looked at my watch. "Time to go, Morgan, we still have some work needing to completed. We can pick something up later."

Morgan nodded and made her apologies over the protests at the table.

"Thanks again, Signore Borgia for allowing Morgan and I to join your group for dinner."

"Think nothing of it, Mr. Rixey."

We left the restaurant and headed for the elevators. We were soon outside our door. As usual, I listened for any noises and hearing none, I slid the keycard in the slot and pushed the door open. On the floor, just barely inside the room, was a white envelope.

Chapter Forty-six

"There is no victory at bargain basement prices." Dwight D.
Eisenhower.

November 8, 20xx, Westin Hotel Denver International Airport, One
Thirty A.M. MST

The envelope had been slid into the room about a foot from the
door. I signaled Morgan to check the place out. She nodded and fished
out the electronic device detection wand she normally carried. It was so
useful in the past. While she went about her business, I went about mine.

I tossed the envelope on the table by the couch and went to the
minibar, debating what to drink. I finally decided that coffee was the way
to go. After the champagne and the Macallan double, I didn't need any
more stimulation for one evening. I looked into the fridge under the
minibar and took a bottle of iced coffee from there. I then took my seat
on the couch. Morgan came out of Fingers' suite and gave me thumbs up.
I nodded and made a motion for her to join me on the couch.

I looked at the envelope. There was no name on the front. I opened the envelope and showed the letter to Morgan.

Sir:

I sent a man, a simple messenger to peacefully ask you to reconsider taking me on as a client to aid me in gaining the Chalice of Power. You responded with violence that resulted in the death of the messenger. Accidents do happen and the man was of no account anyway. I am currently staying on the twelfth floor of the Westin and would like to discuss a plan that will make you wealthy beyond your wildest dreams and will fulfill a lifelong ambition of mine to have one of the key artifacts from the Renaissance Era. Please consider stopping by. Wilmer and Alfie are very anxious to meet with you and your girlfriend again. Just come down to my floor; my guards will know who you are and you will be promptly escorted to my suite.

Hanover Fiste

"I'd love to meet those assholes again. I have some unfinished business with both of them," Morgan growled. She looked at me strangely. "Whom did you murder? You never told me anything about murdering someone."

"Yeah, I sure did. He was the guy who jumped me in the men's room at the airport. It happened at the airport after you left."

"The guy who jumped you? It sounded like self-defense to even Stanton. Mr. Fiste has a little problem with reality or the truth."

"Simple messenger my ass. He got a gun and a silencer through TSA. Remind me to write TSA a thank you and well done letter."

The whole situation was so absurd. I began laughing.

I took a sip of my coffee. "I'm going outside for a smoke then I have some calls to make. People need to know the players are present and ready to go the day after tomorrow."

"You sure the exchange is going down at the meeting? I'm not so sure Crypt will even be here."

I smiled sardonically. "Crypt has fifty million reasons to be here. I don't care if the airport is closed and the roads are crappy. He is highly motivated. He'll be here."

I took the elevator down to the ground level, walked through the teeming crowd and into the storm, as well as the ongoing protests against the World Bank. I took a cigarette out of a pack, lit it, and inhaled deeply. The burn felt good. I made a mental note never to stay in another non-smoking hotel. I enjoyed the cold. It was one of the things I missed living in Southern Illinois. As I stood and watched the protesters, I saw that some were out there to merely protest and some were out to cause a riot.

I was surprised that Fingers soon joined me. He would fit right in with the marchers decked out in his black beret, a very colorful winter jacket, and sporting a goatee. "Mr. Rixey, how's it going?"

I took a puff and nodded. "Fine."

"You got a smoke, Mr. Rixey?"

I silently handed him my pack and just as quietly took it back. "Before you go out tomorrow morning, make sure you take my phone. It's still the only working one in the hotel I'm aware of. I can send the picture of the courier North Korea sent to make the final payoff for the Chalice to someone who has a face-recognition program. My guess is the problem with the internet and cell phones will continue until after the OTO meeting."

Fingers nodded. "Sounds good, Mr. Rixey."

We stood there in silence watching the protesters. Out of the corner of my eye, I saw Eldor Jamieson Crypt. He was walking next to an Asian male who carried a satchel and four of the biggest men I had ever seen. I got over my shock in time to pull my phone and snap a nice picture of the group. I snapped a second picture and got a great shot of the still-unknown Asian male. I slid the phone back in my pocket.

I turned to Fingers. "You just got most of tomorrow off. The last pic completes my set. I know exactly who is here now. Meet Morgan and me about five P.M. and we can discuss our plans for tomorrow. Meanwhile, I need to get back upstairs and send these pictures to Stanton and let him run them. I'd like to know who the North Korean is and I have a funny feeling Stanton doesn't know how bad our situation is once we recover the Chalice."

Fingers doffed his beret. "Thanks, Mr. Rixey. You know where I am when you need me if you need me earlier."

After Fingers left, I lit a second cigarette. The cold doesn't particularly bother me. I spent most of my life in northern and central Illinois. Unlike Carbondale, it does get cold up in that part of the state. *What the hell,* I thought, *what's a few extra minutes one way or another in my sending out the pictures.* It turned out to be the luckiest cigarette I have ever smoked.

Six very large and very mean-looking men who were decked out paramilitary style approached the hotel. No visible weapons. These men were pros. The man they encircled was of more interest to me though. He was five foot eight or so with a very slight frame. I couldn't shake the feeling I had seen him before. He carried a small black case, according to Stuart, matching the approximate size of the Chalice. I casually took my phone out and did my best "I'm not looking at you" act while I snapped his picture. The man was nice enough to turn his head at the moment guaranteeing a nice clear picture of him.

The picture taken, I waited for Crypt and his group to clear security before I headed toward the checkpoint. I flashed my FBI cred pack at the harried security guard and he quickly waved me through. I was glad Morgan had secured these things. I didn't want to have to wait in line for a long time.

I took the elevator back up to our suite. Morgan was lying on the couch watching the Weather Channel. She looked up as I entered.

I smiled. "I took some nice pictures out there."

Morgan sat up and stretched. "While you were outside smoking and taking pictures, I was finding out some valuable information."

"Well, lay it on me."

"With the weather, internet problems, and the phone problems, the World Bank meeting has been canceled. The weather is supposed to break tomorrow. No one knows when the electrical problems will be fixed. As a result, DIA will be closed to commercial flights until the problems are resolved."

"None of this is any good. The World Bank's meeting being canceled, it means large crowds of people to hide amongst won't be here. If the airport is still going to be closed, I need to get Stanton to find a way to get us out of here after we snatch the Chalice."

Morgan nodded. "So what all did you find out?"

"I saw Crypt and the Chalice arrive. It looks like the weather won't be changing the OTO meeting schedule. All the major players in this caper are now here. Crypt, unlike in Mexico City, has heavy security with him this time. He doesn't want a replay of what happened down there. He didn't get to where he is today by not learning from past mistakes."

Morgan responded, "I'm not saying it will be easy, but with the various devices we have like the grenades and the sonic screamers, we will pull this off."

"I hope you're right."

She smiled. "I know I am. Now we both have things to do. I'll be back in an hour or so." She kissed me and left.

I sent the pictures I took to Stanton. He seemed to have taken charge of the project to recover the Chalice. He would be able to run the photos through a facial recognition program to which we didn't have access. I'd call him after I spoke to Mr. Chen.

When I dialed his number, there was a lot of static and background noise. This wasn't very surprising considering I was even lucky to be able to make a phone call with all that had transpired.

"Miller, good to hear from you. I've was told things are pretty wild up your way. The blizzard and the electronic attack make for interesting times, don't they?"

"So, you think it's a calculated attack like I do?"

"What else could it be? I know neither of us believes in coincidences."

I sighed. "Very true, Mr. Chen. The purpose of this call is to let you know Hanover Fiste, Carlo Borgia, and the representative from North

Korea have made it here. Naturally, Crypt and the Chalice are here too. We knew it always was going to be, didn't we?"

I heard a tone of excitement in Mr. Chen's voice. In the relatively short time I'd known him, he never got flustered or excited. He was always a very cool cat. In his line of work, it's a commendable trait. What I was telling him must be very big. "Fiste is there? This was not expected. Has he attempted to contact you? Sad to say, we have no reports on his current location."

"He has. He sent me a letter telling me he is staying in the same hotel I am. He wants us to meet. I'm passing on the meeting as I never betray a client and I'm sure he wants to convince me to do so. I doubt I'd live long enough to enjoy the money he has promised me." More static and noises came on the line. I didn't know if the static was merely a bad connection or if someone was trying to eavesdrop on my phone. *Good luck trying listening in,* I thought.

When the noises diminished, I heard Mr. Chen. "You are wise beyond your years, Miller. Fiste is a very dangerous man and it is most unlikely he will survive the year. Accidents, crime, and suicides can take their toll on people."

"Yes, Mr. Chen, I am well aware the world is a very dangerous place. I do have some other people to contact."

"I understand. Thank you so much for keeping me in the loop."

I clicked off and then dialed Stanton.

His voice sounded a little hoarse as it exploded over the phone. He must have been yelling at people again. "Rixey, you do good work. We identified the Asian as Kae Du-Ho. He holds the rank of Colonel

General in the Reconnaissance General Bureau (RGB). I will assume you know what the RGB does."

"Yes. We have crossed paths before."

"Be very careful in your dealings with him. He is very dangerous and is a nephew of Kim Jong-un. As for the person carrying the case, his name is Phillip Vandamm. His father is Eldor Jamieson Crypt. We can't be certain of his rank in the OTO, but it seems pretty certain he is a member. In this case, the apple doesn't fall far from the tree. Are you familiar with him?"

I mulled the question and finally decided there was no reason to lie to Stanton, as much as I wanted to. "Yes. You're correct. He was involved in an attempted attack on my office."

"How do you know?"

"The person he shot was able to wrest the ring from him. The ring was engraved with his name. This guy is a really bad actor. I can tell you this. The OTO is little more than a well-run and well-organized criminal ring."

"Yes. He sure sounds like one."

"If the regular plane cannot land or take off, how are you planning on getting us out of here once we snatch the Chalice?"

"We'll have a chopper parked in the same area where the plane is. Make sure when you leave the room tomorrow, you have all you need. You won't have time to go back to your room. The same driver and vehicle who brought you to the Westin will be waiting for you out front tomorrow. Are we clear?"

"Sounds great, we take the helicopter to an open airport, fly back to DC, then I turn over the Chalice to either you or Stuart, and you lay a nice check on me. Right?"

There was a long pause. This is never a good sign. The way the conversation is supposed to go is the question I just asked is answered with a snappy yes. The pause told me there had been some changes of plans and suddenly your life or your plans just got tougher.

"Stanton, are you there?"

Stanton stammered, "Um. I don't know how to tell you this, Mr. Rixey, but there has been a slight change in plans."

Chapter Forty-seven

"God gives every bird his worm, but He does not throw it into the nest."

P.D. James.

I inwardly groaned. I hate being right all of the time. "What's the change in plans?"

"Now, now, Rixey. It's just a minor change of plans. The President has decided since there are so many security leaks about your mission and because this artifact is much too powerful for humanity at this time, it needs to be delivered to a certain place for safekeeping. Perhaps in about two hundred years or so, we will be able to use the Chalice for good and not evil. Many people fear it would be much too easy to destroy the world with it."

"You're the boss, I guess. Where are we supposed to take this?"

"There is a deserted Mayan temple located in the Yucatan Peninsula. I'll send you the GPS coordinates and the details once you have secured the Chalice."

"This sounds dangerous. I need a larger fee."

"Sorry, Rixey, no money for larger fees. By the way, our government has been dealing with this group since the early days of the Republic. These people are very reliable and there has never been a breach of security. Now what I want from you is a nice quiet and discreet plan to guarantee to get the Chalice away from the North Koreans and the OTO. I will be sending a black SUV to pick your crew up tomorrow morning. It will take you to DIA. The vehicle will be there from eight thirty AM to ten AM. If you don't make it out by then, we're going to assume you failed."

"Quiet and discreet is my middle name, Arch. I'll call you once we are on the move. You better have the chopper at DIA and that SUV in place." I clicked off.

I knocked on Morgan's door. "We need to have a chitchat. Stanton has thrown another curve into our plans."

Morgan sleepily replied, "I'll be out in a few minutes."

"Put on something warm. We're going outside. I need a smoke."

Morgan opened the door, yawning, clad in jeans and a jacket, and stumbled to the minibar. She poured a cup of coffee. "You want one, too?"

I nodded.

As we walked to the elevator, Morgan asked, "What's so important you needed to wake me up? I had a wonderful dream."

"Stanton changed the plans on us. We aren't going to DC to deliver the Chalice. He is sending us some other place. I don't like it."

We stepped into the elevator and headed for the lobby floor. With news spreading about the cancellation of the World Bank's meeting, only a few people milled about the lobby. The security checkpoint was taken down. The doorman opened the door for us. "You folks heard?"

I shook my head. "What about?"

"They canceled the World Bank meeting for a few weeks. I guess it was due to the weather and the electrical problems we have been having here."

Morgan smiled. "Good guess."

We walked out of earshot of the doorman. I noticed the protesters on both sides left as well as the police. "I guess they will need to find a new place and new cause to protest," I smarmed.

Morgan handed me my cup of coffee. "So, what was this about? Stanton wants us to go to another place other than D.C.?"

"Yeah. He says POTUS doesn't think the Chalice is safe in anyone's hands at this time and they want it dumped to a secret location. For once, I agree with POTUS. It's much too dangerous for humanity. He claims they have been doing things like this since we became a country. It sounds like they have been dealing with the same group for centuries and haven't any problems."

Morgan looked at me strangely. "I normally don't like sudden plan changes. An item like the Chalice makes any plan to keep it hidden well. Did he say how are we supposed to contact the Mayans?"

"The Mayans?" I asked as I lit my cigarette. "Stanton said he would send us the particulars like GPS and whom we are supposed to meet once we are in the air."

"Yes. You said Yucatan Peninsula. There is only one group I can think of capable and honest enough to hide something like the Chalice. If it's the tribe I'm thinking of, they escaped the Spanish conquistadors and simply vanished. They can trace their bloodline to the Mayans. With a few exceptions, they live like they did centuries ago. POTUS and Stanton have to be worried about abuses of the Chalice to go to these lengths to secure it."

I looked over at the door when I heard the doorman say something I couldn't make out. I saw Fingers and motioned him to come to join us.

"Hi, Mr. Rixey and Colonel Burke. I figure we are alone so I can at least call you by your right names."

Morgan said, "Fair enough. It's not going to matter much after tomorrow. You heard the World Bank conference got called off?"

"Yes, ma'am."

"Well, as long as we are out here, let's discuss our plans. It's going to be pretty basic. We have skin masks, nose filters, and ear plugs." Morgan pulled out a map of the second floor. "The meeting room is here," she said as she pointed to it. "I want Julian standing by the elevator."

She looked at Fingers. "We need you there just in case the hotel or one of the other players try to send security people quickly via elevator. As soon as you see Crypt appear, toss two sonic screamers."

She turned to me. "Miller, two flashbangs for anyone not down on their knees. I'll toss two smoke bombs to finish it. Julian, I need you to grab somehow the case the Chalice is in. Can you?"

Fingers nodded. "Yes, Colonel."

I put my hand up as some people were coming up behind Morgan from behind.

Once the people passed, she continued. "In case we get separated,

Miller said there would be an SUV, the one we rode over in originally, parked out front waiting to take us to DIA. A helicopter is supposed to be waiting for us at DIA right where the airplane landed with Miller and me. I mean it seems simple enough. What can go wrong? Let's plan on being on the second floor at seven thirty."

Chapter Forty-eight

"When you can't make them see the light, make them feel the heat."
Ronald Reagan.

*November 9, 20xx, Westin Hotel Second Floor Conference Area, Seven
Thirty A.M. MST*

We were waiting for one hour before Crypt, General Hyono,
Phillip Vandamm and the rest of the OTO entourage arrived for their
meeting. We did some prep work like putting on vests in case shooting
broke out. It turned out, except for the World Bank meeting being
canceled, it was still business as usual at the Westin. Enough people were
around so we didn't stand out like a sore thumb, which was a relief. There
was shouting from the half dozen or so groups who were getting ready for
their meetings. People began queuing at tables to receive their name tags
and other registration materials. None of the convention goers realized
that very soon, they would have an experience they would talk about and
remember for the rest of their lives.

The OTO contingent finally arrived at about eight thirty. They were divided into two groups. The first group was composed of Crypt, General Hyono, still clutching the same leather satchel I saw him with yesterday, and Vandamm, who was carrying the Chalice. An Asian man, I was guessing North Korean, shadowed the General. A dozen very obvious security men surrounded the entire first group. Just in case one doubted their intent, the bulges under their suitcoats cleared any doubt. The second group was made of members of the OTO board, I guessed as I saw the man who ascended to the Board by murdering the person Crypt accused of working for Hanover Fiste was in the second group. I put in my earplugs to protect me from the sonic screamers and nose plugs to defend me from tear gas. I saw Morgan and Fingers doing the same. So far, so good.

I pulled my ski mask down and saw Fingers and Morgan do the same. It was the signal for Fingers to begin the attack. I saw Fingers roll the sonic screamers toward the OTO group. The effect was instantaneous. The silent sound waves sent people either to their knees or screaming as they sought to escape whatever they thought they were terrified of. I saw Vandamm drop to his knees and drop the case as he covered his ears from the horrible sound waves he was hearing. Two members of the OTO security group were not affected by the screamers and drew their weapons, looking for someone to shoot. Crypt and the General were not affected and I heard Crypt screaming orders. Just what the orders were, with all of the noise on the level, I couldn't hear. When I saw them draw their weapons, I pulled mine. Morgan tossed two tear-gas canisters and they began shooting off a noxious fog that would immobilize anyone without a mask or filters to the ground, weeping and choking. I saw

Morgan draw her pistol after tossing the canisters. The chaos was incredible to view.

Suddenly, alarms went off and lights began flashing all over the floor. I saw Fingers start for the dropped case. The guards began coughing. The rest of the entourage was out of it by then. One of them got his bearings and aimed his weapon at Fingers. I fired three rounds into the guard, aiming for the head. I knew these guys wore vests. I couldn't hear my suppressed shots over the noise from the people and the alarms. The guard jerked violently and I saw his pistol fall from his hand as his body crashed to the floor. Morgan opened fire on the second guard and he collapsed to the ground dead.

The elevator door opened and five men dressed in Westin Security uniforms piled out. They were immediately affected by the sonic screamers and fell to the floor, clutching their ears. Julian ran up, kicked Vandamm in the head to pry his grip of the case loose, and grabbed it.

"Stairs," Morgan screamed.

I didn't hesitate. I followed Fingers and Morgan down the stairs to the lobby. I saw the black case on the first-floor landing. I kicked it and found it was empty. Good man, I thought, Fingers put the Chalice in a new bag. I tore off my ski mask and stuck it in my jacket pocket. The first floor was mobbed with law enforcement officers and firefighters. Hundreds of guests also packed the lobby. I lost sight of Morgan and Fingers. I hoped they had made it out. As I pushed toward the door, I was stopped by a policeman.

"Where do you think you're going, buddy? Nobody is leaving until we figure out what all happened."

I flashed my FBI cred pack at him and he nodded and waved me on.

I made it outside and saw Morgan and Fingers standing at the curb, but no promised black SUV.

Chapter Forty-nine

"Fortune favors the bold but abandons the timid." Latin Proverb.

Ten Minutes After Taking the Chalice of Power

"What the fuck? Stanton assured me we'd be met. Jesus." I've experienced low points in my life: this was going to be a top-ten one. I heard gunshots come from the hotel and turned around and saw a group of angry people charging out of the Westin with weapons drawn. I drew my pistol. *I guess this is how it ends,* I thought.

I heard Morgan shout, "Hang on, Miller, the SUV is pulling up the driveway."

Shots bounced all around us. I saw Fingers with the Chalice secured in an airline carry-on bag. I fired some rounds, aiming high and attempting to slow the crowd down. It worked. I try not to kill people until I know their level of guilt.

I heard the screech of the brakes and a voice said, "Get in if you want to live."

I emptied the rest of my magazine at the crowd and dove into the front passenger seat. Morgan and Fingers were already in the back. The SUV began moving even before I closed the door.

"Sorry, Mr. Rixey, I got a text message telling me the mission was scrubbed. The proper authorizations were on it. I called the number back to confirm and got sent straight to voicemail. I figured something went wrong and decided to get over here and see for myself."

I looked at the driver. He was the same one who initially dropped us off at the Westin. I had paid no attention to him on the way over, now noticing he was a young man, I'd guess in his twenties. I reached over and shook his hand. "At least you got here. How were you able to get a text message with a cell phone blocker program running?"

He grinned. "I got a special phone from my dad, Arch Stanton." He kept his eyes on the road. "Get your FBI cred packs out. We are coming up to an airport security stop. It's the only one we'll pass before we get you to the chopper. Once we get by the checkpoint, we're, or rather you're, home free."

He stopped the SUV and a man wearing sunglasses and a TSA uniform stepped out of a guard shack. He carried a semi-automatic pistol of some type and two other men stood near with semi-automatic rifles. These guys were serious. "Papers, please."

All of us showed our cred packs and he waved us on.

A few minutes later we were at the place we had been only a few days ago. Our jet sat ready. We weren't going to be taking a plane today. I saw the helicopter with a pilot and copilot standing outside.

"Thanks for the ride," I said as I shook his hand.

"My pleasure."

We got out of the SUV and ran to the chopper. The pilot and co-pilot nodded when they saw us and gestured for us to get aboard. A few minutes later, we were strapped into the helicopter.

Once airborne, I poked Fingers and gestured for him to open the bag. The rotors made conversation difficult. He opened the carry-on bag and I was transfixed by the beauty of the Chalice of Power. It was six inches high, made of gold, and covered with precious stones. Even if the Chalice didn't have its reputed powers, it wasn't hard to see why people would kill for it. The fact its powers were so incredible made it all the more desirable. Control of this item meant world domination. More than one person had died because of men seeking the Chalice. I didn't want my name or anyone's in my group being added to the list. I motioned Fingers to zip the bag closed. I looked at Morgan and she shook her head.

I felt a tap on my shoulder and was given a headset by the co-pilot. He also handed them out to Morgan and Fingers. He motioned for us to put them on.

"Who is Miller Rixey? Press button A to talk to me and B to talk to your other party members," the pilot stated in a clipped southern accent. He smiled as he shook his head.

I pressed A. "I'm Miller Rixey."

"I got an Archibald Stanton who wants to talk to you. He is pretty unhappy with you." I heard a chuckle come over my headset.

Chapter Fifty

"There's a difference between standing up and telling people what you're planning to do and standing up and going and accomplishing something." Paul Stanley.

The co-pilot handed me a radio. "Press the red button to talk. Release it to listen." He pointed at my headset. "There's an auxiliary slot there. Just plug it in."

I nodded to the copilot and plugged in the radio. "Miller Rixey."

Stanton was in fine form. "I know who this is. Remember, I called you." Before I said anything, he continued his voice rising. "Quiet and discreet? Two dead, a half dozen in critical condition, hundreds of people traumatized, and every law enforcement group in the nation is at the Westin. Luckily for you, our cover story about a terrorist attack is holding. What's with you, Rixey?"

I shrugged out of habit. I knew he couldn't see me. Now it was my turn to get angry. "What the hell did you think was going to happen? Did you think they would just give it up?" I paused to calm myself down.

I still wanted the promised check at the end of the day. I took a softer tone. "Look, someone has infiltrated your little group. Our driver, your son, saved our bacon. He got a message our mission was scrubbed. Luckily for us, he figured out something was wrong when he attempted to verify the message. He showed up anyway. He deserves a pay raise, promotion, and a medal. He said the message contained all the proper verification codes. He told us he couldn't contact the sender. That made him suspicious. Smart boy, you got there, Arch."

Sounding a little mollified, Stanton spoke. "You did succeed in getting the Chalice, I'll give you that. Like I said before, your body count seems awfully high. Can you dial it down a notch?"

"I'll do my best, but don't hold your breath. What I need from you are the coordinates for the meeting."

I wrote them down as he gave them to me. I repeated them back to him and he agreed. I thought we were on easy street as far as this caper went. It turned out I was wrong again.

"The pilot you are meeting in Colorado will know where to take you. There's another slight problem. I don't like these changes any more than you do. Unfortunately, we have to do the best we can, don't we?"

"Now what?" I asked in an exasperated tone.

"It's very dense jungle where you are going and the chopper will have to drop you off a couple of miles from the meeting place. Also, about a mile from the meeting place, no electronics seem to work. You will be totally on your own."

The pilot cut in. "Mr. Rixey and Director Stanton, we will be landing in ten minutes."

"I got to go, Arch, I'll call you when it's over." I clicked off, disconnected the radio, and handed it back to the co-pilot.

"Mr. Rixey, look," the co-pilot said excitedly.

I looked down and saw our chartered jet surrounded by a dozen squad cars, some black SUVs, and two Mine Resistant Ambush Protected Vehicles (MRAPS).

Chapter Fifty-one

"The battlefield is a scene of constant chaos. The winner will be the one who controls that chaos, both his own and the enemies." Napoleon Bonaparte.

I was forced to think quickly. If this didn't convince Stanton and Stuart we had a security leak, nothing would. How did the cops find out we were going to be here when none of us knew of the plan change until recently? None of this stuff mattered. What mattered was how were we going to get ourselves on our jet and finish our mission. I was going to have to wing it and see what happened.

Before I left the helicopter, I told the pilot, "Wait here until you see me signal for you to leave."

He nodded. "Anything you need, sir."

Morgan and Fingers followed me off the chopper. I held my FBI cred pack over my head and Morgan and Fingers taking my cue did likewise. "Who the fuck is screwing with national security? Who's in charge and why are we having a law enforcement convention right here?"

I broke off my rant long enough to address Morgan and Fingers. "I want the name and badge numbers of every person here. Heads will roll. I want the list five minutes ago."

Morgan and Julian walked over to the various law enforcement officials and began talking and writing. I was almost ashamed of myself. I hate bullying, but based on the way Arch Stanford did things, it seemed the best way to get people moving and to get things done in these types of situations.

A very pale middle-aged man dressed in a cheap suit approached. He looked at my credentials. "Sorry, sir. I don't understand what happened. We got a report from what I was certain was a solid source that the terrorists from the Westin Hotel who staged the attack were on their way here. I'm in charge here. I'm Special Agent Robert Adair. How can we be of assistance?"

I leaned into Adair. "Someone is having some expensive fun with you. What I want from you is to clear this runway and allow my team to continue with its mission. Am I understood?"

"Yes. You are quite clear. I'm sorry about this."

He raised his walkie-talkie and spoke into it. Almost immediately, I saw officers returning to their squad cars and other vehicles and within five minutes the tarmac was cleared.

"Good job."

We shook hands and I saw Adair get into an SUV and drive off. He was looking miserable. Soon we were alone. I motioned for Morgan and Fingers to follow me aboard the jet. Morgan ran back to the helicopter and returned with a large black box. I waved to the pilot of the helicopter and saw him lift off.

The plane began to taxi once the law enforcement vehicles cleared the runway. I saw the door to the cockpit open and a thin, balding, middle-aged man walked out. He was dressed in an Air Force uniform with captain's bars. His nametag said Kinser. He nodded at Fingers and me and then saluted Morgan. She stood and returned his salute. Captain Kinser held rigidly.

"At ease, Captain."

"Yes, Ma'am. I just wanted you and your company to realize we were as surprised as you were when the police cars showed up."

Morgan nodded. "Good, Captain. We understand totally."

"Perfect, Colonel." He saluted and Morgan returned it.

Once Captain Kinser left, I decided to bring out into the open what Morgan and Fingers feared. "There's no way around it. Someone's leaking and if we don't figure it out, it's going to cost us our lives."

Fingers looked quizzical. "We have had some bad luck, man. You think there are leaks?"

"This isn't the first time I thought this has happened. The evidence is piling up rapidly. For one, why didn't the OTO bring the Chalice to Mexico City? For another, how did Fiste and Borgia know where I was going to be when we were in Mexico City during the festival? Remember, they both knew we were at the Westin. Combine that with the attempt to leave us standing at the Westin and our greeting party here. Just way too much information was getting out and I know it wasn't accidental. A direct pipeline on the inside exists."

"Any idea who the leaker is?" Morgan asked.

"It would be a person who gained Stuart's confidence and the person needed to know a lot about the Chalice. My guess is it's the good Dr. Eve Kendall. She has one more surprise for us before this caper is over."

I looked at Morgan. "So what's in the box?"

She smiled. "I'll let you know after I change." She got out of her seat and headed for the restroom. When she returned, she was dressed in her fatigues. She took her place and reached for the box. She slowly opened it up and inside was a cache of weapons, ammunition, and some earplugs. She pulled out a long rifle I recognized as a Dragunov. A Russian sniper rifle and one of the finest weapons in the world for its purpose. She handed Fingers a revolver matching the one he was carrying and handed me a Glock-17. She handed me a couple of magazines of 9 MM ammunition and gave Fingers a box of twenty-five bullets. She took out a scope for her rifle and a Sig Sauer P 229-Legion, her favorite handgun. She pulled out two suppressors and two sets of earplugs and handed them to us. We still wore our vests.

She sat back and began fiddling with the scope on her rifle. "Chances are good I won't even need this," Morgan said, pointing to the rifle. "We'll have a dozen of the roughest and toughest Rangers waiting for us at the drop zone. This rifle is just in case."

I couldn't resist. "Just in case of what?"

"Just in case the Rangers don't show."

I heard Fingers mumble something under his breath. I wasn't sure what he was saying, but I knew I agreed with it.

Finally done with her sight, Morgan looked up. "When the

Rangers show, the plan is you guys walk about four hundred yards ahead of us. When we get to the clearing, all people are going to see is you. This will be much easier than what we did in Argentina, Miller."

"I hope so. I don't need another chewing out from some Under-Secretary of God knows what."

Morgan took my hand and squeezed it. "It'll be fine. Soon we'll be back in the USA, you will be spending your money on me, and we will be laughing about the whole thing."

"I hope you're right."

She smiled. "Deep down, you know I am. Now we need some rest. We'll be there in three and a half hours."

I nodded and dozed off. I felt myself being shaken. I looked up and through my bleary eyes saw Morgan.

"The Rangers aren't here."

Chapter Fifty-two

"Adventure is worthwhile in itself." Amelia Earhart.

November 11, 20xx, Somewhere on the Yucatan Peninsula

Our pilots, local people, dropped us off about two and a half miles from where our GPS device told us to go. They refused to go any closer, citing mysterious disappearances, unexplained attacks, a verified viewing of some demons, and the effects of *la zona muetra* as the locals call it, the dead zone where electronic devices don't seem to work. Once we stepped out of the cool helicopter we were hit by a blast of the hot and humid weather the jungle contained. I couldn't say I blamed them. I could think of only a thousand other places I'd rather be. When we got out of the helicopter, Morgan handed Fingers and me a compass.

"This is not a big deal. We can do this without the Rangers. It'll just be a little more difficult." She handed me a compass. "Keep due north from this point on. You'll run right into the meeting. Your GPS will not work once we get about a mile or so from the meeting place."

Morgan did her best to sound convincing. I'm pretty sure she didn't really believe what she was saying. "This mission would have been more straightforward with the Rangers, but we'll be fine."

Fingers asked a very logical question. "Assuming we make it out of here in one piece, how do we get home?"

Morgan patted one of the pockets on her shirt. "Once we are clear of the dead zone, I have a transmitter capable of sending out a burst transmission. Our rescue party will receive our coordinates."

I looked confused. "Why all the intrigue? Why didn't the rescue team simply drop us off and wait for us?"

"It's bad enough we are here. We wanted to have as little exposure to Americans as possible. In case you thought about it, we are in this country illegally. You don't recall going through customs, do you?" She smiled. "Remember, we aren't in the United States. This country takes a dim view of illegals." Just as quickly, the smile left her face. "Let's get going. The meeting place isn't getting any closer."

"Let's wait until the chopper takes off. I don't even want them seeing what direction we are taking," I suggested.

Morgan said, "I guess a minute or two won't make any difference. Probably a good idea."

The pilot motioned for us to clear the area so he would have the clearance to take off. I hung onto my fedora as the rotors began turning. Moments later, the helicopter took off. I looked up and saw the blinking lights start to fade from view. It couldn't have been more than a minute from its takeoff. The chopper was almost out of sight when it exploded with such force, the sound waves knocked us to the ground. The sky lit up for a moment and then the inky darkness of the night returned. As we lay on the ground, we heard the beatings of the wings of hundreds of birds combined with their screeching at the illumination in the sky and the unknown noises as they were startled. There were no sounds. No bird calls or growls from the other animals. To say it was a little creepy would be a massive understatement.

I took off my stained fedora and mopped my face. The sweat running down my face was stinging my eyes. "You wouldn't want to bet we were supposed to be on board when the bomb went off?"

Morgan nodded knowingly.

Fingers gulped and began to whine. "Gee whiz, Mr. Rixey, I didn't sign up for anything like this." He pointed to the fire burning so brightly in the jungle. "Does this mean I'll be getting some hazardous duty pay?"

Both Morgan and I laughed.

"Yes. There will be something extra for you when we settle up," I said, attempting to reassure him. "All you have to do is survive tonight. I don't think any of us signed up for what we've been through."

We started heading toward the meeting place. As we walked, I said, "You know, while the explosion sucked for the pilots, it may work to our advantage."

Morgan asked. "How so?"

"They probably think we died in the explosion."

"They will continue to think all hands lost until they get to the crash site and discover only two bodies," Fingers analyzed.

"They probably are sending people out to the crash site. We'd better get to the meeting place before they discover we weren't killed and the Chalice isn't there. Luckily, we aren't too far away. We should beat them back. Let's be on the lookout for the mercenaries or whatever Kendall is using for her muscle. I'll start to follow you in a few minutes."

Fingers and I both put our earplugs in and our NVGs on and we were off. We moved slowly through the jungle. No one had thought to bring a machete. We moved liked ghosts. The failure to bring a machete probably saved our lives. We had gone about eight hundred yards when I heard some voices and smelled the unmistakable odor of cigarettes. They were in the process of making a fatal mistake. *Keep your head on a swivel. Just because you don't think anyone is out there, doesn't mean there isn't. That's the number one rule of tracking.*

I motioned for Fingers to get down and joined him there. I drew my pistol and clicked twice on the microphone. I hazarded a look to see how many people were in the group. I counted five. They were within twenty yards or so ahead of us. I drew my weapon and focused on the night's sights. The eerie green glow helped me focus on my potential targets. I was glad I already screwed in the suppressor. I heard two clicks in my ear. I looked over at Fingers. He was ready with his weapon drawn. I saw his suppressor attached, too. Here was our problem. In the movies, I've seen people make incredible shots, quite often from a great distance, and kill the bad guys. In reality, shooting a target with a handgun sixty to seventy feet is quite a shot. I'm pretty good but not that good. We needed to wait for them to get closer. Semi-automatic or automatic rifles versus handguns generally mean a loss for the handgun side. With any luck, they would either come closer to us or miss us entirely.

Suddenly, I heard a curse in a foreign language. I saw two of the men soundlessly collapse on the jungle floor. I didn't speak their language, but their tone told me they were panicked. Now there was a chance. Two of them blundered into my range. I fired two shots at each, aiming for the head as I was confident they wore vests. I heard Fingers' gun go off and saw the final man collapse.

We laid on the ground to see if this group was on its own or if others were following them. After about five minutes, I heard two more clicks over my headset. It was our signal for all clear. Morgan joined us.

"Let's check the bodies."

She smiled at Fingers. "Nice shooting, Julian."

Fingers said, "Aw shucks, Ma'am. It wasn't any big deal."

There wasn't much left of the heads of any of them. I tamped on one of their chests. They were wearing vests. I knelt down next to one of the corpses and searched his pockets. Nothing. No IDs, no wallet, nothing. I would have been surprised had I found anything. Pros don't carry their wallets on missions. Even the sloppy ones. The mercenaries were carrying M-16s. Fingers and I each grabbed one along with some magazines. I checked my weapon, still a full mag. I saw Julian do likewise.

Morgan asked, "Should we move the bodies?"

I snarled. "Fuck 'em. No one's going to be by this way anytime this century. I don't want to waste any time on them." I looked at my Omega. "Let's get going."

We continued our appointment with Morgan still lagging a few hundred yards behind us. About five minutes later, I noticed my NVGs beginning to flicker, and when I looked down at my handheld GPS device, saw the object was beginning to blink. I knew the batteries were fresh in both devices and now knew the dead zone wasn't merely just some local legend.

"I'm having some problems with my goggles, Mr. Rixey," I heard from behind me.

I motioned for Fingers to stop. "Looks like it's time for some old-school direction finding." I fished into my jacket pocket and brought out the compass Morgan gave me. It seemed to be working. This decreased my fear that, if the zone existed, the compass might be affected. Without a regular compass, navigation would be impossible in this area.

I looked up at the sky and saw nothing. The tall trees formed a canopy over the jungle floor. No moonlight or sunlight was going to break through. For the hell of it, I tapped my earpiece, knowing the answer before I touched it. It was totally dead. I didn't see how this dead zone area was created. It seemed like a pretty effective defense against more modernized attacks. We trudged on. We both stumbled a few times. Luckily, no one was nearby to hear our falls or our soft curses. I finally took off my jacket. The heat and humidity were unbearable. I was surprised I didn't take it off earlier. I'd had it since I'd lost mine in Hong Kong, so there was no great attachment to it. I removed the magazines from it and put them where they were easily reachable.

After another few hundred yards or so, I made out a fog-shrouded clearing. I heard muffled voices. It was impossible to make out what they were saying as the fog acted as an effective muffler on the area. I motioned for Fingers to get down and crawl. We made it to the edge of the clearing. I was able to make out five figures. The one who was speaking was a woman who held a knife at the throat of a dark-skinned man. I gritted my teeth when I heard her very nasal and eastern voice. It was Doctor Eve Kendall.

Chapter Fifty-three

"Diplomacy is the art of saying 'Nice doggie' until you can find a rock."
Will Rogers.

"Come, come, Mr. Rixey. You have something I need and I need it now. Now don't be a dawdler. God, I hate dawdlers." She smacked her hostage with a riding crop she carried. He was a dark-skinned man of medium height, who wore a blue feathered headdress, and a most magnificent multicolored feathered robe. "I want you out here with the Chalice, unarmed, and hands up." Eve Kendall, clad in a khaki jacket, pants, pith helmet, and black boots motioned for us to enter. She also wore a large holster on her right hip that I assumed contained a large pistol. She seemed supremely confident. Why shouldn't she be? It looked like game over and she had won.

I looked at Fingers and nodded. We laid down our M-16s and I took off my holster. After removing my suppressor, I put my Glock-17 in the back of my pants. Fingers slid his .38 down the back of his pants. He then quickly concealed the carryon bag containing the Chalice. We walked into the mist-shrouded area where our meeting was supposed to have been. We ambled as I was trying to buy Morgan time to get in position.

There wasn't much to the area. There was a temple I knew wasn't Mayan. A stone table stood about four feet off the ground. I was a little surprised Kendall's hostage, who I supposed was the person we were supposed to meet, was alone. I felt the ground sinking with every step I took.

"Where is the Chalice? You idiots were supposed to have the Chalice with you. Can't you idiots do anything right?" Kendall screamed.

I saw two men emerge from the temple. Both were armed with rifles swung over their shoulders and a pistol on their hips. Just my luck, my pals from Mexico City, Alfie and Wilmer.

"What's the shouting about, love?" Alfie asked. Then he saw Fingers and me and smiled evilly. Alfie whistled. "Miller Rixey, I thought you were dead. Where is the little slitch who sucker punched me? I was looking forward to smashing her face in."

Wilmer couldn't seem to control himself. "It's judgment day, Miller Rixey," he said in a high-pitched and excited screech.

I yawned and shook my head. "A fine lot the two of you are. Like I said in Mexico, the cheaper the hood, the gaudier the patter."

I looked at Kendall with amusement. "This is the best you can do?"

Kendall ordered, "Stop moving! Where is the Chalice? I want to know now. No more screwing around!"

Fingers and I stopped. "I told Fingers to leave the Chalice on the helicopter. I wanted it someplace safe while we worked out if this meeting was on the level."

Alfie said, "He's lying again. How about I just shoot him and his friend?"

Fingers sputtered in a panicked tone, "No! He's telling the truth! I left it behind on the chopper."

Kendall looked thoughtful. "They might be telling the truth. We'll know for sure when our crew gets back." She slapped at a mosquito. "God, I really hate this place."

Alfie asked incredulously. "You mean the Chalice might have survived the explosion?"

"I mean exactly what I said. Mr. Fiste told me, based on his research, the Chalice would probably survive even a nuclear attack. Once our crew gets back, we can take care of these three and get the hell out of here. I need a hot bath. Damnit, where is the rest of the crew? Must I do everything myself?"

In a fit of rage, she struck the man she was holding hostage and the man silently fell to the ground.

I smirked. "So you're working for Fiste. He promised me twenty-five million. What did he promise you?"

She sniffed. "Mr. Fiste is a wonderful man. He is dedicated to world peace. He will be funding the Institute for World Studies. We will work to stop the spread of violence and hate by using common-sense gun control and mandatory sensitivity classes. We will be able to end all wars by having the United Nations governing the world. In short, it will be a world Neanderthals like you despise." She sighed, looking very dreamy-eyed. "Don't worry, though, you won't be around when the changes occur."

I scowled. "Then we have something in common. You know, you and Mr. Fiste have murdered quite a few people in pursuit of the Chalice. He's little more than a terrorist and a gangster. He'll dispose of you once you aren't needed anymore."

Kendall shrugged. "It couldn't be helped. The goal of spreading nonviolence is much more important than anything else. You're a fine one to talk, Mr. Rixey. You are a very violent man yourself."

I took off my fedora and pulled the red bandana out of the lining and used it to wipe my face. My eyes were really stinging from the sweat. *Where the hell was Morgan?* I wondered. I was sure I'd given her enough time to get into place. I eyed Dr. Kendall. "I only kill bad guys, like your boyfriend, Hanover Fiste. You realize using violence to advance nonviolence is like fucking for chastity, don't you?"

She laughed. "How delightfully crude and totally expected from someone of your ilk. Alfie, please go out and see what's happened to the crew we sent out. They are well overdue."

"Leaving now, Doctor." He headed off into the jungle.

She kicked the man lying at her feet and ordered him up. She turned to Wilmer. "Now I fear Mr. Rixey and his friend have outlived their usefulness. Please terminate them. We will hunt down the pesky Colonel Burke at a later date."

I saw Wilmer's lip curl into a snarl as he raised his M-16 and pointed it at me. "I'm going to enjoy this. I warned you what was going to happen when you mess with me," he gloated.

I held up my hands. "Wait a minute, Dr. Kendall. Certainly, someone as civilized as you are would grant a condemned man his last request and a couple of answers?"

She frowned. "What's your last request, Mr. Rixey? Be quick about it."

"A last cigarette and a couple of answers. It won't take very long."

She cackled. "Don't you know cigarettes are bad for you?"

I took out my pack, shook one out and handed it to Fingers. I lit up and inhaled deeply. This sure looked like this was it. Something had happened to Morgan and no rescue would be coming.

"Well, Mr. Rixey, you and your friend have your cigarette. What's your question?"

"Let's see if I can figure this out. You've been leaking information on this case to whatever side suited you the best. Crypt didn't bring the Chalice to the meeting because you knew we would be down in Mexico City to grab it. You told Crypt the board member who was murdered at the board meeting was working for Fiste. The man who took his place was loyal to you. You and Fiste are responsible for the electronic attack on Denver. You called Arch Stanton's kid and told him our mission was off." I looked at her angrily. "How am I doing so far?"

"One hundred percent. It's too bad we couldn't work together, Mr. Rixey. You are quite perceptive." She drew her pistol, pulled the hostage up, and held the gun to his head. "Anything else? I need to get out of this hell hole, with the Chalice," she said in a bored and condescending tone.

"Just a few more moments of your time. You or someone working for you planted the bomb on the chopper we came in. You also called off the detachment of Rangers we needed for security and to help us get here." I made a gesture like I was scratching. In reality, I was reaching for my pistol.

"Right again, Mr. Rixey. I knew the proper access codes. You know OAR really needs to work on their security. Stuart and Stanton didn't have any idea what was going on."

I turned as I heard a high-pitched scream. Kendall and Wilmer were momentarily distracted. I smiled as I drew my pistol. It was a male scream. It sounded like Alfie found Morgan and was getting what's his.

I emptied the magazine into Kendall. The hostage dove out of the way when he saw me bring my weapon out. As for Wilmer, he never knew what hit him. Fingers emptied his .38 into him. The jungle erupted with the screams of birds as they fluttered up from their various roosts. I walked to over to Kendall. Amazingly she was still alive. She looked up at me with a look of total disbelief.

"Oh, yeah, that crew you kept talking about. We killed them all."

Her life was rapidly flowing from her body. She croaked, "I'll see you in hell, Miller Rixey."

"Perhaps. You first," I spat.

Her body shook for the last time and she died.

Moments later, Morgan walked into the encampment, carrying the carry-on bag containing the Chalice of Power.

"Where the hell were you? We might have been killed," I railed.

She giggled. "Quit being such a baby, Miller. You were never in much danger. I had Kendall lined up in my scope the entire time. Well, most of the time. I had to take a brief break to deal with Alfie. You looked like you were handling it. Plus, I heard her entire confession. Good job, Miller," she said as she slapped me on the back.

By now, the man Kendall held hostage slowly got to his feet. He was readjusting his feathered helmet and robe. It was the first chance I was able to observe him carefully. His face and the exposed parts of his arms and legs were covered with Mayan tattoos. I saw traces of his black hair under his helmet. As to his age? It was impossible for me to tell. Let's just say anywhere from thirty to sixty. He had a kindly face and I sensed the good vibes he was sending.

He approached Morgan, Fingers, and me.

"I suppose an explanation is in order." I was surprised by his English accent. He chuckled. "I see you are surprised I sound like a Brit. Like the other members of my family, I was educated in England." He became somber. "My name is Yum Cimil. My tribe has guarded the secrets of the world for more than five hundred years. My ancestors were able to avoid the Spanish when they destroyed our country and spread their diseases. You are Americans, I believe?"

"Yes, we are."

"My tribe's relationship began with your country back in 1791. We have held many items for the United States. Items too dangerous for mankind to be exposed to." He sighed. "We do need to finish our business. You have something for me?"

Morgan stepped up and handed him the carryon bag with the Chalice inside. He gravely accepted it. He unzipped the bag and shook his head as he zipped the bag back closed. "How sad, something of such beauty has caused so much evil in the world." He shrugged resignedly.

"Perhaps one day, humanity will understand this item as I do."

He reached under his robe and pulled out a gold coin. It was the size of an American double eagle. It was made of gold and was covered with Mayan hieroglyphs. It seemed to have a strange glow to it. He handed it to me and I accepted. I didn't have anything to protect the coin. Fingers gave me a handkerchief. I nodded my thanks and wrapped the coin in it and placed it in my pocket.

"When your country desires the item to be returned, you will bring this coin back to this area. Those in charge know how to contact me."

Uncertain on how to address him. "Your majesty, the only place this coin is going is into my private collection. As far as we are concerned, the Chalice was lost in the helicopter explosion."

Cimil nodded approvingly. "You are wise beyond your years, Miller Rixey."

He stepped forward and shook our hands. He took the bag and went into the temple. I never saw him again.

We stood there silently for a few minutes. We checked the bodies of Kendall and Wilmer and found nothing of any value. We left the bodies where they lay. We knew the jungle would reclaim them. I picked up their firearms. I didn't want to leave those behind. It would corrupt the environment. I felt some raindrops hitting me and looked up. It was soon pouring. We headed back to our extraction point. No one bothered to say anything. Nothing really needed to be said. Morgan sent the blast transmission. Thirty minutes later, we were boarding an American helicopter. We were going home.

Chapter Fifty-four

"People who enjoy meetings should not be in charge of anything."
Thomas Sowell.

November 11, 20xx, Washington D.C. National Intelligence Agency
Headquarters, Conference Room A

Five of us sat in Conference Room A at the NIA Headquarters. Morgan, Fingers, me, Stuart, and a balding-middle aged man with thick glasses. *Probably some bureaucrat here to chew my ass out*, was my first thought. We were waiting for Arch. It was his show. Like most big shots, he was running late. People like him always think their time is more valuable than anyone else's.

The room was very nice. I wouldn't expect anything less on the taxpayer's dime. I heard the whopping sound as the ceiling fans worked to move the air-conditioned air around the room. Eleven very nice padded-leather chairs surrounded a highly-polished dark wood table. The same dark wood paneled the ceiling and walls. Each seat came with a work station in front of it and four large viewing screens hung on the rear walls. As I said, it was very nice.

I'd filed a full and extremely detailed report when I got back to Carbondale. Well, mostly complete and incredibly detailed. I didn't see what mentioning my involvement in the death of the late and unlamented Colonel Pong would accomplish. I'd also failed to mention that the Chalice of Power now resided in a vault in the Yucatan. I mean, the President of the United States had determined it was so dangerous we needed to be protected from ourselves by hiding it. Who am I to argue with someone like the President? I never got a chance to see the powers the Chalice held. What I did see were the extreme lengths men would go through to obtain it. That was enough to convince me of the dangers the artifact held. I filed a very detailed expense account report, totally truthful, more or less. I accomplished my mission. I recovered the Chalice and, as an extra, revealed some traitorous activity and wanted to be paid for my work. D.C. doesn't function in any normal way. The bureaucrats must have their meetings to justify their existence. I glanced at my watch and hoped we wouldn't be here much longer. The door blasted open and Stanton was followed by the usual entourage of harried aides. He didn't look too happy.

"Jesus Christ, Rixey. Is there anyone you don't feel you have to kill? Every time you do work for the United States, must you create an international incident? You're in a country illegally and decide to kill seven American nationals and two citizens of the United Kingdom. What's wrong with you? Dr. Kendall was a respected professor and a scholar of great repute," Stanton roared.

I thought he was going to have a heart attack then and there. His face was beet red and I saw some major veins throbbing in his neck. "Listen Arch, did you not read my report? She was working with Fiste to get the Chalice for him and for whatever purpose he planned for it. She killed the helicopter crew, tried to screw up our mission, tipped off the OTO about us being in Mexico City, and last but not least, she was all set to execute us. Both Colonel Burke and Mr. Malone heard her confession."

"You didn't even deliver the Chalice?" Stanton sputtered.

"I told you, the Chalice was destroyed when Kendall blew up the helicopter. We met with Yum Cimil after we rescued him from Kendall and Fiste's men and explained what happened. You surely contacted him to verify those facts?" I asked.

Stanton only nodded.

Stuart stepped in. "Now, Director Stanton, everything Mr. Rixey has said has been verified. I was in the room when you contacted Chief Cimil. Kendall was a traitor and, well, you may not approve of how Mr. Rixey handled the matter, but it's all for the best. We really didn't want to have a trial. A trial would have been very embarrassing to the government. While I agree Mr. Rixey's methods are not what I would use, it was effective. The official story is Dr. Kendall died on an expedition along the Amazon River. We agreed to fund an Eve Kendall chair at her school and as far as everyone who isn't in this room knows, she died a hero. Case closed as a result of a tragic accident."

Feeling frustrated, Stanton turned his attention toward Fingers. "I know where I've seen you before." He pounded the conference table. "You're a suspect in a dozen burglaries occurring in Beverly Hills and surrounding areas, an art heist in Chicago, and a snatch and grab at

Tiffany's in New York City. Tell me, Mr. Malone, when do you have time to sleep?" Stanton asked in an icy tone.

Fingers shrugged. "Mr. Zogg, my new employer, told me those charges will never be proven. I have no idea what you are talking about."

The balding middle-aged man who wore thick glasses cleared his throat. "Gentlemen, I am the Under-Secretary of State for Political Affairs. My name is Mark Denzer. I mention who I am for the benefit of Mr. Malone and Mr. Rixey. I know the rest of the people in the room know who I am. I have spoken to the President. While he agrees Mr. Rixey should have handled the situation in a more, how would you say it, delicate manner, based on his past record it doesn't seem to be the way he does things." He paused and slid an Executive Order in front of both Stuart and Stanton. "He is satisfied Mr. Rixey essentially completed his mission and will be paid. If there are no further questions or comments, I have to meet with the President and tell him you agree to follow this Order."

Stanton looked crestfallen. "Yes, Mr. Under-Secretary, he will be paid."

The man nodded. "Now the President has one more question. How is the OTO reacting to the loss of the artifact?"

Stuart said. "I can address your concerns. Crypt and the OTO really can't do much of anything. If you recall, the Chalice was stolen in a burglary. That's how they came by it. They came to this scene with dirty hands. They can't very well say somebody stole the item we stole, can they? The interesting development will be what North Korea will do to get back their four hundred fifty million they paid for the Chalice. My guess is we have heard the last of the OTO and Mr. Crypt for some time."

"Very good," the man responded. He shook his head. "I wish there were some way we could get Hanover Fiste. It hardly seems fair he escaped from this matter basically unscathed. For that matter, what about Borgia? He needs to be punished, too. I mean calling in a bomb threat on a commercial flight and his involvement in attempting to gain control of the Chalice for whatever purposes he had in mind? Any act of terrorism and an act that threatens the national security of this country needs to be dealt with.

Morgan said, "Not to worry, sir. Mr. Borgia has been taken care of, as you put it, already. According to my sources in the DIA, his private jet exploded over the Atlantic while he was returning home from Denver. There are no suspects. Mr. Fiste is a person of interest. I doubt they will ever be able to prove anything. He is slippery."

Denzer smiled. "Thank you for the update, Colonel Burke. I'm sure the news of his demise will bring a smile to the President's face. Now if we could only find some way to get Fiste."

I decided this wasn't a good time to mention the phone conversation I'd had with Mr. Chen. I was sure by the end of the year, both the President and Denzer would be smiling.

Stanton nodded, took all the information in and picked up a phone at the table. He dialed a series of numbers, and spoke in hushed tones. He hung up the phone. "Mr. Rixey, you will have the money in your account within twenty-four hours. You are to be paid in full per our contract with you. If you haven't gotten it by then, call me." He stood up. The meeting was over.

Chapter Fifty-five

"If you want a happy ending, that depends, of course, on where you stop your story." Orson Welles.

Things have been blessedly slow at the Bishop Agency since my return. Willard and Ms. Nickels stayed on top of everything while I was gone. Willard even went out on a few cases. I never thought I'd say this, but it's good to be back in Carbondale. I've had plenty of adventures recently and now am looking forward to a long rest and recuperation period. As to some rest time, I just got off the phone with Mr. Chen. Morgan and I are to be his guests from December twentieth until January fourth at his hotel in Hong Kong. It seems after what happened in Mexico City, my Hong Kong privileges have been reinstated. Morgan and I plan to take a train ride to San Francisco and fly from there to Hong Kong. We both decided we needed to spend more time together. I know I'm really looking forward to it. Stanton, for all of his faults, did get my fee wired to my account.

Willard has promised to hang around Carbondale and keep an eye on the office. I doubt the workload will be too difficult during the holidays. I looked it up. In the past ten years, we've had a grand total of two cases during the period.

For her especially hard work during this case, I'm flying Ms. Nickels and a friend of hers to Jamaica and putting her up in a five-star hotel for the same time I plan to be gone. For some reason, she has always wanted to go there, but she never seemed to have the time.

Banner has really surprised me. He has stayed sober and will be attending my alma mater, Illinois State University, starting in a couple of months. I really wanted him out of his current environment. Going to school in a new place like Normal will give him a chance to reinvent himself. He shouldn't have too many financial problems as he'll be able to use his GI Bill, the Illinois Veterans' Scholarship, and will receive money from the Bishop Agency Scholarship Fund. Willard and I both helped out in setting up the new fund. The money goes to non-traditional students who attend Illinois State.

Apparently, Fingers made quite an impression on Lothar Zogg. Fingers told me he was hired as "Director of Special Projects." I didn't ask what special projects. Some things you just don't want to know. He showed me a lot during this case and I know he'll do an excellent job for Zogg.

December 20, 20xx, The Ancient Cloak Hotel, Hong Kong

The trip worked out better than I ever imagined. I recommend the train ride if you are into trains and, naturally, it helps to have the perfect companion along. We arrived at Hong Kong International Airport and breezed through customs. They didn't even check our bags. We were informed that the Ancient Cloak Hotel did have a helicopter waiting for us. We were soon at the hotel. Morgan excused herself and I saw Mr. Chen walking up to me. We shook hands.

"You've been staying busy, young man."

"Just trying to survive, Mr. Chen, nothing more, nothing less."

"Nonetheless, you did fine work, Miller. A real man's job."

"You're much too flattering, Mr. Chen.

I hear a squeal behind me. It was from Morgan. Her heels were clicking as she sprinted across the lobby. "Uncle Joe!" They embraced.

"How you've grown, young lady. How long has it been?" Chen asked with a rare smile.

"Sixteen years, Uncle Joe."

Now it was my turn to be confused. "You know Mr. Chen and never bothered to tell me?"

Morgan laughed. "A girl has to have her secrets."

My phone went off in my pocket. I sighed and pulled it out and saw the name flashing on the screen. "Excuse me, you two, I need to take this." I walked to an unoccupied section of the lobby. I fumbled with the security system and once the line was secured, I spoke. "Miller Rixey."

Epilogue

Singapore, December 25 (Reuters): Billionaire recluse Hanover Fiste and his crew of five have been reported missing after his yacht, *The Banker*, was found adrift one day after leaving Singapore, roughly five hundred miles from Singapore in the South China Sea. The Malaysian Maritime Enforcement Agency commenced a search for the vessel after repeated transmissions from the Agency to the yacht went unanswered. Upon their boarding of the ship, they found it abandoned. There is a concern the ship was attacked by pirates, as piracy in the South China Sea is on the rise. The Malaysian Maritime Enforcement Agency and the People's Republic of China Navy have commenced a joint search.

Fiste, who was fifty-five, was attending a Board of Directors' meeting for his banking conglomerate, Fiste Bank, Ltd. The meeting was being held in Singapore. It was his first public appearance in ten years.

-30-

Singapore, December 26 (Reuters): The body of Hanover Fiste has been found floating some one hundred miles from where his yacht, *The Banker*, was first discovered abandoned. No details concerning the cause of his death have been released. The search for his missing crew members has been called off as the very rough seas and storms would have made survival virtually impossible. There will be an investigation.

-30-

Addendum

I initially wrote this as part of the book when Miller was thinking about potential occurrences which would be possible if the Chalice of Power were able to have the ability of time travel in Chapter Fourteen. Miller analyzed one event, the JFK assassination in Dallas on November 22, 1963, and how if it had not occurred what would have happened. Most of my readers liked what I wrote. While they liked it, most thought it did little to advance the story. They were right. So now the Chalice of Power is in supposedly safe hands and the world is right again, I leave you to read this:

I hadn't been totally convinced about the time travel capabilities of the Chalice when Stuart and I first talked. I began thinking there was a good chance it was true when I received information from Kaplan verifying what Stuart showed me about the interruptions of the time-space continuum. The frightening thought was people have no idea how dangerous time travel can be in the current world. I began thinking about how the prevention of one major event would totally change the world.

If somehow, a person was in Dallas on November 22, 1963, and stopped the assassination of President Kennedy, quite a bit would have been changed. First of all, chances are good Lyndon Baines Johnson would have ended up in prison for the various crimes he committed throughout his political career. At a minimum, if Kennedy not been assassinated, Johnson would have been out of power as Kennedy already decided to dump Johnson from the national ticket.

As for American involvement in Vietnam, there is a good chance our involvement would have never escalated to the levels it did under the Johnson regime. Would Kennedy have won reelection in 1964? Despite what revisionists would like to claim, his presidency had been a disaster. The Bay of Pigs debacle, the failure to pass any civil rights bills, and the fact that he led America to the brink of nuclear war would not have been lost on the voters.

The compromise candidate supported by President Eisenhower and Henry Cabot Lodge would have been the likely nominee. Kennedy also made organized crime, the reason he carried Illinois, angry with him from Robert F. Kennedy's continued attacks on the mob. Even with Johnson on the ticket, Kennedy barely carried Texas. The Democrat Party actually lost the special election for Johnson's seat when it became vacant upon his election to Vice President. Losing Texas and not having organized crime boss Sam Giancana stealing votes in Illinois, his chances for reelection were remote.

About the Author

The author is sixty-five years old and has been an attorney for the past fifteen years. He went back to school late in life and received my B.S. from Illinois State University in 1997, my M.S. from the same institution in 1999, and my J.D. from Southern Illinois School of Law in 2002. Williams is an expert bridge player having achieved the rank of Diamond Life Master from the American Contract Bridge League, an avid coin collector, and lover of all things noir.

He has published six books. Four deal with the Zombie Apocalypse. The titles are: *The Trek to Elysium Chronicles: Vol. 1: A Zombie Apocalyptic Tale 1st and 2nd edition, The Trek to Elysium Chronicles: Vol. 2: Survival Guide,* and *The Incident.* The second edition of the first novel arose from the experience I had gained working with the publisher of my third and fourth novels. The fifth book is the first book of The Rixey Files Series. It's subtitle is *The Quest for Caesar's Medallion.* The Sixth book is the second book in the series which is the one you're now reading. It's title is *The Quest for The Chalice of Power.* My WIP is the third book of this series: *The Quest for The Ring of Life* and I have a title and a start for book four, *The Quest for The Spawn of Mayhem.*

Also by the Author

at

Rogue Phoenix Press

The Quest for Caesar's Medallion

Miller is given the chance to run a very exclusive detective agency. The name of the agency is the Bishop Agency. It's named after Miller's employer and mentor. Miller will go anywhere in the world to recover rare items for his client. To the casual observer, the Bishop Agency looks like any other small-town detective agency. The difference is that the Agency, as it's referred to, has "special clients" who employ the Agency when government law enforcement is unable or unwilling to help the clients recover their property.

Chapter One

"Every new beginning comes from some other beginning's end." Seneca

"Miller Rixey?" The ICU nurse called my name.

"Yes." I put down my newspaper and rushed to the counter, anticipating the worst.

"You may see Mr. Bishop now," she said with a smile.

"Is he okay? Is he going to make it?"

The nurse's smile quickly left her face. The bullet has been removed and is still in critical condition... but he is awake."

I rushed through the doors and was escorted to the ICU room. I saw him there, hooked up to all the wires, my heart sunk. The beeping from his various machines did not help my mood any. His eyes were closed and his face was bruised and swollen. I walked to his bedside. "Willard?"

The nurse said. "He may not be very coherent at this point."

Willard opened his eyes and focused on my face. "Hey kid, good to see you." He groaned and sat up in his bed. He looked a little unsteady but in his condition; who wouldn't look that way?

"Glad you are still with us," I said, choking back my emotions. Willard Bishop had been my friend, my boss, and my mentor for the past sixteen years. I always thought he was invincible. He was one of the best Private Investigators that I had ever known and he had taught me so much.

"You cannot get rid of me that easy, kid. "Bishop said in a raspy voice and then began coughing. The commotion brought a couple of ICU nurses into the room. "Kid, come here...," Bishop said, struggling with the ICU nurses attempts to lay him down. "I'm fine, leave me alone," he rasped.

I went up to his bed as he held out his hand. He dropped a set of keys into along with a piece of paper into my hand. "The Agency's yours now. I'm getting too old for this shit."

I started to say something to him, but I thought better of it and remained silent. No one ever won an argument with Willard Bishop. I took the keys and nodded as the nurses pushed me out of the room. At the door, there were other nurses and a doctor rushing to enter.

I held the keys and the piece of paper in my hand and walked back to the waiting area. I flopped down on a couch. My head was spinning. I knew I had to collect myself. I was soon lost in my thoughts. Memories of my first meeting with Bishop came to mind. Sixteen years ago, I was attending Illinois State University where I majored in Criminal Justice. I had always been a big fan of detective stories and had no desire to teach, become a cop or a correctional officer. My degree in Criminal Justice would mean that I would only have to apprentice for one year instead of the usual three years to get my license. I began sending resumes and cover letters to well over one hundred detective agencies. I thought I would get lots of offers since after all, I had excellent grades and strong recommendations. I was wrong. I got one offer. It was from The Bishop Agency. It was an offer for a paid summer internship worth $5000 if I passed the interview and he decided to hire me. My initial excitement at the meeting faded when I saw the Agency was located in Carbondale, Illinois. It was hardly the bustling metropolis I had envisioned working in when I sent out my resumes. I thought to myself, well you aren't exactly flush with offers, why not check it out?

I made the decision to interview for the job and that moment changed my life forever. I wasn't sure what to expect when I arrived in Carbondale, Illinois. I wondered what working in a small town like Carbondale could offer me. I knew from the letter; the Agency was located in a section in the city the locals called "The Strip." I walked up and down the strip finally locating a non-descript building that had "The Bishop Agency" proudly emblazoned on the door. I had been to

Carbondale plenty of times before to visit friends. I guess I had even walked past the building quite a few times and never noticed it. I later found out this was not by accident; it was by design. I pushed the door open and walked in. I shivered as I felt the cold blast from the air conditioning. I heard a bell tinkle.

The reception area seemed rather bleak. A manual typewriter rested on a cheap fabricated wood desk. There was also what looked like a very old and battered landline also seated on the desk. I saw five old file cabinets that looked like they had seen better days. Five folding chairs completed what I would call the "Early Depression" look. I noticed four what appeared to be office doors behind the desk. I wondered to myself if I had made a mistake even coming down to Carbondale since it had been about a four-hour drive for me.

A beautiful red headed woman was sitting at the front desk. Her nameplate read "Ms. Nickels." She appeared to be a forty-something in terms of her age. She looked up and smiled briefly at me. I doffed my fedora as I introduced myself and showed her the letter I had received from Mr. Bishop. She nodded as she quickly read the letter and then she pointed to a door that said "Mr. Bishop Private" and told me to go in and that I was expected. Out of habit, I knocked and when I heard "Come," came the booming voice from behind the door. I entered.

In the large, well-lighted office, a man in his fifties sat behind a wooden desk. He motioned me to a seat as he was talking on the phone. I looked for a place to put my fedora and saw a hat rack. I flipped it toward the hat rack and to my pleasure and surprise, it landed right where I had tossed it. I sat in the chair in front of the desk that was unexpectedly comfortable. I looked around the room to pass the time as I waited for Mr. Bishop to get finished with his phone call. Maybe the way his office was set up would give me some insight into the man I was about to interview? I hoped so.

Bishop's office was in sharp contrast to the reception area. It was well lit. He had two laptops sitting on his desk as well as what looked like two monitors. There was also what looked like a state-of-the-art desktop on a smaller desk behind him. The office was undoubtedly lavishly furnished. The forestry class I had taken during my Freshman year in college told me the desk was made of teak or some other precious hardwood. The walls were lined with cedar. I looked around the walls of the office and saw three oil paintings. It looked like Bishop had a rather eclectic taste in art. Where these really a Pollock, a Picasso, and a Warhol I was seeing hanging on the walls? I thought, perhaps a better time for that question later. I saw three pieces of sculpture that I could not immediately place, but they did look familiar.

I quickly turned my attention to his desk. I saw what I knew to be an expensive humidor. I saw three signed baseballs from Ty Cobb, Honus Wagner, and Babe Ruth. They all resided in plastic cubes with their certificates of authenticity being prominently displayed. I also saw a pen holder on the desk and as I love using fountain pens immediately recognized two Mont Blanc's, a very nice Cross fountain pen and a Waterman fountain pen. I wasn't sure what to make of what I had seen, but my interest had been piqued. There was no doubt that Mr. Bishop was a fascinating man.

Bishop finished with his call and cleared his throat to let me know the interview had begun. He opened a drawer and pulled out a file that was a couple of inches thick. I saw my name on it. I hadn't realized I had been alive long enough to have merited a file that size. Did I wonder what type of person would have the resources and contacts to build a file that size on me? I shrugged, well I was here, let's see what happens.

"Miller, may I call you Miller?" Bishop began.

"Yes, Mr. Bishop." I looked him over and decided I was having a hard time placing this guy. He could have been anywhere from forty to sixty. He had a full head of gray hair and it looked like three days' growth. He seemed to be in pretty good shape.

He smiled at me and picked up a pair of reading glasses. He opened the file and began. "Before we get too far along, I wish to give you an option." I saw him slide a check toward me. It was made out to me in the amount of five thousand dollars. "If you choose to, you may take this check and head back to Normal and there will be no hard feelings. Believe me, I know being a private detective isn't for everyone."

I frowned and said slowly. "Well, your offer is generous to be sure. Don't get me wrong, it would be great to have five thousand in my pocket and to be able to goof off this summer, but I decided I wanted to be a private detective, yours was the only firm that even sent me a positive reply. You must have seen something in me the other agencies didn't. Let's continue with the interview and see where it leads." I shifted uneasily in my chair and looked Mr. Bishop in the eye. "How does that sound to you?" I asked.

Mr. Bishop broke out in a smile. "Excellent. I like your attitude, young man. You can call me Willard."

"Thank you, Willard."

"I see you have excellent grades in college, but shall we say your grades and ACT score in high school left something to be desired. Care to elaborate on this?" Willard asked.

I looked back at Willard. "I hated high school and did not take enough classes to do well on my ACT. The school counselor told my parents and that I was bored and did not feel challenged. I shrugged. "She could have been right. Anyway, my parents are both alums from Illinois State and pulled some strings and got me in." I laughed. "I'm sure you had all of this in your file."

"Yes. You are quite right, but I put a huge premium on talking to people. You know what I mean, gives me a better feel for them rather than simply reading about their records in black and white."

I nodded and adjusted my position in the chair as I awaited his next question.

He thumbed through my file and making a sort of a raspy laugh, continued. "I see you have a Carry Conceal Permit. That's a good start. It shows me you know a little something about basic weapon safety. What is your weapon of choice?" he asked.

I carry a Ruger LCR .38 special."

"Somehow, I would have been surprised if you carried a semi-automatic. It wouldn't fit your personality," Willard replied.

I looked at him, somewhat confused.

He pointed to my fedora on the rack and the fountain pens in my pocket. "You seem like kind of a retro guy. I have the feeling you would have been more at home in the 50's."

Willard thumbed through my file. "You seem like a good kid. Your teachers speak highly of you. You sure you wouldn't be happier in law school or perhaps working on a Ph.D.? I can probably get you into any school you would want. Teaching and the law are honorable professions."

I winced at the "kid" remark. I wondered who this guy was who said he could get me into any school I wanted. "Thanks, I really appreciate your offer, but I want to give being a private detective a try. It may not turn out to be what I wanted, but trying it is the only way I will ever find out," I replied.

Willard stood up and walked over to where I had been sitting. He reached into his desk and pulled out a bundle of paperwork. "Please fill out these forms before you leave. They are pretty standard. The most important is the confidentiality agreement. I'm guessing you want to get college credit for your work this summer. Fill out the enrollment form for Illinois State and submit that form along with the letter Ms. Nickels has waiting for you when you leave my office. You will be getting four hours' credit for your internship. That should about cover everything." He stood up and shook my hand. "Welcome to The Bishop Agency. We will see you back in two weeks. Do you have any questions?" he asked with a broad smile on his face.

"None that I can think of."

Willard concluded. "You are certainly free to tell your friends and your parents that my agency has agreed to hire you for the summer. The only thing I ask is that you refrain from discussing with them about what you have seen in my office and your theories of what is going on here.

Fair enough? I try not to impose too many restrictions on young interns such as yourself. I find that it sometimes inhibits them, which gives me a harder time trying to evaluate them."

I laughed. "Fair enough Willard. I don't know enough to form any type of theories as to what is going on here. All I know is this is a detective agency and that you hired me to work for you as an intern for the summer."

"Good boy," he beamed.

I felt a gentle nudge that broke me out of my reverie. I looked around wildly to get my bearings. I was still at the hospital. That had been one interesting dream.

A concerned looking, motherly type nurse looked down at me. "Young man, there is nothing you can do for your friend here. I can appreciate your concerns. Don't worry, we have the best doctors looking out for him. Go home and get some rest, we will keep you informed."

I nodded and thanked her. She was right, there was nothing I could do for Bishop here. I decided my time would be better spent at the office. Since Willard had now put me in charge of it, I was sure I had a lot of catching up to do. Being in the office and reviewing Willard's files might give me some insight into why he had been attacked. While maybe the local police were all too anxious to write the attack off as a simple mugging, I had my doubts. I got up and rode the elevator down to the ground floor. I barely noticed the hum of the electric door as they swung open as I left the hospital. I spotted by SUV in the parking lot and headed toward it.

FOR THE FULL INVENTORY

OF QUALITY BOOKS:

http://www.roguephoenixpress.com

Rogue Phoenix Press

Representing Excellence in Publishing

Quality trade paperbacks and downloads

in multiple formats,

in genres ranging from historical to contemporary romance, mystery

and science fiction.

Visit the website then bookmark it.

We add new titles each month!

www.ingramcontent.com/pod-product-compliance
Lightning Source LLC
Chambersburg PA
CBHW061936170626
46813CB00006B/2424